'One-Eye came from T
And Two-Eye came fr
But Three-Eye bowed t
Who saw what none w



So ran the ancient heretical prophecy handed down in secret from generation to generation, despite harsh, rigorous attempts by the priest leaders of Phadraig to stamp it out. All who knew the prophecy knew the arrival of One-Eye would presage momentous changes in their world. But just what changes, no-one was certain ...

Stuart Gordon

# One-Eye

Panther

Granada Publishing Limited
Published in 1976 by Panther Books Ltd
Frogmore, St Albans, Herts AL2 2NF

First published in Great Britain by
Sidgwick & Jackson Ltd 1974

Made and printed in Great Britain by
Richard Clay (The Chaucer Press) Ltd
Bungay, Suffolk
Set in Linotype Pilgrim

*For Carolyn*

Table of Contents

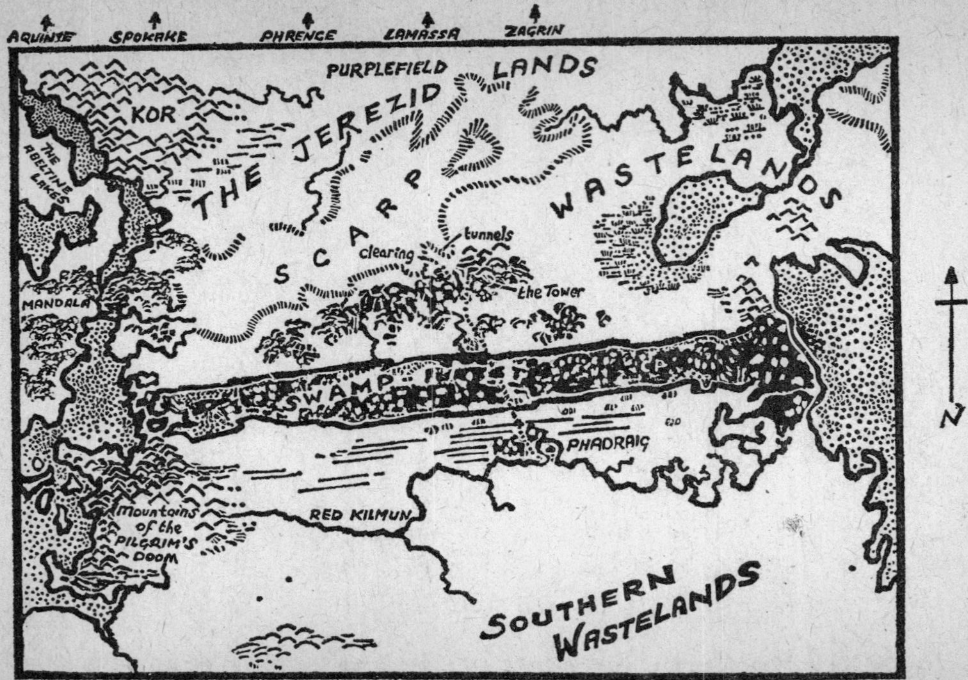
AQUINYE
SPOKAKE
PHRENCE
LAMASSA
ZAGRIN
PURPLEFIELD LANDS
KOR
THE JEREZID WASTELANDS
THE ABELTINE LAKES
SCARP
clearing
tunnels
the Tower
MANDALA
SWAMP
PHADRAIG
Mountains of the PILGRIM'S DOOM
RED KILMUN
SOUTHERN WASTELANDS
N

# Part 1 : Phadraig

## 1 : The Birth Of One-Eye

The dwindling, introverted community of human beings which inhabited the hill-city of Phadraig was obsessed by the problem of maintaining a genetic norm in a world where the norm no longer existed. As the potency of the inbred inhabitants continued to fail, the birth of freaks became the rule rather than the exception. In time it came that the great majority of children born were born deformed, according to the harsh standards of Norm Purity, to be classified as Uncleans of Greater or Lesser Degree. If Greater, they were killed on the spot; if Lesser, they were permitted to live as slaves and pariahs. Increasingly, the ideal of Norm Purity became corroded and unattainable. The society became rigid, superstitious, and bound by taboos. And the failed mothers and their monstrous offspring were not spoken of, save in whispers, at midday, when the hot sun beat down upon the sullen Wastelands which surrounded the lonely city. The failed mothers were not spoken of, and they were never seen out walking on the dusty streets again, while those few women who bore normal children were praised and called true servants of Phadraig. They were called the Witchmothers; it was believed by the citizens of the city that they were under the protection of the incomprehensible Witchgoddess, the planet Earth itself, which gave the gift of life, or took it away, according to its arbitrary whim.

But the Witchmothers were few, the Wastelands were encroaching closer, year by year, as the population of

Phadraig fell below ten thousand. And as the people vainly struggled to believe that all was well and would be well, hate-filled eyes stared from the cover of the Wastelands at the crumbling, declining city. . . .

Salamander was young and beautiful; she was the daughter of Aurum, once the High Witchman, the Protector of Phadraig at the time when the city had last been attacked by hordes from the Wastelands. On that occasion, a decade previously, Phadraig had been saved from destruction and pillage by the efforts of the Company Chatachain, under the leadership of Patrick Cormac.

Now, Patrick Cormac was the High Witchman, and the city was again threatened by fresh armies from the Wastelands under the leadership of the feral Warlord, Khassam, who had vowed to take the city and avenge the death of his father, Kalnakill. Kalnakill had died at the hands of Patrick Cormac ten years ago, and now Khassam was encamped just seven days' march to the north, at the rim of the Metal Forests where his army was gathering.

And now Salamander was about to be delivered of her firstborn.

Her firstborn and, she knew too well, her lastborn too.

Within weeks of the artificial conception she'd known that the child she carried would be judged upon birth as an Unclean of Greater Degree. She endured the knowledge throughout the arid months of this choking summer. She was afraid, but the fear wasn't for herself. This child she carried was the subject of a prophecy which her mother, the seer Gaidhealla, had never allowed her to forget. Salamander was prepared for the birth of a polypheme, a one-eyed child. And she knew that the child must not be allowed to die.

She didn't know the father; fathers were never known in Phadraig. She'd been impregnated according to the usual custom on her seventeenth birthday. Many Phadraig girls never reached the age of eighteen; many Phadraig youths similarly died young on their first hunts in the Wastelands. And those of either sex who stayed alive became old and hard before their time.

She didn't know the father, but often she consoled herself with thoughts of Patrick Cormac during the long summer months as she twisted on her bunk. Expectant mothers were confined to rooms in a high concrete tower on the western side of the ancient, tumbledown city. The tower was almost empty that summer; there were few girls who had come of age. Salamander lay through the long nights, enduring the insinuating mental tendrils of the mutant growing within her. She couldn't think of it as human; her conception of humanity was limited to that taught by the laws of Norm Purity. But she knew it had the right to live. Gaidhealla had made her understand that fulfillment of the prophecy was more important than obedience to laws which represented frightened, wishful thinking. Salamander didn't fully understand what her mother had said, but this lack was made up for by her trust in the old woman, the Witchmother of the Third Eye.

She'd grown large as the months passed in isolation and, when the arid swelter of midsummer was past, it was time for her to be taken to one of the cells deep beneath the city for the birth.

The bare hill on which Phadraig had been built by the unknown ancients before the Great Forgetting was honeycombed by shafts and tunnels cut from the rock. Access to these subterranean levels was by means of metal cages, which ascended and descended the deep vertical shafts. The raising and lowering of these cages was controlled by the pressing of buttons set in their gleaming walls. Nobody in Phadraig knew the origin of the cages, or how they worked. The citizens accepted the explanation that the cages would continue to ascend and descend so long as the Witchgoddess condescended to hear the prayers of the High Witchman.

The Council of ruling Servants explained that the Witchgoddess had provided the cages for the descent of expectant mothers. Thus each new child could be born within the body of the Witchgoddess and so receive her necessary blessing and protection. The citizens firmly believed it was heresy for children to be delivered above-ground, a denial of Norm Purity. If there had ever been a rational explanation of this custom, it was largely forgotten. However, the Council was very much aware of one good reason for it. There was one obvious advantage in hiding expectant mothers far from the citizenry. The morale of Phadraig's people would suffer if ever they discovered just how many of their children were born mutated and Unclean in Greater Degree. Of course, many suspected, but in the lack of proof they could continue to hope, and even to believe in their leaders. Their belief was fanatical, spartan; it could be nothing else. Their sole connection with a recognizable future lay in the birth of normal children – 'normal' according to the stringent definition of the laws. Clinging to their religion of Norm Purity, they despised the rest of the disordered world with fierce, righteous intensity. But their tragedy wasn't so much in their genes as in their minds.

The night came when Salamander's labor pains began.

The narrow window of her room in the concrete tower was set high in the outer wall. The customary anger of sunset was fading into night. There was a spyhole in the welded metal door. There were spyholes all over Phadraig. Vigilance was extensive, if not eternal.

She was alone and under constant observation. Hopeless now, she knew there was nobody, not even her mother, who could help her escape the horrible descent beneath Phadraig into the Witchgoddess. Now she was certain that both she and the eerie child would have to die. The prophecy was vague, ancient, and surely couldn't be fulfilled under these circumstances. How could she hope to escape? And where? The concept of 'escape' itself would have been meaningless except for Gaidhealla's secret, heretical instruction. But her mother was far away, waiting in another part of Phadraig . . . while she was alone. . . .

Shadows grew longer on the heat-cracked plaster wall. A spider paused in its spinning to watch the girl who lay heavy on the bed below. There had been many such girls tossing and turning, though now there were fewer than there had used to be. This one was tall, with long brown hair which would be glossy when in health. Pallor was pronounced beneath her tan. She had been slim. Soon, she'd be slim again.

In the west, the sun was vermillion through dust-clouds which swirled on mountain peaks. Salamander felt the spasm of the first contraction. The physical pain was marginal to her mental torment. The child seemed aware that it was about to be born, seemed aware of the danger which threatened before life was properly begun. It howled in her mind. It thirsted for life. It was new, unnatural. She was certain that Phadraig, which had known many varieties of mutant, had never known the like of this one before. And – the prophecy. Maelnagar the Maker of Outcries had foreseen the coming of a strange child more than two hundred years before. To speak of this prophecy in public was generally a fatal mistake. It was condemned as heresy.

And Salamander found no comfort in prophecy. She could see no way out of the coming trial. *Why me?* she wondered a thousand times. She was convinced that her ordeal was cruel and pointless. She found herself thinking about Patrick Cormac again. But he was imprisoned by his position, pinned by the weight of the Onerous Burdens which lay on the High Witchman.

Pain racked her body unfelt, for that in her mind was worse.

'Oh, mother,' she moaned, 'help me! Please help me!'

But she knew there was no aid. Just a vague prophecy about the power and wisdom of a one-eyed king. She twisted, subsided, hands clasped tight on the linen shift which rode her swollen belly. She didn't hear the opening of the door, or see the black-robed Witchman's stealthy entrance. He wore a belt of double-looped white cord which indicated Initiate status. His sharp young face was pale and emotionless beneath the cowl. For a moment he stood in silent prayer by the bed, eyes closed, hands clasped invisibly together beneath the full, heavy sleeves. Only the sliver of his face was visible. Dressed thus, the laws taught he was protected from the wandering demons of the air. Phadraig's theocracy had reversed the traditional directions of heaven and hell. The air above the planet's surface was hell; paradise was down below, in safe pockets where the demons couldn't reach.

Council taught that imperfect men could descend just twice in their miserable lives.

When they were born, when they died.

Council taught that women were favored above men.

The Witchman fixed Salamander with deadpan gray eyes.

'Fortunate woman, you are given the opportunity to lie within the Witchgoddess and enrich Phadraig. Stand.'

He didn't assist her. She didn't expect it.

But, dizzy in the corridor outside the door, she found a screened sedan chair waiting. The gilded woodwork was splashed with sacred fertility symbols; the hard seat inside was decorated with the Goat, the Bull, and the Virgin; the three Earth Signs. The chair was to be carried by four undernourished Uncleans, who took up the load when Salamander was heavily slumped. The Witchman snapped commands, thin lips curling back in harsh dislike. The Uncleans grimaced, staggered briefly beneath the weight. They had averted their eyes as the expectant mother stepped inside, behind the protecting screens. Now they carried the chair through a bare, dusty concourse, the staves digging into their undernourished shoulders. The Witchman strode behind, his contempt plain. These Uncleans were of Lesser Degree. In most other societies, they would have been called human beings. But not in Phadraig. One had a birthmark on his thigh, a second lisped when she spoke. A third had the affliction of blue eyes; the legs of the fourth were of different lengths. The Witchman was disgusted by such impurities. But the priests were forced to allow an increasing percentage of Uncleans to survive in Phadraig. In former times, they would have been drowned at birth. But the population was falling. Phadraig needed beasts of burden. It needed inferior beings to hate....

Leaving the high concourse, the chair passed doors of frosted glass with strange symbols on the panes. The passage was long. The Witchman didn't know the thoughts of the Unclean with blue eyes, whose brain was working beneath his unkempt shock of yellow hair—

*If we were to fight for Khassam when he comes ...*

They came to a hall which gave access to a vertical shaft. An open cage was waiting. Salamander twisted with pain inside the sedan. But she made no sound. Gritting her teeth, she dug in her nails until the palms of her hands were bleeding. *Lost ... going down!* In the cage, the Witchman pressed the button. He stood as far as he could from the ragged Uncleans, forcing them to huddle in a corner. The cage descended five hundred feet beneath the tower, to one of an intersecting maze of dank passages cut bare from the granite. Though at this level the passages beneath the hill were hardly below the level of the Burning River which circled the steep city, there were no horizontal exit passages. The mazes were self-contained.

The chair was carried steadily along the low, rocky corridor. An oil-lamp glimmered every fifty feet; the deep-set doors of empty cells yawned wide at irregular intervals. Salamander was set on a cot in one of these; it was a contemptible hole, cramped and unwholesome. From one corner, a tallow candle flickered on the slick damp surfaces and dark cracks of the rock. The cell had been incompletely hollowed; there was no definition between roof and wall, it was a hole in the ground. The door slammed, was locked. And she was left to give birth alone. In the eyes of Phadraig, she was privileged. To be alone with the Witchgoddess!

Now the contractions came more frequently. The cot creaked and groaned beneath her; the drab blanket fell aside, across the tin bowl on the floor which held a sharp knife and a length of cord. The surgical facilities were primitive. But there was no need of them. If the Witchgoddess could take care of the rising and the setting of the sun, She could certainly take care of lesser details. If infection or stillbirth was the result, then obviously the child was unfit to live. There could be no interference with the natural process of birth. It must be allowed to take it own course.

The Witchman dismissed the Uncleans, ordered them back to the Citadel for further duties. Crouching outside the door, he watched through the spyhole, and waited for the birth. Night grew over the city above. Down here, it was always night. The Witchman shivered as he waited; the air was dank, and he was young. He was just eighteen years old; it was his first Watch at a birth. He was proud of being a Witchman: he was exceptional; not two in a hundred belonged to the priesthood. He watched the woman's shadow twisting on the wall, ignoring the cramping of his body. He saw her teeth bite deep into the hem of the linen shift which was up around her neck. Her legs were crooked; the candlelight flickered on her swollen breasts and belly. Her back arched as the contractions pursued her more fiercely. The Witchman muttered fervent prayers. 'Let Norm Purity be served, Great Mother!' he intoned. 'Give blessing to this birth.'

He was a pious man, whose thoughts and seed were true. His breath was fast and shallow as the birth began; he crouched in the lee of the door, wrapping his arms against the drafts. And he thought only of Phadraig. As far as he was concerned, the woman was only a method for bringing a new child into Phadraig. Of course he knew that she was one of Aurum's daughters; the knowledge was general in the Citadel. But this was no more relevant to his feelings than the fact that her hair was brown.

The child was coming, but the birth was difficult. The

Witchman peered more closely at the shadowed, convulsive movements. The woman cried out loud, the despairing sound came muffled through the spyhole. Shadows jerked and thrust, skin gleamed, there came the sound of a slap, but no newborn bawling. The Witchman cursed, he couldn't see what was happening, the woman had moved, blocked his view. He squinted harder, his eyes watering, saw her lean for the knife, contorted face momentarily full-on to the candle flame. Still the body she held in shadow made no sound. *Born dead!* the Witchman feared, cursing her, but still watching as she severed the umbilical cord, knotted it as she was trained. The Witchman felt a prickling growth of fear and suspicion. The knife was dropped to the floor; shadows shifted. The Witchman realized that the chill he felt was internal, cellular. 'Witchgoddess, give me your protection!' he gasped, slightly frantic, thrusting the key into the lock.

He was about to enter and confirm what he feared when the woman shifted; for an instant the candlelight showed the face of a —

'Polypheme!' he hissed, thoroughly frightened. 'One eye! And . . .'

And something else which scared him worse. Something alien, cold, which froze his hand. Something Unclean, a wraith of shocking mind.

The glimpse was enough to condemn both mother and child.

Almost grateful, the Witchman fell back from the door.

*If it is more than polypheme,* he reasoned quickly, *then it is not my duty to go in and kill it. This is one for Caltioram. . . .*

His thought was grateful, also slightly malicious. He ran for the nearest available cage and ascended to the exit building, more than halfway up the hill. He wasn't surprised to find that many hours had passed. It was late in the night, dawn wasn't far distant, and the Wind after it. Leaving the building, he crossed a sloping square beneath the dour, cloudy sky. All about, the ascending and descending ranks of towers and crumbling piles were gaunt, lifeless; as yet there were no lights even from the High Towers which crowned the hill. The Witchman hurried through narrow streets, climbed a flight of stairs, traversed the halls of a shabby museum, knocked at Caltioram's door.

The telepath was a small man, dry and withered by age like a blasted grape. Technically, his talent rendered him Unclean. He'd managed to conceal the existence of the unwanted perception until past the age of thirty. Then he'd avoided execution by persuading Council that he could be useful. He could look inside the minds of newborn children to give judgment on the degree of mental impurity, if any. This could be dangerous. On other occasions, he was employed to check the purity of those like himself who'd grown to maturity before being suspected. Several times, this had almost been fatal.

But the mature mind wasn't what he feared most.

The chaos of a newborn mind – that was what would shatter him.

The Witchman was bending over his bed before he'd reacted to the knock. 'Polypheme,' the Witchman stated flatly. 'Get up, old man.'

The Witchman knew how the old man hated his duties. He shook the telepath into wakefulness, holding a lamp above his face.

Caltioram was momentarily dazed, defenseless, mousy.

'What . . . what is it? What are you doing here. . . ?'

'A young mind for you to read, old man. Get up!'

Suddenly, Caltioram found his bed very comfortable. He sensed doom.

'If the identification's made, you don't need me!' he protested.

'I sniffed something worse than polypheme . . . much worse. . . .'

'But you don't need me!' Caltioram insisted again, his voice shrill, his pale eyes wide. If only these sadistic young

Witchmen would stop torturing him; they wanted to see him dead! 'Polyphemes are automatically condemned. I'm not needed!'

But the Witchman was unmoved.

'You'll be condemned as well if you don't get up.'

Caltioram had no option. He rose and pulled on his robe of dyed and woven mewhound hair, hunted for a missing amulet while the Witchman bustled around the room, inspecting it, pulling aside the faded green curtains to let in the dawn. The light was as pale as the old man's face. The Witchman talked compulsively; he was still shaken inside. 'You hate your Unclean talent, don't you, old man?' he spat. 'I don't need to read minds to know how afraid you feel. You fear that one day you'll be sucked into a powerful newborn mind you can't control. Then where will you be, eh?'

Caltioram had no answer. Sensing that he'd never see this room again, he stood with eyes downcast to the floor.

'I am ready to go,' he said.

He felt more comfortable with the amulet in its pouch about his neck, but he expected nothing from it.

'Good. Come. There is no time to waste.'

The Witchman led him rapidly through the deserted museum and into the streets, walking so fast that the weak old man quickly fell back. But Caltioram was resigned; he refused to move any faster. He knew his time was ripe, though there was nothing solid which proved it. Ignoring the Witchman's gestures, he reflected that perhaps it was as well; he'd lived too long, and his life had been Unclean after all. Not just according to the laws, but according to his own definition. He'd used his talent selfishly; his life at the scales was little more than a sum of condemnations. He'd understood beyond the laws of Norm Purity to the causes which underlay them – essentially fear of past, present, and future; fear of life itself. The people of Phadraig would rather die in their illusions than acknowledge their own true characters. Caltioram knew that the world had changed and left Phadraig behind with nothing but history for meat. And he couldn't honestly judge humanity in the false measure called Norm Purity – but he'd spent forty years doing just that. True, he feared the Uncleans of Greater Degree; he feared that one was about to destroy him. But they were not to blame for their deformities, so designated by an artificial standard; he couldn't hate them like the rest of the people. He was one of them himself, though often enough he'd tried to forget it. He felt only sorrow for the poor beings born withered and strange, for those whose minds screamed oddly and thus brought his condemnation on themselves: his pity was greater for the mothers condemned with their Unclean children. Failed fathers were simply prevented from further Breeding by secret Council order, and their identities were never made public. But the women were luckier. They went to join the Witchgoddess, forever.

And his condemnations had been the price of a long life. He followed the impatient Witchman across the still deserted square, Fionnmachair, its flags white and dusty beneath his sandaled feet. Merchants were slowly gathering in the growing light, setting up their stalls and carts at the upper, southern side. Caltioram hardly noticed their eyes on him. His mind was lost in Phadraig, the city of the ancient past, built before the time of the Great Forgetting. When the suns bloomed and the waters died, when the mutations began. When humanity lost faith – save in a few surviving pockets. Phadraig had been one of these. But now, at last, Phadraig was dying. *Perhaps new empires will rise on its bones,* he thought.

The Witchman waited impatiently by the cage inside the hall which he'd left twenty minutes earlier. His gesture was impatient as the old man approached. 'Get inside!' Without answering, Caltioram entered the cage, refusing to meet the Witchman's eyes as the young Initiate followed, stabbing a button. The empty space became the fourth wall, indistinguishable from the other three. The cage descended silently. And Caltioram resolved his fear. He'd lived longer than he could ever have hoped, and to no purpose at all. If he was going to die, he'd do so with his self-respect.

Salamander waited in the cell, alone with her one-eyed child.

The door was locked; somehow she'd remembered to try it. She felt weak, she shivered incessantly, holding the child close with her left arm. She wouldn't – couldn't – look at it; it didn't move, or make a sound, hadn't so much as broken wind. It was alien, she could hardly believe it had come from her body, it seemed no part of her. But in her right fist she gripped the sharp knife; she was prepared to use it for a horrifying, unlawful purpose. Gaidhealla had warned her it might come to this. It wasn't unknown for crazed mothers to resist the destruction of their Unclean children. But it was unheard of for one of them to attack the Witchman who came to kill the child. Her mother had told her the Witchman would enter, suspecting nothing except a weak submission to the purity of fate. Gaidhealla had said that Caltioram would be called, that Salamander must take her chance, and strike....

But such a reality seemed impossible to her. The birth had been agony, difficult despite all her mental and physical training for the event. The child's head was unnaturally large, had come through only after unbearable pain; for a moment she'd passed out. Now she waited, shivering in waves as though caught in tidal vibrations. She heard the scrabbling in the lock, her heart pounded, the child stirred in her arms, she found herself looking down into the well of its eye....

She stood without stumbling, went behind the door as it began to swing open – but so slowly, as if in a dream, a widening wedge of light from the passage falling on the empty cot. Salamander's pain and tension escaped in quick, shallow breaths; she crouched beneath the level of the candle, found herself raising the sharp knife to her shoulder, poised, ready to deny Norm Purity forever, unaware where her strength and purpose came from. And the child was silent.

The Witchman cursed when he saw the empty cot.

'Stupid woman, come out; there's nowhere to hide!'

Caltioram hung back. And the Witchman's right arm came ahead of his body, reaching for where he imagined she'd be cowering with the hideous child. But instead of flesh he met with sharp steel. Salamander shut her eyes and stabbed downward with a dagger; the point passed through robing and flesh and jarred on bone. The Witchman yelled out loud in horror and fell back, unable to comprehend. Salamander, sobbing, threw herself around the opened door and collided with the wounded man who clutched his right arm incredulously. Her mind hysterical, she stabbed a second time, deep into his body. He stumbled back, eyes wide, half falling against the withered old man behind him. Salamander was scarcely aware of what she was doing, but she recognized Caltioram. She remembered an occasion as a child when the old man had been kind to her. Now she saw him trembling, trapped against the wall of the passage, the whites of his eyes staring with anguish, the horror of a burned brain printed on his lined face. Forgetting the Witchman who'd fallen to the ground, she shook her head, tears starting from her eyes; she stopped dead before her flight was even begun.

'Please ... please ...' she implored.

Behind her back the wounded Witchman pulled himself up onto his feet, reaching left-handed for his own knife tucked beneath the blood-stained front of his black robe, grimacing with determination. But the girl was immobilized by her sense of guilt, for the old man now began to crumple, clawing at his chest, his heart unable to withstand the force in the child which Salamander held so tight. He was overwhelmed by his proximity to such raw, chaotic forces. He realized that the child, if allowed to live, would become the fulcrum of immense changes. The realization was killed by a numbing breathlessness as the child looked at him full;

its face was smooth, ageless, it stared from its one black eye, curious, soundless. The laboring of Caltioram's heart threatened to burst his paper-thin chest; he knew that at last his abnormal receptiveness had killed him. Beginning to fall, he sensed vague movement behind the distraught, confused girl; saw the wounded Witchman stumbling forward, knife raised high. Caltioram tried to warn her, but no words emerged, only rattling breath which hissed out into her frozen face. With the last of his bodily strength, he succeeded in collapsing forward against the Witchman's arm, diverting the knife-thrust aimed at her back; the blade sliced across Salamander's ribs as she turned, as the Witchman screamed and fell again. Pain flared across her left side, blood welled against the linen of her shift, and she cried out. And Caltioram died.

The spell was broken by the hate she read in the Witchman's eyes.

The man started to crawl toward her feet; she fled, gasping.

She didn't realize she took the direction opposite to that in which she'd been brought to the cell. One thought, one command possessed her mind: she had to find a cage to take her and the child to the surface! On borrowed energy she stumbled faster; the Witchman pursued, breath rasping, uneven gait absurd but menacing. She fled for her life, closed cell doors flickering past her distended eyes, the ugly wound fretted by her blood-soaked shift. She'd dropped the knife, and her steps along the rocky rough-cut corridor were uneven with the child held against her breast. Slapping feet, whooping breath. Past a deserted intersection and to an open cage! She threw herself inside with the gaining Witchman not six feet behind; she pressed a button at random before falling exhausted to the cage's floor, body burning, child instinctively cradled. And the empty space became solid wall even as the Witchman threw himself desperately at it.

Salamander lay unconscious. She was spared his choked scream, didn't see the severed arm which fell to the floor of the cage. The arm terminated in a fist which still clenched the stained knife. It was followed through the air by a shred of black hood, a few drifting wisps of hair, flakes of flesh and bone.

Silence in the cage.

On the other side the Witchman was mortally wounded; he pulled himself away on his remaining arm. Blood ebbed fast from the stump of the other. A section of his skull was laid clean open. His eyes were already glazing with weakness, but fanatical purpose dragged him along the dim passage, a crawling creature which left a blood-trail in its wake. The alarm. Before he died, the alarm.

In the cage. The one-eyed child stared unblinking at the severed arm. It lay silent, couched against its fallen mother's body. Its skin was oddly tinted, an olive-yellow, smooth. Its face was strangely beautiful beneath a down of dark hair. Its eye lay in a slight declivity where the bridge of the nose should have been. The nose itself was little more than a nostriled mound, disturbing the plain of skin which stretched from cheek to cheek. Lips hardly existed; the mouth was a slit, yet the whole added up to weirdly perfect symmetry. The abnormality of other polyphemes – which, in Phadraig, accounted for perhaps one birth in every one hundred and fifty – constituted gross and ugly affliction. But there was something beautiful about this one-eyed, large-headed child, Caltioram's doom. It was not a human beauty, according to the standards of Norm Purity.

There was neither sound nor motion. There was a second button to be pressed before this cage would ascend. But Salamander was quite unconscious as blood continued to spread against her shift. The wound was deep; her mind was nebulous and murky with exhaustion. But presently, she was conscious, seemed to feel a tentative probing, the tremor of another will. The child's eye never left the severed arm.

Salamander's eyelids, malachite green, drooped up.

A sea of strain; she realized she shouldn't be conscious,

that in her condition unconsciousness should be natural. She had no volition.

But her horror was driven out by an obsessive purpose. Groaning, body throbbing, she dragged herself to the wall still holding the child; inch by inch, she pressed herself up toward the second button. 'Give me strength!' she hissed, not knowing where she sent the prayer, or whether it was she who sent it. It was answered. Her finger found and stabbed the second button. She slumped.

The cage rose. The polypheme ascended with its wounded mother to the surface of the Witchgoddess. This was the cage which the Witchman had descended in with Caltioram, and its exit was in a high old hall overlooking Fionnmachair. People gathering there to bargain and gossip had no suspicion of the approaching danger to their lives. For other than a protected Witchman to look on an Unclean of Greater Degree, or on its failed mother, meant damnation and expulsion from Phadraig as a Fallen One.

The cage carried an Unclean of Greater Degree and its failed mother toward pure citizens who would destroy them both.

Toward impure individuals with other intentions....

## 2 : Patrick Cormac

Now the dawn was full on Phadraig. The old city rose from the honeycombed hill like a bleached skeleton. On three sides, it was bounded and protected from assault by the corrosive reek of the Burning River, Red Kilmun. The fourth side of the hill fell to the narrow, liquid-locked neck of the peninsula formed by Red Kilmun. The rising ground up from the neck was barricaded by recently-built granite walls. They glared across the southern Wastelands at a dun range of low hills on the horizon.

The steep-sloped city exuded an aura of decay. The lower extremities of the avenues radiating down from the High Towers were greedy with weed. The surface of the Culane, the lowest of the horizontal ringways which circled Phadraig like quoits around a cone, was almost impassable in places. The banks of Red Kilmun had eaten closer through the centuries; now the air above the road fumed; its surface was littered with cindered slag. Most of the flatter, outlying areas close to the turgid chemical soup were abandoned to heat-cracked fields of mud carpeted with ash deposits. The peripheral buildings – mostly brittle towers and disintegrating warehouses – glowed red and gaunt like skulls at night, reflecting the river's glare. But dawn showed broken windows and jagged cracks, light fell on long-abandoned floors covered by concrete rubble and wind-shaped piles of dust.

Phadraig had been built for millions.

Now it was a ghost, retreated up the hill.

Only the High Towers retained a degree of faded glory.

The five slim pillars were the focus of Phadraig. Four were set in a square around the fifth, the highest, the Central Tower, exposed to the elements on the summit of the hill. The unknown makers had aimed at grandeur, punctuation, and other forgotten principles.

*One of these days, the Wind'll bring them down on top of us....*

Setting up his stall in Fionnmachair, Galmis Taskvaig looked up at the towers and thought his customary morning thought. To him they seemed to brood in shame, their summits caught in rising sun as yet invisible in this lower district. But the Tanner was biased, and he kept his blasphemous thoughts to himself. He spread his supply of pelts and cured leather on the trays before him. The pelts were verminous, and the leather wouldn't hold through a season. Taskvaig knew it. It was evidently the fault of the Servants. They couldn't be praying hard enough for righteous citizens like himself. Life was getting harder. Rivals and other traders bustled in the growing light, setting up their booths, running through their sales pitches, conversing and exchanging gossip with much head-shaking. At other stalls, early-risers bargained meat prices, hurrying the exchanges, keeping an eye on the sky's shifting colors. The Wind would come soon. Their warning would be the descent of haze which invariably preceded the short, vicious northern blast. Though the Witchgoddess was temperamental, the Wind was dependable throughout the summer. In other years it had been customary even for traders to remain indoors until the Wind was gone. But the hunters were returning empty through the Southern Gate this summer. And the spring harvest had been blighted. The scarcity was such that those who came to Fionnmachair after the Wind usually found the stalls and shops around the side quite empty.

But the Tanner, allotted two wards to support, was not selling any more pelts because of the food shortage. Impatient, pessimistic, he stroked his bushy muttonchops fiercely, wondering how he could grab customers from his competitors. He knew he could bellow out rock-bottom prices until he was hoarse and attract nothing but the derision of youths of sixteen and seventeen. Due to go out on their first expeditions in the autumn, they met here to pester the surly mew-hound hunters for information. They were a plague on his life; he had no sympathy for youth. It was hot already! He mopped his shaved brows with a cloth taken from a pocket in his striped overall. 'After the heat, the Wind, after the Wind, more heat!' he grumbled.

The wells were dry, the underground reservoir almost empty. No rain would fall for at least another two months. Then Phadraig would be a quagmire, despite its slope in all directions. The climate was extreme. But the citizens of Phadraig regarded it as the latest of their worries; Phadraig was an ancient jewel set in a greedy wilderness. The time was never long between one assault and the next. Ten years since the last siege. The Tanner had seen the signs and heard the rumors of a new invasion. His attitude was fatalistic. He would fight ferociously, if and when it became necessary. Until then, he would continue trying to sell his merchandise. He shrugged philosophically, and his eyes fell on a robed citizen inspecting leather at a rival stall. *He's almost plump; he must be rich,* the Tanner decided.

The prey seemed displeased, he pouted, and shook his head.

'It's to the credit of your taste that you're disgusted, sir!' Taskvaig bellowed at him. 'Come here instead. I've got what you're looking for; my trapper has not returned empty-handed yet this summer!'

But the barefaced lie interested the prey, and left his rival with a curse of an expression. With his most polite smile on his face, the Tanner sized up his prospective customer. He was unaware of the cage ascending its shaft to the exit in the hall directly behind his broad striped back.

Hands clamped on hips, Patrick Cormac strode up the north side of the Central Tower's flat concrete roof. A tall, powerful man in his late thirties, he was alone on the roof. There was nothing visible which explained his apparent agitation, the preoccupation on his face. Abruptly he stopped pacing; he stood introspectively. His pale, wide-spaced eyes wandered over Phadraig's north quarter, the steepest and least populated; his gaze slid northeast across the endless Wastelands to the horizon's mist-bloated sun. The Wastelands. They rolled away in all directions. From here, he could see no sign of life; bogs, plains, forests, and distant scarp appeared still and void. The apparent lack of activity was the illusion of distance, but the High Witchman was tense with expectancy and feverish calculation.

*Everything is still,* he thought, *waiting. . . .*

It was five days since the *eala* sent by Khassam had last been seen in the sky, hovering and buzzing in the middle distance, spying on Phadraig. Council had acted fast: the people were ordered not to look up at the sky if they wanted the Witchgoddess to receive them when they died. But it didn't make the ancient machines fly away. And if the Warlord had discovered and successfully activated these devices, there was no telling what else he had at his disposal. Or when he would strike. The Council had sent out scouts. But none returned. The High Witchman's eyes hardened on the north.

Somewhere out there, Khassam the Warlord approached, sworn to revenge the death of his father, sworn to replace Norm Purity with the Jerezid Dogmas, sworn to unite the whole of the old Middle Kingdom under his rule. The High Witchman turned away from the parapet.

'Grandiose ambition,' he mused. 'But he may take Phadraig.'

He shrugged. It wasn't the threat of invasion which preoccupied him. It was another matter which furrowed his drawn forehead so deep. He wasn't a handsome man. His features were irregular and pale, his hands were too big.

He'd escaped classification as an Unclean by a hair-breadth. Now, he was High Witchman. The titular ruler of Phadraig. The father of children by many women, none of them conceived in pleasure. The conception of children was too serious an affair to be left to chance or pleasure. Certain biological techniques had been preserved; insemination was artificial, carefully planned. But the proportion of those born according to the Norm continued to decline.

Patrick Cormac was tired of his stud captivity.

Political expediency disguised as the will of the Witch-goddess had overcome arguments which rejected his election as High Witchman on the grounds of genetic unreliability.

He knew now what he had to do.

He'd have abandoned Phadraig years earlier if Gaidhealla hadn't persuaded him to wait for the proper time – the time of the prophecy's fulfillment. Maelnagar's prophecy. The fulfillment was due. At last, he would be free of the Servants, of Council, of his prison. But the freedom, he knew, would only be relative. The yoke of fate was about to lay its burden on him. He remained still by the parapet, thinking of his dream from the night just past. The dream that signaled the setting in motion of long-awaited events.

*The child is born!*

His momentary exhilaration was dimmed by thought of Salamander.

A sudden puff of breeze tented the hems of his black cloak, but he made no move to hold them down. He heard a cough behind him, a deliberate sound, but he refused to turn. He knew it was the First Servant, parched and pedantic old Gobhan, who waited impatiently. He felt a brief amusement; he could imagine the expression on the old ascetic's face, could see those knotted silver eyebrows as though they were before him. He took every opportunity to insult the First Servant, who'd been chiefly responsible for forcing the Onerous Burdens of office upon him. The Council had feared the popularity of the Company Chatachain after Kalnakill's defeat. They'd had no option but to force the Company's leader to accept the greatest honor Phadraig could offer – the Onerous Burdens. The High Witchman was the embodiment of Norm Purity; the office was a harness for the strongest man. From that day on, he'd been the old man's prisoner. From that day – until this day.

Abruptly, he decided on his course of action. Without turning, he stepped up onto the parapet, stood exposed above the city, cloak wind-swirled around his neck. He heard a sharp intake of breath from behind. But the old man was too proud to call him down, though for all Gobhan knew the High Witchman was about to jump. Patrick looked down past the toes of his boots, down three hundred feet to the leaden dome of the Citadel which squatted at the base of the Central Tower. The Servants' barracks. The fifty senior Witchmen, and fifty Witchmothers. He never saw it without bitterness. But now, his expectation overrode the feeling.

*Iubhar should be in the Citadel now....*

Balanced against solitary puffs of breeze, his gaze went out to be withered by the glowing horseshoe of Red Kilmun; he shook his head very slowly. The people of Phadraig were doomed; their minds were rigid and tyrannized by belief. But now Salamander's child was born, Maelnagar's vision was firming into reality, everything was changed. It didn't matter if Phadraig was destroyed. It was a corpse already. He owed it nothing! His blond-bearded jaw thrust out in anger. His Company had saved Phadraig from pillage, and look how they'd been rewarded! The Company disbanded, and himself forced into a life of meaningless boredom. He'd never have accepted the election had Gaidhealla not sent warning that Gobhan's assassins would answer his refusal, that men of the Company were being watched, night and day. Gobhan! Behind his back, waiting like a vulture. Let him wait!

The First Servant came to the roof to confer with the High Witchman. The consultation was a daily formality, marred by the younger man's bitter tongue. Gobhan was quite capable of bearing the insults, though he felt that the High Witchman's lack of dedication was a insult to the Witchgoddess. He couldn't understand the man even now; he was violently emotional, as Gobhan could never be. Hadn't the Council done him a great honor? What did the man want to do with his life, rot in the Wastelands with his bloody playmates? There was no place in an ordered society for the Company Chatachain. True, the Company had saved the city. But only because the Witchgoddess approved it. Wasn't that obvious? But the Company had been proud and overbearing – many of them had gone so far as to deny the Witchgoddess any part in the victory whatsoever, had instead boasted of their own strength and courage. Mindless children, with brawn and steel where their brains should have been. Many of them were lucky to have escaped classification as Uncleans. Including Patrick Cormac.

Gobhan knew how much the High Witchman despised him. But he didn't take it personally. He took nothing personally: he was the First Servant, a channel of the Witchgoddess.

Angular, he left the cockpit and strode across the flat concrete.

His face was stiff beneath the heavy brown hood; he disliked exposing himself to the unclean air. He suspected this was why the High Witchman invariably chose the roof for these meetings, exercising one of his more petty prerogatives. He detoured around the rim of one of the giant cooling fans which once, in a forgotten time, had circulated air within the now largely deserted Central Tower. The High Witchman stood by the northern parapet, looking into the sun, perhaps watching for the *eala*. He didn't seem to hear the First Servant's approach. It was possible that Gobhan was being deliberately ignored. The First Servant coughed. The High Witchman continued to ignore him before, deliberately provocative, stepping onto the narrow parapet.

Gobhan's thin lips tightened. His eyes narrowed to see the ring which clasped the High Witchman's straight fair hair at the nape of his neck. The First Servant had seen it before. It was gold, embossed with the emblem of the Company Chatachain – a snarling wildcat, generously fanged.

*What does this mean?* he wondered, cold, calm.

He decided not to mention the ring. No doubt the High Witchman was merely looking for new ways to try his patience. He waited, tiring of the game. But he refused to plead like a mother with a tree-climbing child! However, this could not go on forever. 'The view is pretty,' he commented acidly, 'but we have urgent matters to discuss. The citizens must be mobilized and armed to withstand the barbarians, as the sacred laws lay down. You are required to approve our schedules.'

The High Witchman turned and stepped down, smiling curiously.

'Give me back my Company,' he said. 'We defeated Khassam's father when the ancient defense schedules failed last time. Doesn't it occur to your sagacity that the same could happen for Khassam?'

Gobhan's eyes glinted like icicles on either side of the bridge of his long, thin nose. 'There is no Company,' he stated flatly. 'You are the High Witchman. There will be no Company.'

'Patrick Cormac had a Company. Or have you forgotten him?'

'Patrick Cormac has no existence in the Witchgoddess!'

'But perhaps he has existence in Patrick Cormac?'

'You know there will be no Company! Council directs!'

The High Witchman shrugged; his face was slant and masked. But the old man thought he detected a nervousness, a hint of strain, and again he wondered about the ring. What was he playing at now? And the light in those pale eyes was odd – proud, mocking. . . .

'What if we fail to repel the barbarians this time?' he demanded, almost lightly. 'What then, First Servant?'

'The Witchgoddess will protect us!'

'Of course. Forgive me. I forgot we have fate on our side.'

The faintest of angry colors were stealing into Gobhan's cheeks.

'Why do you taunt me with your heresy, your mockery, your —'

'Not heresy,' Patrick interrupted, 'only the doubt of a reasonable mind. Phadraig is weak – and Khassam is determined. And the people are sullen, Gobhan. They won't put up much resistance; the Uncleans will probably defect altogether. But of course – the Witchgoddess will protect us....'

The sky grew sullen and heavy, seemed about to settle on their heads. Before the First Servant could reply, Patrick's attention left him, was drawn past the cooling fan to the access cockpit. He saw a figure scrambling onto the rooftop, come running toward them. Iubhar! Patrick Cormac was racked on tension. If his friend should bring the news he expected....

'Why are we being interrupted?' Gobhan snapped. 'The man runs, approaches without any respect at all! It's your servant – I insist that you reprimand him!'

But the taller man gazed up at the sky. The haze was starting to descend, limiting their eyes already, blotting out the sun. Wind puffed tentatively, experimentally. By some trick of the atmosphere, the glowing slap-slap of Iubhar's feet approaching sounded almost deafening in Patrick's ears. He glanced down at Gobhan.

'If his news is unimportant,' he said, 'then I'll censure him.'

## 3 : Iubhar

Many people had been fooled into believing that Iubhar was as slow and dim-witted as his customary indolent expression suggested. On occasion, some had died because of this mistake, learning too late how fast and sure he could act when the situation demanded it. Wiry and compact, his swart face was framed by a neat fringe of beard which grew from one ear to the other via the underside of his cleft, aggressive chin. The illusion of indolence which he fostered so carefully was accentuated by pronounced facial bone structure. His eyes lay deep and heavily-lidded behind a shelf of high cheekbones. Customarily he wore an amulet of banded onyx about his neck; not that he had any belief in its efficacy.

But it kept his woman happy to believe he was protected.

Patrick Cormac had always valued Iubhar above his other comrades.

He could be pompous, loudmouthed, self-righteous, and sulky, but his grasp of practical reality was greater than Patrick's. The High Witchman had refused to accept the Onerous Burdens unless Iubhar came with him from the disbanded, disarmed Company, answerable to him alone. The wrangling had been interminable. The demand was eventually conceded. Iubhar joined him in the Central Tower. Ten years he'd stayed at hand, countering Patrick's frequent depressions and rages with sour, mordant, good advice. He knew Patrick Cormac better than Cormac knew himself. They'd grown together, fought together, saved each other from fates which included death. The First Servant had always intrigued to drive them apart, without success. If anything, their mutual trust had grown. Patrick depended on Iubhar to keep him human, to drink with him, jeer at his morbid fantasies, and bring him news of their old Comrades, of the Company. But as the years drifted past, the news grew thin. And by the end of the decade the Company was dispersed, driven from the strength of its former collective identity by the persecution of time and Council alike.

This summer saw a change in Patrick's moods, never stable at the best of times. The High Witchman became withdrawn and contemplative; spent many hours closeted alone with a reading lamp and books – books which nobody in Phadraig, let alone the High Witchman, could openly quote. He resisted every effort by Iubhar to draw him from his shell, merely shaking his head and smiling quietly at every new attempt to make him explain. When he had the mind for it, he held his counsel so close and tight that not even Caltioram could have read the oblique, intuitive currents of his mind. Iubhar became totally exasperated by his exclusion from Patrick's confidence. Finally, he rejected conscience and confronted his leader with the rumors going around the Citadel. It seemed very possible that the advancing pregnancy of Aurum's daughter had a lot to do with Patrick's withdrawal. And current scandal suggested that he was not only the father of her child – but the father by natural means. One night, Iubhar blurted it out. To be hurt and infuriated when the silk-robed High Witchman turned from his meal and burst into raucous, totally unexpected laughter.

'Why do you laugh, Patrick? I'm only reporting what's openly said in the Citadel. I find nothing to laugh at!'

'Iubhar, what else do you expect from such witless minds? The truth? You could give them truth on a plate, but they wouldn't recognize it!'

But there was something harsh behind the humor, and

the answer was no answer; it was an evasion of the question.

Iubhar became grim and silent like the High Witchman, affected by the cloud which shrouded Patrick this summer, unable to break through.

Until the night before, when Patrick had at last burst through the clouds which embroiled him, opened out, taken Iubhar into his confidence.

They were alone in one of the innermost of Patrick's extensive, largely deserted apartments on the third floor of the Central Tower. He employed this wide, cluttered, pungent-smelling, windowless room as a laboratory. Sometimes he turned to the ancient mother science of alchemy for relief from the pressures of his imprisonment. This curious hobby was an ill-kept secret. Iubhar didn't believe that Patrick hoped to transmute anything other than his own black moods. The endless process of distillation, sublimation, and combination was an absorbing, mentally-soothing ritual. Patrick once told Iubhar that the hoped-for physical transmutation was a secondary aim of the work; that the prime aim of the ancient alchemists had been the transformation of the spirit. Iubhar had merely grunted, and advised him not to speak about it outside these locked and guarded doors.

'One day, you'll goad Gobhan into ending the pretense,' he'd warned.

The High Witchman had affected to find the prospect amusing.

'It would embarrass the old devil to charge me with heresy!'

'He can always arrange for an "accident,"' he was answered, dourly.

Last night, they were in this room at the same time as Salamander was being taken into the Witchgoddess. Patrick was heating a mixture of nitrates, sulphur, and carbon in a sealed rock crystal receptacle. He was over on a bench beside the athanor set in the bland-paneled wall. Iubhar was well back on the other side of the room, puffing at his pipe, deceptively phlegmatic. There was a good chance of the mixture exploding. It was a miracle Patrick hadn't killed both of them yet. Frequently, he didn't seem too interested in what he was doing. Last night was no exception. For suddenly he'd turned down the flame, swung around on Iubhar, and sought out where the wiry man lounged in the shadows.

'Iubhar, you must do something for me tomorrow morning.' The High Witchman chose words with care. 'Go to the guard-house in the Citadel. Be there by sunrise. Be very alert for news of anything . . . unusual. If you hear of something which has . . . never happened before, bring it to me on the roof at once, before anybody else.' Then he paused, he left the bench, crossed the room and leaned on a table stacked with jars.

'This'll be for the Company, not the Council.'

Iubhar heard the words. He placed his carved briar very carefully on the nearest flat surface. He scratched his brown bush of hair; an amazed, lopsided grin spread across his indolent face.

'The child is due?'

Patrick's answer was an evasion.

'I want to leave Phadraig forever. I want you to come with me, into the Wastelands. I can't tell you the reasons yet.'

Iubhar eyed him cannily.

'This has been going on for months. Why so secret?'

He shook his head with disgust. But he couldn't suppress his joy. And he couldn't hide his disbelief at words only now sinking in:

'Did you say – *leave Phadraig forever*—?'

So many emotions fought for the High Witchman's face that his expression was fearful.

'Forever!' he affirmed harshly. 'No coming back. Yes?'

Iubhar leaned over the other side of the table, over jars of green and orange and purple powders. 'This isn't a joke?

Is it to do with Khassam? But you know how I feel. I'll come, if you ask me.'

Part of Patrick's face relaxed into a smile.

'Good! Who else? Who's left of the Company? Gnorl? Liam? Scalaman? Or is the rogue too comfortable in his brothel? Are there others? You must find and alert them tonight, say the Company lives and has need of them. Tell them to be ready at dawn. I cannot tell you what will happen on the roof tomorrow. Trust me, whatever happens, but act surprise for Gobhan's benefit. This affair is long-awaited. Now, before you go, one more thing I must show you. In the athanor.'

And Iubhar was exhilarated to see him draw from the back of the salvaged ancient electric furnace, a potent slice of memory.

'Your torchblade! Kalnakill's spit! All this – is really real!'

'Yes – now go. You'll know where to find this tomorrow. Be ready.'

They drank to it. Iubhar left the Central Tower. Quickly.

So Iubhar was lounging about in his usual invisibly receptive fashion as the sun rose on Phadraig, a wiry man half melted into the dark brown paneling of the guard-house lobby. But within five minutes, his pretense of inaction had deserted him and he was making for the roof of the Central Tower. A distraught Witchman had rushed into the duty office with an incredible story. Iubhar made sure he was within earshot; it wasn't difficult. It seemed the man had answered an alarm sounded from Level 9, Corridor 16. He'd found the sender of the alarm dead on the floor beneath the bell in a pool of his own blood. The dead man's right arm and part of his head were missing. The Witchman had followed the blood-trail to the lip of the nearest cage-shaft. The cage was gone. Farther down the passage, he'd discovered the telepath Caltioram lying dead beside an open cell door, an expression of peace on his face. It was quickly established with much shouting and contradiction that the dead Witchman had been observing the birth of a first-time mother; the mother was known to be Salamander. Their knowledge of the rumors contributed to the growth of consternation. The implications were terrible. A failed mother at large in Phadraig, with an Unclean of Greater Degree which had already killed. And the Wind about to hit. It was the first crisis of this kind those in the duty office had experienced; they didn't know what to do, and they jabbered contradictory orders and recommendations at each other. Nothing could be done without the authority of the High Witchman, or Council, which meant the First Servant. Nobody dared to take an uncommanded initiative. Iubhar slipped away, without anyone having asked what he was doing there. As he went, he shouted at several Witchmen that the Duty Officer had sent him to find Gobhan. With luck, it could add to the confusion. For he began to understand what was going on, or thought he did.

Grit scurried, lodging in Iubhar's beard; the color of the sky was dreadful. Iubhar delivered the news to the High Witchman, paid the First Servant no more respect than a cursory nod.

Gobhan heard out his rush of words with outraged disbelief plain on his sparse face. But he was given no opportunity to speak his mind.

'It was well-timed.' The High Witchman's voice was flat; he nodded at the sky. 'The Wind is due. This is Khassam's doing. His agents have infiltrated us and abducted the woman and the monstrous child – just as they kidnapped Ranza ten years ago!' His hard voice rose in a sudden controlled passion, and he turned on Gobhan. 'The laws are in danger. If this child lives, they will collapse. There is only one course of action. Cuyahogan must be released immediately.'

Iubhar's heart missed a beat; his mouth went dry. And he forgot completely that his outraged surprise was supposed to be an act.

'Cuyahogan? You're insane! There are no spies in Phadraig. This is one woman, alone. A squad will be enough, surely!'

The First Servant, completely taken aback, suspected complicity.

But the Servant of the Voice was genuinely horrified. Gobhan eyed the High Witchman uneasily. Not even he would have suggested releasing the malign, ferocious golem. The step was extreme. Could he have misjudged the High Witchman's zeal? He doubted it. Spies in Phadraig? He doubted that also. But what if it were true? Certainly the city faced a major crisis; it might in any case become necessary to release the feral golem, the artificial creature of the ancients, even though it would mean the death of as many people as invading barbarians. True, the situation was unprecedented. No mother had ever escaped before. Which lent a certain credence to this talk of spies and agents. And the unfortunate citizens fated to look on the mother or the child would have to leave Phadraig as Fallen Ones, to die in the Wastelands. Perhaps therefore it was better to be sure, and set the golem on the woman's trail. But the last time Cuyahogan had been used to track down fugitives, it had run amok, killing forty people before being brought back under control. And it hadn't been animated since.

For the first time in his life, Gobhan found himself arguing a course of moderation. The confusion this created in him was as Patrick Cormac had calculated. Iubhar waited silent to one side, unable to believe that Patrick knew what he was doing. Cormac waited while the First Servant spread bony hands, almost in supplication, too surprised to argue forcibly. 'Surely it's not necessary to release the golem. One woman! It's as the Servant of the Voice said! We can take care of her and the child without such extreme measures!'

'The laws, Gobhan,' grated the High Witchman, face glaring broad and inflexible. 'You're sworn to protect the laws. You're always lecturing me about the laws. Now the laws are threatened, you contradict me, you waste time. My order is given; it will be carried out!'

'It will be countermanded in Council!' flared the First Servant.

'By which time Khassam's agents will have escaped with the woman and child, you idiot! Release Cuyahogan now! I order it!'

'There's a trick here!' Gobhan shouted up into his face. 'You'd never do this, not to her; it's well-known how you feel for her!'

But the High Witchman ignored this sneer and turned toward the southern parapet, as though reacting to something the other two hadn't heard. The air was uncertain, dust swirled and eddied over the city, the sky was almost on top of the Central Tower. They followed him with some difficulty. And were stopped by thin, distant cries which drifted to them from far below on the western side. 'Listen!' snapped the High Witchman, motioning them to the lip of the parapet. 'And look!'

Gobhan and Iubhar obeyed reluctantly. They eyed each other suspiciously, mutually embarrassed and perplexed by their seeming agreement.

*I trust you, Patrick,* thought Iubhar, *but where are you going?*

Then he looked down toward Fionnmachair, following the panicky sounds. The square was already indistinct through the growing haze which gripped the city, blotting the leprous bogs of the Wastelands from view. But Iubhar could see the scattering ant-figures of Fallen Ones clear enough. He scratched his brown shock of hair, glanced uncertainly at the High Witchman, who leaned so close into Gobhan's taut face that the old man felt physically threatened. 'See? While you waste time arguing, the Unclean child is taken across the city! And Khassam's vicious agents expose its face for our citizens to see. Many damned Fallen Ones will leave Phadraig soon. And you stand here, Gobhan, quibbling about Cuyahogan's release while their miserable numbers mount!' His cheeks were flooded with color, his eyes burned like ice, his anger mounted. 'Waste no more time; order Cuyahogan set on the track of our enemies. Or Phadraig is dead. Do it – I have the authority – Council isn't met yet – do what you like then!'

Iubhar hadn't heard Patrick shout for a long time. And the only time he'd ever seen his face so contorted was in battle. He was baffled. He could see the First Servant trembling in confusion, almost broken by the rage. The moment stretched. Wind moaned, tugged, making their situation atop the Central Tower more perilous by the instant. And Gobhan had taken enough. He stepped back, his lip curled. 'It will be done!' He lashed Patrick Cormac with the words as he spun on his heel. 'Cuyahogan will be released but you will answer for it. Mark my word!'

He departed furiously, feet attacking the weathered concrete.

Iubhar withheld his questions until Gobhan had disappeared into the cockpit. Then he started forward. 'I know what you told me last night, Patrick,' he said, very carefully, as though humoring a madman. 'But – what are you doing? You evade my questions, but I know how you love that woman. Cuyahogan will destroy her! And many others!'

His voice trailed off, puzzled, as the murk closed in about them.

Patrick had stared wrathfully at the cockpit for a good many seconds. Then the anger melted swiftly and he heaved a sigh of deep relief, turned to Iubhar, clapping both hands onto his friend's shoulders. 'I didn't think I could persuade him, but you must admit, his expression was marvelous to see. . . .'

Iubhar lost his temper with Patrick's mannered, conversational tone.

He stepped back, throwing Patrick's hands from his shoulders.

'Why are you playing these games?'

'Games are all we ever play.'

'Explain! Or may I be cursed if I don't throw you down to Fionnmachair!'

'I told you not to be surprised. I did warn you.'

'But you can't control Cuyahogan!'

The High Witchman's face became sober again.

'The golem's part was planned long ago. I had to engineer its release. No – I can't control it – but I know another who can.'

Iubhar was unconvinced; they confronted each other, close.

'And these abducting spies of Khassam's?'

'A pretext.' Patrick shrugged. 'To confuse Gobhan.'

'You knew that Salamander would escape? You arranged it?'

'Do you remember Maelnagar's prophecy?'

The smaller man snorted. 'Prophecies! Give me an answer!'

'I think you know it,' replied Patrick equably. They were now shadowed in the haze. 'But I'll jolt your memory —

*'One-Eye came from Two-Eye*
*And Two-Eye came from Three*
*But Three-Eye bowed to One-Eye*
*Who saw what none would see —'*

'Heretical gabble,' insisted Iubhar. 'Meaningless rubbish.' But he couldn't conceal his worry or his curiosity. For the High Witchman was shrouded in penumbral gloom, his voice had echoed in the thickness of the sinister pre-Wind calm, and he had invested the words of the prophecy with an ominous weight of importance. And when he spoke again, his voice was simple. 'Not so. Two-eye has just carried One-Eye across Fionnmachair, as we vaguely saw and heard. They go to meet Three-Eye, who will bring Cuyahogan under control. Shortly they will leave Phadraig. We will follow in support, to join them where and when we can.'

Iubhar stood. A curious, fateful shiver ran through him. Briefly, dimly, he sensed an abyss of cause and effect beyond his capacity to understand. But he sensed that they trembled on its brink. His mind felt dizzy. He moved a step away from the parapet.

'And who is Three-Eye?' he demanded, voice hushed.

'The seer, Gaidhealla. Her wisdom is of the Third Eye.'

Iubhar made a disgusted sound. 'Typically oblique,' he commented. 'I'm glad to lack your faith in prophecy. But – how did you know what would happen this morning? You are isolated, except for me. Who told you?'

'I dreamed,' said Patrick Cormac, coming closer, grinning. 'And last night, I dreamed again. It was the end of a long battle. The High Witchman is dead. I am alive again. And so is the Company.'

The Wind hit Phadraig. It whipped without warning from the dull purpling sky, destroyed the silence, snapped at the hems of their cloaks. In their intensity they'd almost forgotten about the Wind; Iubhar was taken off-balance, the Wind swooped and swirled and wrenched greedily at him, threw him staggering at the parapet. He roared with anger, Patrick dived, took him low around the knees, slammed him down flat on the concrete. They lay there, recovering, while the Wind shrieked like a flock of banshees. Iubhar, wide-eyed, nodded frank gratitude. They crawled for their lives to relative safety behind the two-foot-high rim of the nearest cooling fan. Visibility was down to a few feet. To hear each other, they had to shout. The sky raved purple-black about them; ragged streamers of vapor shot across the top of the Central Tower. The concrete vibrated perceptibly; they were shaken on top. Crouching low, Patrick Cormac brought his mouth to Iubhar's ear and started yelling instructions until he was hoarse.

'Listen well! I must go down to Council shortly. You must go to my room, gather clothes and equipment suitable for the Wastelands, take my torchblade – there is no danger from the coils! Then take what you need, go to find Gnorl, and Liam the Songmaker, drag Scalaman out of his whorehouse, take any others we can trust who are left. Meet me at the porch of the Black Bear Inn in Madadhmachair an hour from now. I'll come disguised as a penitent Fallen One. I have an excuse to leave Council; my route is prepared. Be ready to leave immediately! But move carefully, Cuyahogan will be on the streets, and deadly until Gaidhealla brings it under control! Now, no more, no time. Say no good-byes! None!'

'My woman!' bawled Iubhar, aggrieved. 'I must ...'

'No!'

Patrick turned to go. The din was ear-splitting, the demons howled. Iubhar pulled him back. 'Wait!' he screamed. 'This one-eyed child. We are going to *protect* it? What is it? What will it see that nobody else will see?'

'How do I know?' shouted Patrick, tearing himself free. 'How can I? It's the only one who'll know! And it won't – if we fail it. My visions are limited; I don't even know where we're going. But forget Phadraig. It's meat for Khassam. And good riddance. If I'm here any longer Gobhan'll send up a squad. Only Uncleans can withstand the demon Wind. It might even be so! But do as I say, and we'll get out of here with our skins intact!'

And he was gone, crawling away on hands and knees to the sanctuary of the cockpit and the stairs below, swallowed up before Iubhar could interrupt again. The smell of scorched earth lashed out of the Wind, a sign that it was nearly over. Iubhar was left in the lee of the cooling fan, riding out the storm with the expression of a sphinx. With Patrick Cormac gone, his mind began to function again. Rueful, he realized he wasn't going to get answers. Somehow, he was into Patrick's new cause without knowing what it was. It had been like that in the past. Since his youth, Patrick Cormac could sweep people along on his tidal enthusiasms. People tended to abandon their own causes when they saw his. The Company Chatachain, flamboyant and heretical, had been a one-man band. It had died when he was trapped by the Onerous Burdens. Now, it might live again. For some obscure, disturbing purpose. Iubhar realized that he'd committed himself to the protection of a newborn being whom, a day before, he'd have seen dead without a qualm. One-Eye? Polypheme? Unclean of Greater Degree? A denial of Norm Purity? But what was Norm Purity? He'd never bothered to question it deeply. Now that he did, it was clear. Norm Purity had died of old age, Phadraig was a corpse, with people who pretended they were alive and the rest of the world was dead. It *was* good riddance. Phadraig was sterile. The Wastelands were fertile. There was no more to be argued. It was time for something new. As for his questions, the whole world was a question. Iubhar shrugged.

Shortly, the Wind died as quickly as it had risen. The building stopped vibrating. Iubhar continued to sit for a while, thinking.

*She'll curse when she finds me gone. But I've stayed with her a whole decade; what more could she expect?*

He snorted with sardonic humor, stood, scratched particles of dust down his back, shook them from his tunic, scratched grit from his hair. 'The world's mad!' he insisted vehemently at the sky. 'But why should I worry? I'm protected by prophecy. What more could a bad man ask for? And Patrick Cormac is reborn! Why, I truly believe I could face Cuyahogan, and jeer, and spit at those monstrous razor-lined limbs with impunity!'

An instant later, he wondered if his satirical boast might not have been thrown too soon. For the warning klaxons began to wail their mournful two-tone notes out over Phadraig, ordering the people off the streets.

Cuyahogan was at large.

## 4: Cuyahogan

Up the cage had come, up, up, rising up to Fionnmachair. . . .

Within it, two eyes were shut; one was open . . . unblinking. . . .

At his stall the Tanner had the plump man where he wanted him, picking over the trays with a petulant, supercilious expression. But the prospective customer evidently thought no more of Taskvaig's material than he had of the pelts presented by the Tanner's rival. Shaking his head, he started to turn away. Taskvaig reached after him, sweating freely, ignoring the chatter of idling youths nearby.

'Feel the texture of this leather, sir; tough, but pliable, last a lifetime. . . .'

'. . . But Khassam claims sisterhood for Ranza's daughter . . .'

The Tanner, cut off, regarded the loudmouthed youth with mounting irritaton. The boy paid his glare no attention. The Tanner tried to pick up his pitch again before he lost the plump man to the crowds. But the sharp voice cut right through. The Tanner turned to regard the loudmouthed group with hands on hips and fire in his eyes. The door into the cage-shaft hall was to his left. But he had no reason to be aware of it.

'Ranza was pregnant with Aurum's daughter when she was kidnapped before Cormac drove out the horde. Now Khassam claims a precedence here on her behalf!'

The red-haired youth in mottled suede was incredulous.

'Pretext, what do you think?' demanded a crop-headed companion.

'Just another of many,' grunted a rake-thin boy in shabby green vest and trousers. 'He also flies the Jerezid banner and claims he will liberate Phadraig's Uncleans!'

'Of course, the Witchgoddess will save us, as She did before!'

The fourth youth's voice was derisive. Roguishly, he looked around for approval. Taskvaig felt his blood about to boil; the plump citizen on the other side of the stall was a study in contempt, pudgy beringed fingers curled on a tray. The argument grew more animated, attracted more attention. 'Cudrun,' interrupted the youth in suede, greatly ironic. 'You forget Khassam's armies of men and unmen assembled in the Metal Forests! You forget there is no Company Chatachain! You forget that Patrick Cormac is . . .'

'Keep your voice down, fool!' hissed the shaven one, anxious.

'. . . And what will the Witchgoddess do about the *eala?*' continued the red-haired mocker. But he lowered his voice. 'It is prophesied that Phadraig's last days will be attended by giant metal swans roaring from the sky with the voices of angry hounds. . . .' He laughed, raised his head and saw the Tanner's wrath, and called out impudently, 'How would you like to fly in one of the *eala*, Tanner, up there in the demon sky, just like the ancients did. . .?'

'Go!' shouted Taskvaig, his whiskers bristling. 'Go and tell Council what to do! Your inane jabbering drives my customers away. You waste my time, and the Wind is almost due!'

The rake-thin boy gaped with theatrical astonishment. And the one in suede jeered. 'There's no customers for vermined pelts like those! And it would be an insult to an Unclean to be made to wear your leather. Why should we stop speaking for your bad temper?'

The Tanner started around the side of his stall in a fury.

Heads turned and eyes lit up at neighboring stalls. 'I'm going to give you the hiding you deserve!' howled Taskvaig, flinging a hairy fist which the youth dodged easily, laughing. But then the boy stumbled and his red head slammed into the plump man's chest, taking them both to the ground. The citizen pulled himself up rapidly, dusting himself off as he did, mouth pursed into an angry dimple. The Tanner rounded on the cornered youth, murder in his eyes. The redhead was dazed by the collision; his friends were edging through the crowd, ready to rush the Tanner and hold him off —

A woman screamed.

The sound burst shattering from a neighboring stall. It cut through heads; it froze the Tanner, who'd bent to drag the redhead to his feet. It jerked many eyes first to the screamer, then to the cause of her terror. It was fatal. The sudden babble of crazed fear rose, then trailed off as the owners of these eyes went rigid, trapped numb in realization.

They were Fallen Ones.

They included the angry citizen and two of the youths.

The Tanner and his enemy were surrounded by onlookers who screened them; their eyes had been locked in hate. The Tanner dropped the boy and turned away, trembling, hardly daring to see the reflections of disaster on so many faces about him.

Silence.

Just a puff of breeze, the sound of faltering footsteps....

The haze grew slow on those hiding against the dirty tiles or behind the stalls, fighting the insanely attractive impulse to take just one look. Those already lost stared without movement; the image of wounded Salamander and her Unclean burden was lava in their minds.

It meant that they were Fallen.

Certain that they were damned, they were damned, thoroughly damned according to Norm Purity.

Now they had nothing left to do but abandon Phadraig

and life itself.

They had nothing to take but memory of the one-eyed child, memory of the piteous horror on the woman's face.

On his knees by his stall, the Tanner was jellied by fear. He could hear the unsteady footsteps closing behind him. His conscience was bad. He became sure they were feet of fate, directed toward him in particular, bearing a special damnation. Hastily he implored the Witchgoddess to recall his many donations and symbolic purifications. 'No closer!' he insisted tremulously through clenched teeth, his eyes shut tight. 'I don't have the practical experience to survive in the Wastelands . . . please, lady . . . no closer . . . I fear . . .'

The feet passed him by in the midst of his babbling.

The haze was fully descended. The Wind would hit them at any second. Though weaker here than on top of the Central Tower, it could still tumble a grown man down the streets and break his head against a wall. Many roused themselves to flee to safety, keeping their eyes well down. The sound of the uncertain feet faded into the distance, haze-concealed. Taskvaig pulled himself beneath his stall as he usually did for the Wind. His heart pounding, he tied the flaps down securely. The Wind pounced, keening into Fionnmachair, sweeping along this western side of the hill, swooping, gusting, flinging rubble through the air. The square emptied save of those who didn't care whether they died in or out of Phadraig.

Up the hill, beyond the arid gardens which surrounded the High Towers, a squad of Witchmen waited behind the gray walls of the Citadel. Waiting for the Wind to drop. Waiting for Cuyahogan to be brought out.

If the Tanner had known they were bringing Cuyahogan, he wouldn't have stayed where he was.

Salamander had reopened her eyes, dragged herself to her feet, left the cage, and stumbled to the exit from the hall: all against her will. She fought, she hung back, she held onto the carved doorposts, resisting the urge to walk out on

Fionnmachair, to doom the many. But she was dizzy and weak, without control; it took most of her own strength to hold the child firm against her. The wound bled fresh with every violent movement; it sapped her. And the command to go out was too powerful to fight against for long.

*The Witchmen will have you. Go to Gaidhealla. Run! Now!*

Her feet refused to obey her, they were dragging her from the shadows, she wasn't moving: she was being moved! Her thoughts were veiled and weak. What good was it? How could they escape? What could Gaidhealla do? Now she was in the doorway, looking out on the ranks of stalls and barrows, at the energetic crowd. They gestured, bargained, and argued as if life were too short to waste an instant. Sick with despair, her green-rimmed eyes brooded on the Tanner's back, on the plump man facing, on others facing who hadn't seen her and her burden yet. She should hide the child! It wasn't possible. The external compulsion to move out was too pressing. It wasn't a compulsion of prophecy; it was this thing in her arms, she was sure. It was making her do this! She heard the youths arguing, but got no meaning from their words. It made her miserable beyond her own misery to think they'd turn unlucky eyes upon her, and thus be damned according to the laws. Condemned to the Wastelands in futile search for the mythical Savior of the Fallen Ones. His abode was said to lie high above the volcanic peaks called the Pilgrim's Doom. Storms raged incessantly there; electric energies flayed reeking mires in the bowls of steep-sided valleys.

Her command? – or the child's?

She didn't know. All she knew was her pain, the forward movement of her bare feet coming down heavy on the tiles of Fionnmachair, and the child in her arms. All she saw were those she was about to doom – to plains of matted weed riding sluggish on the lifeless eastern sea, into glowing quicksands, poisonous clouds of dust, into waiting jaws. Some would stumble into crumbling ruins inhabited by spiteful, aberrant beings. Many would fall at the first hurdle – Red Kilmun.

There was Khassam with his army.

And the one-eyed child she held.

Then the woman saw Salamander, saw the child, and screamed.

Salamander limped out through the rabble and into the frozen silence, her mind naked, feet taking an unchosen direction. She heard and saw nothing of the people she passed; her body was forced into a broken half run in order to reach the square's southwest corner before the Wind hit. Racked by unbearable physical pain, she sobbed, for the first time cursing the creature silent in her arms as her flesh screamed to be let down on the ground.

The one eye remained open.

Her body reached the protecting lee of a ruined wall which had once carried colorful mosaics; she fell for rest as the Wind raved through the descended purple. Walls loomed and were lost above her, but she was collapsed, the driving, destructive compulsion to move was temporarily lifted from her.

In Fionnmachair, the Tanner huddled beneath his stall like a frightened dormouse. The spell on the Fallen Ones remaining was broken in the wake of her passing. Many of them stampeded into the teeth of the Wind as though its violence could exorcise their culpability. Others stumbled wherever their feet took them, unaware of the Wind until it hurled them to the ground.

In the wake of the wind, the warning klaxons began to howl.

They broke into Salamander's head, horrifying her with their meaning. That two-tone note meant Cuyahogan! How could Patrick command it? Only he could order its release at such short notice. Her despair was slashed away; the creature in her arms mindscreamed a vicious survival demand. She found herself back on her weary feet; they dragged her past vertical walls through still-swirling dust, down the hill.

The Tanner also heard the klaxons. He started to sweat more freely than ever. Heart thumping, he peered through a chink in the canvas flaps. The square seemed empty. But he didn't dare move. So he was still kneeling there when he heard the approaching stamp of ordered feet. And sensed something worse than an Unclean.

Cuyahogan.

Unprotected, the Tanner was stranded.

Cuyahogan was coldly efficient with those who were unprotected.

But the Tanner wasn't without courage. No reason, he thought, why he shouldn't remain safe, so long as he did nothing to betray his presence. Through the chink, he saw sandaled ankles, bare legs, gray robes kilted up around Witchman hips for greater ease of movement.

He saw the colorless ankles of Cuyahogan, and the feet.

The feet were perfectly formed, from vein-ridges to toenails.

It was said the golem could spit these toenails as far as a man could shoot an arrow. They were venomous razors. The Tanner tried not to breathe too loud. He realized that the golem wasn't yet wholly released from the binding spell. With great daring, he shifted his bulk to get a better view, taking care not to disturb the flaps. He saw, with mouth open, the creature's pale flesh – an unflesh, pallid and hairlessly sleek. The deadly golem was nine feet tall, cold bald perfection, with all human characteristics except external sexual organs. It towered above its Keeper, who looked up with unease. The order to animate the golem had virtually paralyzed him. His office was hereditary; he'd never expected to have to release the golem during his tenure. Cuyahogan knew nothing of sacred laws. The ancients had installed no morality of Norm Purity within its loathsome dome; only that of efficiency. The Keeper looked around at the squad. He was given his order to complete the activation.

He spoke the word which released the golem. The Witchmen were all protected. Or so they hoped.

For a moment, the golem didn't move. Then it twitched – and was still again, as if considering. Then it swung around so suddenly that the Keeper fell back in alarm. Cuyahogan was pent with energy stored through decades of waiting. It twitched again, spun on the balls of its feet, as if casting for scent – this way, a quarter-turn that way, a flick to the left. Then it moved – a sudden dead-white blur which bent to the canvas flaps beneath a nearby stall. Before anyone could move the Tanner was ripped out, sick with death which came immediately, without time to realize his mistake, that Cuyahogan could do more than see with its burning ruby eyes. The golem reacted to the vibrations of life. Life-forms with identity patterns unscreened from the icy efficiency of Cuyahogan's scan, they died. In Phadraig, only the elite were screened, and the secret of the process was known to the Council alone.

The Tanner's neck was severed, his body torn, his blood stained the tiles.

Cuyahogan stood twitching, jerking, its perfect face blank.

It turned toward the southwest corner of the square.

'Cuyahogan! At a pace we can follow!' called the Keeper, fearful.

The golem began to flow across the tiles. The Witchmen followed past the Tanner's body, eyeing each other with furtive relief.

Their protection, at least, seemed to be effective.

*But will it seek out the woman as ordered?* worried the Keeper. *Or will it kill whoever's unprotected... ?*

## 5: Gaidhealla

Salamander flinched. Something feral blew hot through her mind. The golem's searching tendril! It knew her pattern. She shivered in her pain; she was finished. It was impossible. Her body half slid down the quickening slope past old three-story buildings; her wound was slow fire, tearing her apart as she reached the gap in a wall which she remembered from childhood. It was covered by a casual sheet of rusted corrugated metal. She wrenched at it, sobbing, tearing her fingernails, no longer fighting the compulsion which kept her moving, left arm holding the child and pressing against the wound as the golem bayed closer, hotter in her mind. It had her scent. Half clearing the gap, she ducked through the ragged brick hole, tearing her shift, and emerged into a dark and dusty room. She staggered across the worm-eaten planking toward light which filtered down an arched corridor opposite. Down this she fled past other rooms to an open doorway, tripping over the sill into an abandoned courtyard which was full of cracked erotic sculptures overgrown with moss. Grabbing for each breath, head swimming, she pulled herself along, her legs scratched by the brambles and stung by the nettles which sprouted between intertwining limbs of stone. The graveyard gave way to ruined garden and to a jungle of tangled metal plates and dead machines with flywheels and levers which struck across her shins. She dragged herself across crumbled walls, past huge flowers which sprouted from vertical walls covered in creeper festoons; their stamens were ugly maroon, their pollen was choking. Distant shouts and hoarse orders echoed from the skull-facades of the buildings about her. But the clamor was nothing compared with the baying in her mind.

The golem was now much closer, but she couldn't look back.

She was a shivering wreck, dragged on by unknown energy.

The heat was intense, cell-draining. The heavy saffron sky was streaked with faint whorls of shredding rust. And her mind was rotten with uncomprehending despair.

Where was her mother?

And why had Patrick done this to her?

Gaidhealla was very old, almost sixty. For ten years now, since Aurum's death, she'd lived alone somewhere in the middle of a maze of old buildings far down the western side of the hill. Council had made numerous attempts to bring her back into the Citadel, where as senior Witchmother she belonged, but the old lady had no such intention. Her reputation in the city was powerful; her last child had been the seventeenth, and she was Salamander. It was remembered by the people what influence she'd had on the former High Witchman, and how Gobhan had tried and failed to oust her. Gobhan had always feared and resented her; had made incessant efforts during the last decade to spy on her solitary activities down where the stench of Red Kilmun was foul. But she was too well-respected for Council to pillory her for evading them. It was generally believed she knew the future and could lay maledictions on those who crossed her path. It was not known whether the First Servant believed this. At any rate, apart from periodic harassment, she'd been left alone.

Left alone to prepare for this day.

She'd always known that Salamander was fated.

Perhaps for this reason, she'd never opened herself wholly to the growing girl. Though she was Witchmother of the

Third Eye, she was prey to human weakness. And she'd never found it possible to open herself wholly to the daughter destined to be a pawn in the great game of which she had dreamed – of which Maelnagar had dreamed. Only with herself had she ever given way to despair. She could not show any weakness. Too much depended on her, if this game was ever to be played on Earth. She had never, for so much as an hour, even in childbirth, laid aside the knowledge which came when she was young, before she met Aurum. Knowledge that a one-eyed child would one day be born to a daughter of hers, and that the birth would signal the spelling of changes in reality, the dawn of a new age. Knowledge that the daughter would suffer. But no vision of the daughter's fate. No certainty of the child's survival. Only the basic situation of the one-eyed child's birth to her daughter had been preestablished in her foresight, like a landmark in the uncoordinated future. But no connections were established with whatever reality lay about the landmark. Just the birth of a great potential, like a punctuation mark in time.

What happened to that potential would depend on those around it.

Gaidhealla had determined then that it must survive. And that she must see to it that it did. Her life became a devotion to an event she could never speak about – except to a very few people. In pursuit of understanding to explain the origin of the knowledge which had come on her, she learned much of the ancients' wisdom.

She knew Salamander was the one before the girl was born.

She treated the girl with a strict compassion, sent her away as a ward of the General Purity when Aurum died; Kalnakill attacked, and she moved down the hill. She didn't want Salamander to depend on her; she rejected her own feelings. And then there was Patrick Cormac. He was the other one. He was the first to hear all of what she knew. Over the decade, the plan evolved.

And its hinge was Cuyahogan.

She was picking her way through a network of steep, twisting alleys when she heard the klaxons. She stopped for a moment.

'I coached him well,' she murmured, 'but he's a strange man.'

Early-risen, she had sat in meditation till dawn, when she left her concealed apartment forever. Now, she was calm and prepared; she moved diagonally up the hill with an ease which denied her age. Her face was elfin, sharp, unlined, her eyes deep-set. Her hair was still black, though gray-streaked at the temples; it was cut to her earlobes, from each of which hung small jadestones, the color of her eyes.

Now all lay in speed and control. She emerged from the network, crossed one of the ringways which ran around the hill. There was no sign of life in either direction. The dust in the air was choking. She ducked her nose into the deep hood of her cloak, pushed herself on up the hill, away from the stench of Red Kilmun, up a steep flight of steps, onto a level of wasteground bounded by an empty granary.

Shouts rang through the air. The klaxons sounded again. She turned the corner of the granary, entered an overgrown alley bordered by the gray granary walls to one side, a sagging fence to the other.

She saw her daughter, thirty yards away.

Salamander couldn't focus her eyes. She staggered a few more feet forward as her mother cried out, her knees gave way, and she dropped in slow motion, crumpled with the child held out for her mother.

She squeezed words from the dried husk of her throat.

'Run, Mother! Cuyahogan! Prophecy ... destroyed ... run....'

But Gaidhealla dropped to her knees on the hardpacked grit. She took the one-eyed child, found her gaze held in its depths. 'Yes,' she murmured, as though lost in recognition. 'He is as I foresaw. I sense his aura. . . .' And there was awe and salutation in her voice. For a moment she seemed to be in a daze, but then Salamander sighed out her last shreds of consciousness, slumped down on her right side, wound exposed. Her mother saw it; something jumped inside her, her face froze, and, holding the child tight, she reached out.

Then she knew there was no time.

The heat of Cuyahogan's proximity shriveled her mind. She stood, composed herself, breathed deep.

The golem appeared at the other end of the alley. Stopped to twitch and juggle on the balls of its feet. Then it was a blur of unhuman movement. For the first time, the child opened its mouth and wailed, face puckered and red with instinctive terror. The blur was upon them, a savage wind. Gaidhealla screamed the word-sequence she'd coaxed the Keeper's predecessor into revealing, years before.

'*Met*, seven, *met*, eleven, abort, seventy-seven. . . .'

Hurricane blur, razored edges flashing —

If she'd inflected it wrong . . .

The golem stood arrested above her, momentum and intention denied.

Gaidhealla found she was shivering like a leaf; the child was bawling, struggling in her arms. The shadow of the golem's upraised right arm lay across her face. The nails of its right hand were extended into five-inch slivers, pointed at her heart, their downward plunge canceled with not a moment to spare. The golem's face was totally neutral, the face of the perfect androgyne. Cuyahogan awaited her commands, its program of killer reflexes scrambled by the correct sequence and pitch of sound vibrations. During its last rampage over fifty years before, this word sequence had been shouted, but the pitch was not correct.

Gaidhealla was weak with reaction. Breathing deeply, she allowed herself momentary relaxation, knowing that Witchmen wouldn't be far behind the golem. She examined Salamander's wound swiftly; it was deep, the girl had lost a lot of blood. To survive, she'd need rest and constant treatment. It was impossible; there was no time. Stay in Phadraig and they'd die anyway, besides betraying the one-eyed child's potential. Swiftly, the old woman padded and bandaged the wound with healing herbs; she'd come prepared, half expecting this.

She wondered how Salamander had managed to get this far.

Then she looked at the one-eyed child; her face was grim.

But she'd known for many years that high prices would have to be paid. It was one of the reasons she rarely smiled anymore. She rose calmly, still holding the child. She could afford no excitement; her actions now were too important. Nevertheless, she still trembled when she spoke to the immobile golem again. Her initial words were furred and thick.

'Eighty-four ... new ... program....' She took fresh breath, keeping an eye on the far end of the alley. 'You will ... Cuyahogan will carry the child and these two women ... to the Southern Gate by Madadhmachair, away from Phadraig ... to the Fiststone Crossing of Red Kilmun, into the Wastelands, to the north, beyond the Swamp Forest, past the Scarp, the Jerezid lands, and Kor ... past the Black Lakes ... and north to Comraich Inbhir Dhobhrain, the sanctuary town at the mouth of the river which flows through the Land of the Briars to the Neotirik Sea. The name of the other woman is Salamander. She is very ill; carry her gently, protect her. The name of this woman is Gaidhealla. Protect her, and the child, whose name is not yet known. Cuyahogan will obey the orders of Gaidhealla instantly at all times. Cuyahogan will harm no other beings unless it is ordered ...'

She heard the sound of feet, of voices —

'Cuyahogan, signal reception and acceptance!'

And she felt the brief pulse of the golem's affirmation of her control. It sparked in her head, at the same moment as the Witchmen burst into view at the upper end of the alley. She picked up the broad emanation of their collective hatred very clearly. They were desperate to see the Unclean exterminated, to see the golem locked away again. Unaware that the programmed attitudes against which they'd been screened had been canceled, they came around the corner, wondering where Cuyahogan had vanished in its speed and fury.

Then they saw the stilled golem, its right arm upraised.

Shielded by its body, Gaidhealla hesitated to give the order she knew would be necessary. Salamander remained unconscious beside her.

The Witchmen were thrown into confusion, confronted by Cuyahogan immobile above an old woman some recognized as the Witchmother of the Third Eye. They swung around on each other, disbelief in their eyes. Their lieutenant drew his issued powertube slowly, uncertain, his eyes alternately flickering from the horrified Keeper to the golem and back again. He took a step forward. And another. But stopped when the old woman's voice came clear down the forty steps separating them.

'Stay back! You are no longer protected. The golem is under my control! Let us leave; stay alive to fight Khassam!'

She knew it was futile.

To the Witchmen, a death at the hands of the golem was small beside the judgment of the Witchgoddess.

Frozen, she watched and heard as the lieutenant exhorted his men.

'What are you waiting for? Haven't you been issued with weapons of the ancients? So many, and you hang back? If you die, you will die in Purity. The Unclean child must be destroyed, and the spoiled mother ... and the old woman has betrayed Phadraig ...!'

Slowly, cautiously, they advanced, their bravery a frozen compulsion, forcing their unwilling bodies forward. In a dream they brought up their tubular sidearms, came sideways forward. But Gaidhealla could not bring herself to give the order which could end twenty lives....

*The crucial moment, and I am weak!*

The child bawled into the crushing silence, its mind oppressed.

Its urgency shattered the spell; a powertube flared.

The finger that studded the button was trembling. The yellow sizzle burned high past the golem's left shoulder, expended itself in empty air. Somebody shouted a curse, and Gaidhealla's tongue was freed. 'Stop them!' she cried at the golem. 'Cuyahogan, drive the Witchmen from us; return the instant they're in flight! Hurt no more than ...'

But the golem had already blurred. Before human reaction was possible, there was deadly confusion among the Witchmen. Their low-charged ancient weapons sizzled uselessly wild, flaring on the dull granary wall, burning their comrade's flesh as the flickering shadow cut them down. In four seconds, half were down, and the rest were turning to flee.

'Back, Cuyahogan! Return!'

The sinuous wrath slowed down into solidity, returned past eleven bodies. The old woman was sorrowful. Then she looked at her unconscious daughter, at the one-eyed child. Its small fists were closed over its stomach, its eye was lidded shut, its face was red and tearstained.

'If you live,' she whispered, 'will you remember this?'

The golem stood pallid before her, nails retracted. But there was blood on its flanks. The old woman's voice was urgent. 'Cuyahogan, now you must take these people to Madadhmachair as this one told you. Descend to the Culane, thence to the square. Gaidhealla orders your route. Now take us up – first Salamander, gently....'

The golem bent smooth from unboned hips, lifted the unconscious girl into the crook of its right arm, transferred her to its left shoulder. She lay on either side, legs down its chest, head and arms down its back, hastily-bandaged wound against the golem's neck. The old woman held the child more tightly, her feelings in conflict.

'Now these ones, Cuyahogan.'

The touch of its unflesh was too smooth; she fought brief but automatic revulsion as it swept them up in its right arm. She lay back, passing her left hand around the back of its neck to cradle her daughter's head. The child opened its eye. And began to wail again. But she paid no heed. Salamander's forehead was ice-cold. And from beyond the alley came sounds of argument and angry orders.

'Cuyahogan, go. Cross the wasteground beyond this alley; keep to the southern side. Be quick – but don't jolt us.'

The golem executed these and successive commands with rapid and chill efficiency. *I fear it; it has no soul,* Gaidhealla realized, *but we must depend on it until Patrick catches up – if he escapes.* Cuyahogan held her firmly. Its motion wasn't unpleasant, it darted through Gaidhealla's maze, from darkness through pools of light on rotten floors to darkness again. But the child wailed inconsolably, gripped by rage and fear. Gaidhealla's nerves were stretched by this howling; she crooned and rocked and comforted as the golem took them diagonally down the hill, but she was ignored. Now the stench of Red Kilmun attacked her strongly as they emerged onto the broad, pocked surface of the Culane. On this gentler southwestern slope the avenue was passable, with ashen ground between it and the red-glowing river. Gaidhealla did her best to protect Salamander, buried her own face and the child in the depth of her hood as the golem took them past the rotted verge where the liquids had eaten closest. Here, the fumes were vicious. They were fully thirty feet from the verge of Red Kilmun. And they would have to cross the Burning River in order to escape to the north. It ate its way too far to east and west; detour was out of the question. They had to cross at the Fiststones, and soon.

Approaching Madadhmachair, the Culane left the Burning River and veered up the relatively gentle slope of the broad ridge which flattened down to the neck of the horseshoe. Gaidhealla focused her stinging eyes. They were among occupied buildings again, the rotten periphery of the Chahd, ramshackle shanties. But no faces showed. All lay low in prudent fear of the golem. Its feet moved swiftly across the crumbling surface when the avenue widened out into the Plain of the Dogs, Madadhmachair, a squalid and normally bustling place so-called because of the hunting packs kenneled nearby.

Many drunkards staggering late from the Black Bear Inn had mistaken the mournful howls of the hounds for the wailing of departed Fallen Ones, returned to corrupt and chastise Norm Purity.

The child was quiet at last, as quiet as the square itself.

There were sounds in the distance, but they were far behind.

Salamander's mind remained dark. Gaidhealla crouched lower in the golem's arm, pointed.

'Past that inn, Cuyahogan, to the Southern Gate.'

The golem took them through the deserted square.

But it wasn't quite deserted.

Passing the porch of the Black Bear Inn, Gaidhealla saw four shapes in shadow, watching. Then the golem took her past.

*All that's left of the Company, waiting for Patrick,* she realized.

Then they were at the Southern Gate. It was solidly closed.

## 6: The Company Chatachain

Iubhar moved fast, reached Patrick's apartments unobserved, collected torchblade, clothing and equipment. He went to his own rooms with the bundle wrapped beneath his arm. His woman made no fuss, because she wasn't there. It was a relief, but also a source of guilty worry. What if she were one of the Fallen Ones, and they met outside Phadraig? Would he be able to meet her eyes?

He took what he needed and made another compact bundle. Then he joined the two with a leather strap and slung them around his neck. He clasped a hooded black cloak about his neck, eyed himself dubiously in a mirror. Bulky – but it would pass. And who would have eyes for him, anyway?

Hood up to conceal his shock of brown hair, Iubhar left the Citadel unchallenged, passing a squad of Witchmen who were being harangued and issued with powertubes as they waited for Cuyahogan.

He went the way he'd been the night before. Through the cobbled Place of Fists with its furled pennants, ducking the overhanging gutters in a steep alley, he crossed the first ringway, padding across the naked surface, wondering if Cuyahogan was going to run amok.

He couldn't believe that the golem would be tamed.

*But who am I to judge?*

In the next section, he mounted a flight of steps up past a wall blazoned with discordant, disturbing swirls of color. His face registered automatic amusement; the Songmaker's notions of urban decoration were extreme. But then the Songmaker himself was extreme. Only Liam's popularity as a clown kept the Council off his back. He'd clowned the night before when Iubhar came. Jabbered with a sort of demented relief until Iubhar left to find Gnorl. And on into the night, for all Iubhar knew. The Songmaker was his own best audience, was always nodding approval at his own wit, ruddy hair bristling like a scarecrow's. Iubhar crossed the carved bridge which led over an alley to the Songmaker's door. Three-eyed gargoyles grinned at him, left him sad in memory of their creator. Rix would have come with them. But he was a year dead – some said Gobhan's agents had poisoned him.

Some also rumored that Liam's wit had been infected by bitterness following his close friend's death. He had been thought an incurable optimist. Now something was changed – if not his eccentricity.

Iubhar knocked sharply on the lemon-yellow door. The grotesque red face painted on it stuck a wooden tongue out at him through a slot. A bell jangled inside, muffled. Iuhbar wiped his brow; the sound of the bell was drowned by the klaxons, signaling the squad's going-down.

He waited, impatient and exposed in the heat, until the door opened.

'Liam! Ready?'

The Songmaker wore a dark blue cloak, almost black; the hood was down. He was Iubhar's height but thinner, light-boned, easy-moving, madcap, his sharp face quizzical and sometimes vulpine. He gave the streaky saffron sky a cynical eye, chewed at drooping red-brown bristles of moustache, shifted an angular bulk beneath his cloak, then nodded.

'I'm always ready; I live in the present, my friend!'

And he smiled like an eager simpleton, making Iubhar uneasy.

'Your sirena – well-charged?'

The Songmaker patted affectionately the object beneath

his cloak.

'Phadraig will never hear my finest songs.' His mood changed. 'It makes me sad. I wanted to poison Purity like it poisoned Rix....'

'Come on!' exclaimed Iubhar, already halfway across the bridge. 'Khassam will do it for you. And you know what Khassam does with songmakers who displease him!'

But Liam stood, rubbing his brow in apparent perplexity.

'What is it? What have you forgotten? We've got no time!'

The Songmaker wasn't distressed by Iubhar's impatience.

'Ah!' he announced. 'Yes, I've heard. No, I've no wish to entertain such a philistine. I've heard he allows his songmakers no improvisation – only lays of the Divine Mutant, and strict renditions of Middle Kingdom tales....'

He cast a half mocking, half serious farewell at his door, and followed Iubhar with alacrity, down the steps past the swirling colors, into silent, deserted alleys, muttering all the way down the slope, over the next ringway, past the College of General Purity with its grim walls and cast-iron gates. Iubhar had taken as much as he could by the time they were at the place Gnorl had agreed to wait. The area was crowded with rough-built houses, their roofs steep slate, their windows shuttered, their doors closed.

'... makes me feel naked ...' the Songmaker was complaining, peering cautiously around a corner. 'I could never trust this golem; it likes music even less than Khassam. And Patrick says it will be our ...'

Iubhar cut him off with a sense of relief.

'Quiet – Gnorl's meeting us here.'

The city was silent. They waited in the narrow courtyard. And the huge, gaunt-faced trapper materialized silently out of shadows. Hands were grasped. Liam's disappeared into Gnorl's weathered hams. There was no smiling. Gnorl had never been an open book. He had great physical strength, and muscular coordination to go with it. But he also had eyes to scan and mind to learn the Earth's encyclopedia. He understood men through nature, not society; these ten years he'd worked silently, solidly, tracking the Wastelands for a living and a reason to live, keeping his mouth shut and his eyes sharp. His temper was violent and he let it be known, so he rarely had to lose it. Liam smiled shrewdly as Iubhar led them from the courtyard. Gnorl could move like a ghost while he stuck out like a sore thumb wherever he was. He kept it to himself. Gnorl wasn't noted for his sense of humor. While Liam was so tense with expectation it was difficult for him not to joke and jabber. The sky shifted above the silent city. They came to a richer quarter farther down the slope. The buildings were well-kept, rambling, and self-indulgent with embellishment and decoration. Advertisements, crests, signs, and colorful baroque carvings vied with the occasional spiritual exhortation. But ethics were hazy in the Chahd, whether in this richer area, or in the slum by Madadhmachair. The Council deplored the activities here, enforced nominal restrictions, but knew very well that human nature couldn't be totally suppressed. The taverns and sweatshops of the Lower Chahd were the safest places for Uncleans of Lesser Degree to live – the Witchmen regulated the impure activities only so far as they dared, and frequently indulged themselves. In the Chahd, Upper and Lower, laws were flouted without penalty as long as a well-understood double standard was maintained.

Scalaman's notorious brothel was in the Upper Chahd. It was a labyrinth of multileveled excess, surrounded by columns and fretted archways, topped by spires and architectural confections. Scalaman wasn't a businessman. He simply enjoyed throwing parties, every night. Iubhar doubted Scalaman's willingness to join them. Last night, with wine, women, and song in attendance, he'd looked much too comfortable to consider the Wastelands again.

But his excitement had seemed genuine enough.

'Even the Chahd's deserted!' Liam whispered. 'Even here, fear of the golem binds them down!'

Through an archway, they entered a delicately-columned courtyard.

The building before them was crusted with ostentatious overdecoration. Liam's lip curled as they came into a stone corridor beneath a fretted arch. His contempt increased as they passed coupling cherubs in flower-bordered panels frescoed on the walls. 'It's not the subjects I dislike,' he burst out spontaneously, 'but the utter tastelessness of the man! What use is Scalaman to the Company? He plunders the emotions of others. Moreover, he owes me money for my entertainments at his establishment. He swore most firmly that I wouldn't go unrewarded, but the snake tried to fob me off with the pick of his boys and girls!' The Songmaker snorted with immense derision. Now they were at hanging curtains which concealed a heavy door set deep under a stone arch. White marble nudes stood on either side of the curtains, overlit by wall-bracketed candles. One was a drunken, potbellied old man, half squatting, with a bottle tilted to his lips and whiskered ecstasy on his face. The other was a woman, her breasts pendulous, her flesh beginning to sag, her stance and smile an invitation to the door. But Liam paid no attention to the art. 'Of course, I told the sleek buffoon that I didn't need his fodder, I knew better troughs elsewhere; then he had the nerve to ask me if I wanted something special! "Yes, Scalaman," I told him, "I would crawl with gratitude if you would supply me with a telepathic Triple O, but since your only one's reserved for Gobhan, you can't, and Witchgoddess rot if you don't pay up!" He's a snake! We don't want him!'

Iubhar pulled a bell-rope, softly. He didn't show his grin.

'Scalaman wasn't altogether happy when I mentioned your name last night, Liam.'

Gnorl grunted with annoyance, folded his arms.

'Oh, we love each other,' said the Songmaker carelessly, 'dearly. We're like positive and negative; we find each other repulsively fascinating. You know I keep my most moral games for Scalaman. And . . .'

A door opened – not the one behind the curtains, but one they'd passed already, fifteen feet down the corridor. Well-oiled, it made no sound, but they sensed it, and turned. They saw Scalaman. He was tall, still looked imposing, but closer inspection showed he was in danger of going to fat despite the food shortage. His features were good, though his large brown eyes looked liquid, almost soft, or indecisive. His pale skin was framed in a waved mane of hair, which was uniformly bleached from roots to shoulder.

He eyed the three of them plaintively, was obviously reluctant to close the door behind him and abandon his comforts and his ladies.

He was held by the distant, faltering sound of prolonged lament.

Gnorl moved forward, lithe despite his bulk.

'Friend, the Company needs you.'

Scalaman nodded, cast his eyes down to the stone flags.

'I didn't sleep last night after you left,' he told Iubhar. 'I cannot reconcile what you told me with loyalty to Phadraig or Norm Purity.' He made a self-effacing gesture, attempted a smile. 'I am, after all, a respectable man, with many responsibilities, and . . .'

The Songmaker howled with laughter; Iubhar looked irritated.

'Scalaman, Scalaman, Scalaman!' Liam cried. 'You can't know how happy it makes me to hear you groaning again! It's been so long! Of course, I can't ask a respectable gentleman for the money he owes, but surely I can ask you to stop being so idiotic!'

Scalaman flushed angrily, took a step away from his door.

'I owe you no money!' he snapped. He appealed to Gnorl and Iubhar. 'Has this liar been spreading more fantasies about me? Of course he wasn't paid. He agreed to accept praise as the only payment!'

'. . . And a meal or two,' interrupted Liam, moving past Scalaman with an exaggerated gesture. 'You never fed me as agreed – agreed?'

'He agreed to accept praise!' Scalaman insisted, leaving the door. 'When my customers booed the paucity of his imagination, he demanded money instead. And that is the truth!'

'Ohhh!' Liam crooned, wide-eyed with mock horror. 'Truth is relative to the soundness of memory, conscience, and wisdom, and you're endowed with none of these, Scalaman! Naturally some of your customers were inattentive, but I expected that. As for the rest, I had to restrain my inventiveness, or I'd surely have driven them mad with ecstasy. There was praise aplenty from the discriminating, but I couldn't buy food with it, or shelter beneath it....'

'Enough, surely ...' groaned Iubhar.

But Scalaman had been drawn well away from the door. His doubts were momentarily erased by anger with the Songmaker's mockery.

'I'll be civil with the madman,' he muttered thickly at Gnorl, 'so long as his mouth is stitched.'

'He talks too much,' agreed Gnorl, loud, abrupt.

They descended toward Madadhmachair. The slopes seemed still deserted. But there were faces behind windows, surreptitious; and occasionally, an exhausted figure slumped in shadow against a wall.

'Fallen Ones,' remarked Iubhar harshly. 'They cannot believe ...'

'... damned by Norm Purity? By their own imaginations, more like!'

The Songmaker's interruption was too quick to carry conviction.

And Scalaman cast frequent glances back up the hill. Sounds of distant confusion carried to them from the sun's direction. They came quickly to Madadhmachair's filthy, deserted cobbles. No carts, no filthy trappers, none of the usual riffraff of hawkers, Uncleans, astrologers, and fortune-tellers. Even the dogs were silent in their kennels, gripped by the prevailing mood of fear.

They skirted the square, then came to the Black Bear Inn, to the porch.

'I'll watch here,' Iubhar was whispering. 'You go downstairs.'

Gnorl led Scalaman and the Songmaker down the stone steps into the dim, low-vaulted basement. His hood was down; he was too well-known here to attempt concealment. Every one of his Wastelands expeditions had ended with him blind drunk in this basement. They stopped at the bottom of the steps. The place appeared to be empty; the landlord wasn't behind the bar. When their eyes adjusted, they saw the customers, crouching behind overturned trestle tables in the corners.

Gnorl fingered his spade-shaped black beard, scratched tight black ringlets of receding hair, located and crushed a bug. He grunted.

'What's going on?' he demanded, striding to the bar, slamming down his right fist. 'Landlord! Come on out!'

But the door behind the bar didn't even quiver. Voices whispered behind the tables, but none of the early-morning drinkers spoke up.

Scalaman joined Gnorl, studiously ignoring Liam, who was still at the foot of the steps. 'We've been recognized,' Scalaman whispered with slight alarm. 'The idiot, too.' Gnorl didn't answer. He could feel Scalaman's uncertainty. The sensual man wasn't sure if he could accept the old comradeship on the old terms. He couldn't throw off his luxurious respectability just like that. But he could always call for drink. He took his place at the bar; his plump hands struck out.

'Come out, landlord, we need drink. The golem won't come down here! Serve us, or I'll make your indiscretions public!'

Not even this threat had any effect. Scalaman was sour; he could maintain a devil-may-care pretense only with effort. Even thought of the golem made him nervous. Gnorl shrugged massively, and reached across the bar with a bulging arm in red cotton sleeves to the wrist; fingers like discolored bananas closed around a bottle's neck. He pulled the cork with his teeth, spat it accurately at the doorknob. He drank. Seven watched from behind the tables. Liam laughed. Perhaps it was a stutter of tension. He brought the sirena out from beneath his cloak. Tapped derisive notes which wavered and curled, cut them off with a discord, eyes sharp and mischievous. The sirena flashed scarlet and silver reflections. The low-lying drinkers knew all about the Songmaker's strange instrument. He'd discovered it on one of the Company's early expeditions, in the ruins of a sorcerer's stronghold on Comrie Isle to the south. He had established an immediate empathy with the ancient device. The sirena was a flat instrument, shaped like a figure 6. The fretboard, polished curve of underside inlaid with filigree silver design, was the arm of the 6 – five inches wide at the base where it met the intricately-decorated body, diminishing to scarcely more than an inch at the top, where six strings converged over the frets and met. A difficult, temperamental instrument; it was part of Liam's very soul. The scarlet body of the sirena was virtually a controlboard of knobs which controlled the instrument's stranger functions – the direction, pitch, tone, and wavelength of vibrations transmitted from the sound grids set flush with the curving rim of the solid body. A panel on the back opened to reveal a microminiaturized maze within. Liam rarely opened it. He wasn't interested in the nature of the apparently inexhaustible power source; it mattered not at all to him how the sirena amplified and broadcast the sounds he could conceive. With the sweetest music he could persuade enemies that they loved each other. He could growl like hunting animals, roar like angry crowds, and wail like the autumn sky. He could converse, with droll, polite little notes. He could spew inaudible misery, paralyze the nerves, or bring about epilepsy. Ten years ago, his lips were wide from teeth, his sirena sang in the heat of battle. And he grinned now as Scalaman reached sullenly for a bottle—

'Remember your delicate stomach, Scalaman!'

But then Iubhar was gesturing at them from the stairs.

Uneasy in the shadow of the porch, they watched the golem pass, except Scalaman, who refused to look. It was amazing. Cuyahogan didn't react to them at all. They saw Gaidhealla look at them; they realized she controlled the monster. Then it was past, turning into the short avenue leading to the Gate, Salamander's head and hair hanging down its pallid back. Liam suppressed his fears, jumped to the cobbles, ran to the corner. He saw the golem halted beneath the Gatehouse. Iubhar joined him. They heard Gaidhealla's voice, thin, calm.

'Open the Gate – or the golem will come and destroy you!'

'So strange . . .' muttered Liam as the Gate creaked open and the golem left Phadraig with its crew. 'This smells like a stranger affair than any I ever knew. It may dominate us completely.'

Three returned to the basement, leaving Iubhar with his pipe. He watched. They were too amazed to speak until Gnorl roared out:

'You can cringe out now. The danger's gone.'

Patrons started emerging sideways from behind the tables.

The door opened; there was a whispered consultation before the landlord came around the edge, eyes first.

'What did you see, sirs?'

He was nervously eager, a thin ferret with hollows beneath his haunted eyes.

'We'll sell you the information – if your luck's in!' Gnorl growled, disliking the whispering in the background.

'In exchange for bottles of your tawny wine!' flashed Scalaman.

'The half of them for us, the rest to comfort his good boys and girls,' interrupted Liam, grinning wickedly. 'No doubt you'll want to make the delivery yourself!'

The landlord fingered his ear, reluctant to take offense

with these three. He didn't dare ask the questions uppermost in his mind.

'The information – for the drink you've taken already,' he wheedled. 'Nobody can deny the justice of that!'

Bored by this haggling, the Songmaker let himself be taken by fantasy. He struck an absurd declamatory pose, swirled his cloak, and his fingers found the strings and controls of his sirena. 'Hear, landlord. I'll play you how it was!' A menacing bass drone grew to reverberate in the basement; several hands found ears. Into and over the drone came riding a rhythm smooth at first, but it began to splinter awkwardly, to buck and jangle in the landlord's head. He made an impatient, worried gesture; he felt like he had sand beneath his skin. Then came the Songmaker's voice.

'The monster stood poised before us, trembling with desire to rend the succulent flesh it saw, its eyes of ruby burning, martial orbs the twain, slippery and shining it was with the blood of the Unprotected. Its aura was blinding, its mind like lightning came stabbing for our brains—'

He cut all sound off dead, swung to acknowledge Scalaman with a generous hand. Gnorl made a face and reached for another bottle. The landlord made no objections; his jaw was hanging from the shock of the images. But several of the customers, sensing a joke, were moving closer, beginning to grin. Scalaman waited, simmering.

'But then Scalaman stood out upon the cobbles!' Liam announced with dramatic chords. 'His Purity like a shield, a mirror which threw back the monster's evil intent upon itself. And so it fled, mewling like a frightened kitten!'

The heavy sound-picture transformed into farce and dissolved.

Liam gestured mock acknowledgment on behalf of Scalaman and himself.

A customer laughed. 'Landlord, drinks on the house for that!'

But Scalaman's eyes were dry; he was furious, his cheeks

mottled.

'No more!' warned Gnorl in an undertone, drawing them apart.

Scalaman moderated his intention to hurl an insult; instead he hissed bitterly into the Songmaker's face: 'This affair is idiotic. I am an idiot. I expect to die for my idiocy. If it is so, it is so. But I refuse to die for a madman with the mind of a parrot!'

Liam smiled innocently, plucked at his moustache.

'No harm meant – no harm done. It was a joke,' he said heavily to Scalaman, 'just a little play to lighten our mood.'

'Your tongue – too sharp!'

Liam regarded Gnorl above him, took the derision from his voice.

'I am tense.' He made an offhand gesture. 'I joke when I'm tense.'

'Then turn your jokes against mutual enemies!' muttered Scalaman.

The customer who'd demanded free drinks joined them, threw familiar arms around Liam and Scalaman.

'Then where are you going? Why are you here at the Gate?'

Both Liam and Scalaman divested themselves of his arms.

'We are going nowhere,' drawled the Songmaker.

'That is truth,' Scalaman supplied with conviction.

Gnorl's eyes persuaded the intruder to go away. Left to themselves they were an arguing group, resentfully eyed by the landlord as his customers returned to the bar and the tables were uprighted. A buzz of conversation was lit and spread; heads nodded cautiously at the three who waited at one end of the bar. Their speculation was interrupted by a hard-faced young man with a trapper's fur leggings. He skidded down the steps, shouting: 'Cuyahogan's gone! I dared to look. The Gate was open, and I saw its legs, white as death – they walked out of Phadraig! The monster has left us!'

The Company didn't share the general astonishment.

Liam was about to interrupt when Gnorl stuck a thumb in his back.

The trapper stalked to the bar, reveling in his moment.

'There's more! A failed mother is at large in the city with her Unclean of Greater Degree. There are many Fallen Ones from Fionnmachair; the miserable sinners are already on their way out!'

'Then let's get up there and have a look at them!'

'But where's the mother and the Unclean child?'

The second voice was frightened. The trapper grinned.

'Perhaps behind your shoulder!' And he made a hideous face.

There was a shocked silence. The Songmaker was pained.

'Didn't you look any higher than the golem's legs?'

The trapper turned and glared. 'What's it to you?'

Gnorl moved into the trapper's line of view; he knew the man.

'The Songmaker doesn't mock you, friend,' he explained, lying baldly. 'We also saw the golem. What he means is, it carried the mother and child in its arms. Out of Phadraig.'

'There is no danger?' asked the landlord. 'None?'

'Nothing but a sad procession,' said Liam. 'You'd better hurry if you want to see it.' He grinned at the trapper, who spat, and turned for the steps. He was followed by six of the seven patrons. The seventh was the shrewd one who'd questioned the Company. He stayed at the bar, nursing a beer. The Company went to a table.

'No more jokes!' Gnorl pushed Liam backward into a seat.

'A joke is all there is!' The Songmaker was aggressive. 'Our lives are jokes! Patrick wants us to pursue the escaped woman to protect her and this one-eyed child, a mutant prophesied. And the golem is turned into a carriage; half Phadraig believes itself damned, which indeed it is with Khassam on the horizon. It's all a joke!'

'Your mind's sick if you believe that!'

Scalaman's contempt was fluid. He was getting impatient,

waiting for Patrick Cormac, whom he hadn't seen in six years. And he was conscious of suspicious eyes from the bar. What if Witchmen were called to investigate? Could Iubhar outrule them?

And did he have to go to the Wastelands with this babbling fool?

He felt the dismantled pieces of his crossbow beneath his cloak.

And Gnorl rumbled angry assent to Scalaman's contempt.

'Reject laughter,' insisted Liam fiercely, leaning over the table at them, 'and you say good-bye to life! Laugh when you can – take your chances – especially now! We're ten years older, grayer, slower – the Wastelands are ten years different from what we knew. Our brains are three thousand seven hundred days more addled than they were – and the times are worse.'

But the thread of a fresh joke had attached itself to his theme, destroying its pure seriousness. He sat back and grinned. 'Why, the years are even more to endure than they were in ancient times! Before the Great Forgetting they had it easy. Only three hundred and sixty-five days in *their* year!'

'Your mind's disordered!' Scalaman exploded. 'A year of three hundred and sixty-five days is physically impossible; there have always been three hundred and seventy days in the year, you lunatic! The laws clearly explain all references to three-hundred-and-sixty-five-day years as symbolic; it's romantic nonsense to infer actuality on symbols! Note the character of those who believe such rubbish – mystics, poets, singers, and similar riffraff. ...'

Gnorl buried his head in his arms and appeared to go to sleep.

But the Songmaker's eyes sparkled with delight.

'In even more ancestral times,' he hissed meaningfully across the table into Scalaman's outraged face, 'the year held a paucity of three hundred and sixty days; and in former ages, fewer still.' Beneath his cloak, he struck a hollow sirena chord. 'For the Witchgoddess swam closer to the sun, and east and west were not where they are now. It's said that once the sun used to rise in the west, that the days were even hotter and bloodier, as if the same quantity of heat dispersed over our three hundred seventy days was crammed into their three hundred and sixty. Disbelieve it if you will, as the ancients disbelieved the legends of their own ancestors. Say it's not a monstrous joke, Scalaman, that we forget so much we know, that the laws call our true history symbolic, and our symbolic history true. So drink the rest of that bottle, Scalaman; the Witchgoddess will smother before she freezes, there'll be many more changes, many more whorehouses of far greater luxury and generosity than yours. So – laugh! What is there to worry about?'

And before Scalaman could react the Songmaker pulled out his sirena, its graceful curve glinting. A glissade of sparkling firework sounds popped and burst around Scalaman's head, roused Gnorl from his arms, and the two at the bar from their talk.

Scalaman hunched his shoulders pugnaciously.

'I'll show you what there is to worry about, you mental leech!'

But before his hand reached the knife, Iubhar's hand fell on his shoulder.

'Scalaman! Liam! Stop squabbling! Patrick's here. We go.'

## 7: Red Kilmun

The great Southern Gate, posted by twenty-foot timbers paneled with wrought iron molded in heroic bas-reliefs was winched open.

Back from the great bay window which overlooked the inner approach to the Gate, Jarpo Sibbel shook and couldn't speak for fully a minute.

But at a window in the attic above, his daughter was fascinated.

Officially, Adeline was his lawful, unrelated ward. Jarpo had to do a lot of favors to important people to keep his open secret. Adeline was most of the favors and one of the important people was in her bed, yellow-corded black robe crumpled on rush matting. His chest was hairy, his face was dark, impatient, and righteously horrified.

'Come away from that window, idiot woman. You'll fall!'

Adeline pretended she didn't hear; she leaned on the windowsill, rosy naked bottom wriggling with excitement. 'It's into the Fringe, I can't see them anymore!' Disappointed, she came to her lover of the hour. 'Will it kill them? I think the old lady has bewitched it!'

The Interpreter of the Mysteries ignored her, went naked to the opposite window. He watched the downcast, cloak-shrouded Fallen Ones come stumbling from Madadhmachair to the Gate. He wondered why he was so angry. Perhaps he resented her lack of fear and guilt. He turned.

'Take care! You'll end up in the Wastelands too!'

Indignant, she shook generously, pushed him in the chest.

'Just like my father; he can't sin with a clear conscience either. I don't care what you do, or my father. I hate the pimp!'

'He's your guardian, not your ... *father*! Never speak the word again!'

'You'd be in trouble if I did!' she gasped; he was crushing her so hard against him she couldn't breathe. His desire infuriated him.

'You have been claimed by damnation, girl!' His fingers pressed.

She managed to break loose, stood back, and shouted her scorn.

'The whole world's damned and, if I know it, it can't be secret. Phadraig's finished. You know it. And I'm not staying here for the Warlord, or my ... *father*! I'm leaving. And you'll come with me. We'll go to the south – from where my father brought me!'

The Interpreter couldn't believe it. He stuttered angrily.

'Get on the bed,' she ordered, pushing him. 'I know half the Citadel here. I know you best. You don't believe in the Mysteries. You just like to feel important. But that won't do you any good when Khassam comes, will it?' Her eyes gleamed on him; she knew she'd read him right. 'Now. Can you get any of those powertube things ... and maybe ...'

'Great Mother!' swore the Interpreter in astonishment.

Adeline started to laugh; chuckling, she pulled him on the bed.

His mind was turbulent; he started making love like a machine, his eyes vacant, his thoughts racing. Because every word she'd said was true. And he'd thought her a ... He began to wonder. Was it possible? He'd heard of communities in the far south – perhaps they ...

Without warning, Adeline lay back, looking curious.

'Have you ever been to Scalaman's brothel?' she asked.

She had to repeat the question before he responded.

Reluctantly, he nodded.

'Am I better than his girls? Do you enjoy me more?' She peered closely at him. 'Enjoy? You know what it means?'

He swallowed his confused wrath, gripped her more tightly.

'Yes, I do,' he said harshly. There was a pause.

'Yes, you are,' he added, less harshly, stroking one cheek.

But she looked thoughtful, not complimented.

'I thought I probably was,' she said.

Thirty feet beneath the bed, the Company was leaving Phadraig.

With the pace of a running man, Cuyahogan moved along the well-worn trapper's trail through the middle of the Fringe. The city and much of the hill behind was already blotted out by the thick screen of unhealthy-looking cycads all about. The Fringe grew off the ridge which passed through the narrow neck of the horseshoe formed by Red Kilmun's course. The vegetation struggled to breathe. Gaidhealla held the child tight, her eyes tingled, and the vapors attacked her lungs as the golem took the fork in the path which led to the Fiststone Crossing. And Salamander's face was white as milk; her eyes were closed. Now they left the Fringe. Cuyahogan's feet crunched through a layer of corrosive black ash; it was sodden with the acid liquids which overflowed the river banks at each full moon. Here, where the vegetation was transient and withered, the biting stench grew more distressing with every step the golem took toward the verge. Cuyahogan took them across a mat of rootless, stemless red weed, finely specialized to survive the monthly floodings. Its swollen lobes popped and crackled beneath the golem's feet, but the tiny explosions were lost in the serpentine hiss of the vapors which jetted up from Red Kilmun, lazily coiling and hazing the sky.

Her eyes streaming, Gaidhealla darted a look. She saw the Fiststones black beyond the verge before them, surrounded by iridescent bubbles which swirled on the liquid surface and burst against the smooth sides of the table-topped stones.

These were the only way to cross Red Kilmun from Phadraig.

Attempts had been made in the past to build bridges. But it was impossible to work close to the verge for more than five minutes without being overcome. Materials rotted in the vapors: wood, metal and stone alike. The only span ever laid across lasted two months before collapse. And even the Fiststones had been eaten smaller through the centuries, so that now the crossing was more treacherous than in the past. The seventeen stood up through the liquids in a straight line from bank to bank; nobody had ever stopped long enough to chip loose a piece of the stone for analysis. Plenty had tried, wearing masks and protective clothing. But even a fully-charged powertube had no visible effect on the Fiststones. Only Red Kilmun and time together would ever wear them down to nothing.

It was Red Kilmun as much as the Company Chatachain which had saved Phadraig from Kalnakill. Khassam's father had underestimated it as an obstacle. Too eager, he'd grown impatient; his vanguard attacked Phadraig with the better part of his army still queued up on the northern bank. To be driven into a burning graveyard by the Company. Kalnakill died, but Khassam had escaped with the kidnapped Ranza. And Khassam was an altogether different man, spurred by elemental ambitions.

Now the golem was poised by the burning serpent's flank.

Gasping, the old woman searched for and found the masks she'd taken in her pack. Little more than protective vegetable gourds, they were minimally effective, but better than nothing. With one cupped in her mittened left hand, she protected Salamander's face as best she could. With her right hand she drew the choking child into the cocoon of her hood behind another mask. The third she almost dropped before she succeeded in wedging it over her own face with the help of Cuyahogan's shoulder. Lungs burning, she hunched herself and the child as far into the golem as she could, earlier distaste forgotten. And her order was a choked sob:

'Cuyahogan . . . go. . . .'

The golem responded immediately, smoothly, setting its left foot on the first black surface. Two feet from the verge, the stone's diameter was similar; it was worn dangerously smooth by the nervous feet of generations. The liquids slid and hissed around about it; colors slid like oil on their surface. Already she was giddy. The child struggled to dislodge the gourd-mask, tried to bawl, sucked in a tendril of searing vapor, choked. She hugged it closer, drove her own face deeper as Cuyahogan took another easy step, and another. The light about was ghastly, a gelatinous soup shot with crimsons, purples, glowing sulphurous vapors which slid off the ever-combining chemicals and lit the golem luridly. The albinic unman took seven steps, eight, nine, without human fear or weakness, without need of the oxygen which was charred from the atmosphere, firmly holding the two women and the child. Their lungs were ablaze; unconscious still, Salamander whooped. Again and again Gaidhealla's supporting hand felt her shaking; the old woman herself was scorched, knew they could never have made the crossing on their own. Thirteen steps, fourteen . . . the hissing was a clamor. The child struggled, but it seemed the worst must be over.

Then Salamander twisted violently in agonized delirium, threw the golem off-balance in the middle of a step. Gaidhealla felt Cuyahogan lurch, momentarily hang suspended, off-balance.

*We're dead!*

But then some inner flash lit her mind in sharp relief.

Simultaneously, the golem recovered its balance, denied gravity, took the last three steps with faultless precision, gained the northern bank, took them across oily ash and weed and out of the poisonous fog.

It stood, awaiting fresh orders.

But Gaidhealla was working out what had happened.

The flash in her mind which had coincided with Cuyahogan's readjustment hadn't originated from her. It was the side-effect of a beam projected from another mind – a beam which had realigned the golem before it could fall. Salamander was unconscious.

That left the one-eyed child.

She considered implications. Not as a matter of lives taken or saved. But the child – or something else – intended to live.

Beside her, now, the baby struggled for breath.

She forced open her eyelids into heavy slits of vision.

Through a blur she saw an irregular vegetated skyline; dimly, the outline of a crag. She ordered Cuyahogan to set them down in the shadow of the crag, away from Red Kilmun, and out of sight of the city on the hill which loomed above, directly north. She dressed Salamander's wound, more carefully this time. It was ugly and gaping, though no major organs seemed to have been damaged. But the girl was very low indeed. Then Gaidhealla thought of the baby. It hadn't been fed. Whatever its constitution, it had to be hungry. And Salamander's breasts were full of milk which wasn't doing any good where it was. The old woman commanded her thoughts toward hard practicality. If Salamander died, feeding was going to be a problem.

She guided the child's mouth to a nipple.

It discovered it was hungry.

'Your name,' mused Gaidhealla. 'What's your name? One-Eye's not enough. . . .'

The polypheme was avid. The old woman continually looked back at the glowing haze above Red Kilmun, at the hill which rose from the vapors. The High Towers were caught in hazy sun; the saffron was beginning to clear into cobalt. Though she couldn't make out any activity on the streets, she knew that pursuit was being organized. Gobhan would want them killed or captured even though it meant leaving Phadraig defenseless. It was time to go. Quickly, she performed a divination in the soggy earth at her feet with a stick. Eyes closed, mumbling a repetitious chant, dissociated, she stabbed sixteen parallel lines of dots, each of random length. Then she drew hexagrams from each group of four lines, drawing one X by each line with an odd number of dots, and a double X by each with an even number. She studied and correlated the four hexagrams, holding her question as a base of interpretation. The two central formations were the same – odd, odd, even, odd. The ancient name for this hexagram was *Puer* – the Boy. The ancients believed it to be under Mars, in Aries. Gaidhealla wondered if perhaps her state of mind wasn't right, if she might have influenced this outcome. Together, the four hexagrams suggested a disquieting but inconclusive picture. Chance refused to be tempted. Taking up the child, clasping a spare cloak around her daughter's neck, Gaidhealla turned to the motionless golem. Its ruby eyes were watchful.

'Now take us up again, Cuyahogan, as before. Take us into the Wastelands through the ravine in front. Do not set us down if plant or animal attacks; use speed to get away. Obey Gaidhealla's commands immediately!'

Cuyahogan set a rapid pace into the gloomy ravine, past spidery trunks sprouting from the infertile floor. They webbed up into ciliated ocher fronds which fluttered in the restless streams of air. And, lurking between trunks and the vertical rockface, a family of prowlers. Perhaps they rooted here every day, but more likely it was only an overday encampment. When the sun fell away to night, they'd strike roots and hump off in search of flesh. Though now the squat purple cones were motionless and inoffensive the darkness hid different tales. But they were simple monstrosities compared with others.

The ravine filtered out northwest of Phadraig, into wide steppes of dried mud, with tangled, rolling hills to the north. Beyond those hills, half a day distant, lay the great barrier of the Swamp Forest. Once beyond that, they were effectively beyond Phadraig forever. The old woman had to decide what to do. Where should they wait for Patrick Cormac and his Company? This side? – or that? On this side were none of the herbs which might heal Salamander wholly, while Khassam's vanguard was surely approaching close to the other side of the Swamp Forest; at least by now the Warlord must have reached the Scarp.

But if she ordered the golem to wait on this side of the gloomy forest, they ran the risk of meeting pursuing Witchmen instead of the Company. And if they did wait, Salamander would certainly die. Gaidhealla made up her mind. They would make the crossing of the Swamp Forest without waiting for the Company.

She wondered how Patrick would react if her daughter died.

His attitude to Salamander had always been strange, as though to him she were a principle, and not a woman at all.

The golem flowed smoothly out onto the wastes, pallid beneath the glaring sun, its pace causing a cooling breeze to flow around the old woman's head. The baked land roundabout seemed inert and lifeless, but she could sense the myriad thin tendrils of energy emitted by sluggish leeches and worms, and she knew they were being watched.

In the Wastelands, everything watched.

If it didn't, it was dead by definition.

The events threw Council into a confusion which threatened the First Servant's authority. It was now nearly an hour since the High Witchman had excused himself from the octagonal chamber on grounds of sudden sickness. Gobhan's first belief was that he was escaping Council censure – the twelve of them were irritable, nervous, and the session was obviously going to be stormy. And the scalloped stone wall of the chamber in the Citadel didn't hold out the keen of the klaxons.

The golem's release infuriated some Councillors more than the escape of the mother with her child.

After a stormy ten minutes, Gobhan sent a secretary to check that the High Witchman had indeed gone to his apartments. The man returned saying the doors were locked; there was no answer. Gobhan ordered the doors broken down. Cuyahogan, semianimate, was already being led to Fionnmachair. The doors were broken, and the rooms were found empty. Search of the Citadel and the High Towers was ordered. The First Servant strove to grasp the connections in the High Witchman's strange behavior. He couldn't forget the man's references to the Company, his wearing of the ring, his calculated provocations, his insistence that there were spies in Phadraig, that Cuyahogan must be released.

Where was the man?

With mounting fury, the First Servant realized he'd been tricked – somehow. But what was the connection between his disappearance and the golem's release? The search was unfruitful. It was realized the Servant of the Voice was also missing. Several Councillors stormed out of the shadowy room in disgust. The First Servant made a note of their identities – the Tribunal might be interested.

But then news came of the golem's capture by the Witchmother of the Third Eye and the squad's massacre.

(By this time, the golem was already at Madadhmachair.)

The First Servant raged amid the confusion – raged without once raising his voice. Men were sent to the Songmaker's home, to Scalaman's house. But these dissidents of the Company were gone. A few minutes later, reports came in that Scalaman, Liam, Gnorl and the Servant of the Voice had been in the Black Bear Inn. And that Cuyahogan had passed through. The storm burst around the polished table, six men alternately or all at once standing to shout in each others' faces. Karnel Dearg was impatient to lead men out into the Wastelands to capture or destroy the traitors. The

First Servant was in agreement. But it wasn't that simple. The issue required a vote. And three of those left around the table established their opposition. The High Witchman's legacy – he'd grouped these men around him, now they protected him with their procrastination. The obese merchant, Cham Tyron, obstinately refused to believe that the High Witchman would desert Phadraig. The dark-faced Interpreter, Hatabel, refused to commit himself, waiting to see how matters went. Gobhan had him labeled as an unprincipled opportunist. But it wasn't these two he had to watch. They'd follow the lead of the third – Chenil Anka.

The last of the Councillors remaining was Phadraig's official historian – Daniel Humbold.

The First Servant knew he could depend on the bald, thin man.

But even Humbold was objecting to the proposition. While Karnel's scarred face grew more baleful and impatient by the instant, Gobhan calculated. Anka was the one – slumped in his seat like a bag of bones, his eyes on the frescoed ceiling, apparently far away. Gobhan had learned respect for Chenil Anka – though he'd been the High Witchman's man, it was out of convenience. The sharp man could pinpoint objections to every course of action the First Servant proposed. He was ambitious. He reminded Gobhan of his own young self in many ways.

Despite appearances, Anka was in serious danger of being liked by the aging First Servant.

Anka knew it. He also knew that if Gobhan ever realized it, his life would be worthless. Several times in the past, Gobhan had liked younger men too much for his own sense of security. He could afford no favorites who'd usurp his power. One and all, they'd had a Fall. Anka had no intention of following them. The High Witchman, never at ease in this atmosphere, had proved a convenient umbrella. Judging the old man's mind correctly, Anka opposed him on every issue, sometimes falling into line, sometimes not. He forced Gobhan to dislike and respect him, which was safer than being liked and despised.

He knew the First Servant was waiting for him to commit himself. He was annoyed. It was difficult. With the High Witchman missing, the balance was altered. And, as the High Witchman's man in Council, he was tainted now. He thought swiftly. What attitude to adopt? The old man would pounce on servility. And Karnel Dearg glared restlessly, daring him to deny a militant course. While Hatabel was waiting for his lead, and Humbold looked upset. Tyron alone didn't seem too interested in what he had to say. Anka was glad he was in the shadow beside Gobhan, whose face was frigidly lit by daylight slipping through a narrow window. And when his eyes came down, his voice was assured:

'Maelnagar's prophecy,' he said briskly. 'A subject barred by Index, but it must be discussed before we deplete our defenses by sending off our most able military leader on a wild-goose chase. We must also examine ourselves. It appears that the High Witchman has betrayed Phadraig – according to the sacred laws....'

'You deny them?' pounced Gobhan, eyes gleaming.

'Would I sit here and deny our laws? I only want to make the point that they are *our* laws, the product of *our* understanding. To understand what's happening, we must think more broadly. The High Witchman's a curious man; he could never control his spirit. It flies in places that I, personally, don't care to dream about. He's restless, temperamentally the least fitted of men for the Onerous Burdens. We have ourselves to blame for turning the office into a prison – we can't be too self-righteous when the prisoner breaks out.' Anka was conscious of furious objections about to burst. He dared to extend his play further, shaking his head. 'We all knew he has no belief in the sanctity of Norm Purity. I for one did my best to persuade him, but ... Phadraig is beneath his considerations, except so far as it gives birth to them. He's no more Khassam's friend than our enemy. He's enmeshed in something else, some affair we know nothing about – except through ancient words we choose not to think about!' Anka was surprised and increasingly nervous about the lack of interruption, though he could see Karnel Dearg simmering like a volcano opposite. He realized Gobhan was giving him rope to hang himself with, and he ended more cautiously.

'It seems he has left us to protect the life of a . . . creature . . . which we would rightfully destroy, according to our laws. And the old woman too – *Three-Eye* – she has stolen the golem for their own protection. The golem is a questionable ally, even if Phadraig is attacked. They have escaped. We are beneath their considerations. Let them be beneath ours. Recognize this before stripping Phadraig of Witchmen to pursue them! Khassam's close. We have to prepare our defenses.'

Silence.

Gobhan didn't move or remove his eyes.

Karnel Dearg clamped the table with his hands, furious at being held from his duty by all this gabbling.

Humbold vacillated. He'd nodded with unconscious agreement, then realized what he'd done, and changed the nod to a shake.

Hatabel's eyelids drooped; he seemed to be asleep.

Cham Tyron stared angrily, flanked by three empty chairs.

Then Gobhan's words came squeezing out at Anka:

'You say you do not deny the laws. Would the Tribunal agree? I wonder. In any case, your suggestion is ridiculous. The laws have been flouted. And, as the High Witchman took such pains to remind me this morning, what is Phadraig without laws? If we fail to prevent them, fail to kill or capture them, then the laws are truly voided and Phadraig will fall to Khassam. The Norm must be defended. An Unclean of Greater Degree lives, has gone out . . .'

'. . . to its element,' Hatabel interrupted quietly. 'Let it be.'

'Your brother Interpreter!' flashed Gobhan. 'Where is he now? Would the Gatekeeper know? Would his *ward*? Would you, Hatabel? Would you break the laws to protect a brother?'

Hatabel paled but otherwise gave no sign of discomposure.

But the First Servant was satisfied; he studied the merchant, who shook his head and followed Anka's eyes to the historical scenes on the ceiling. The First Servant laid his gaze on Humbold, who stared fixedly at the table. Karnel Dearg heaved an explosive breath.

'Word to leave.' It was a statement, not a question.

The First Servant turned stiffly to the soldier.

'Take who and what you need. Take the golem's Keeper. Take them alive – if you can.'

Karnel Dearg strode out in silence.

Anka's eyes didn't leave the safety of the ceiling. He knew how far he could push. Not that it mattered any longer. Phadraig was going to fall because the old man was out of touch with reality. And because Gobhan gripped them as firmly as ever, with the Tribunal and Karnel Dearg in his pocket. Because his illusions were consistent with Phadraig's unreasonable conservatism, he retained the power.

And would do so until Khassam came knocking at the Gate.

Anka wondered what the others were thinking. Whether the same obvious action also occurred to them. Four of them – momentarily alone in the Council chamber with the old man – Anka's knife was sheathed at his waist. He looked down and around.

Tyron sat, flexing his fingers against each other.

Humbold looked mournful – he wouldn't help.

Hatabel scowled, and looked away.

Then Anka met the old man's eyes. Old lips curled back from rotten teeth, cheeks creased and cracked, sallow skin crinkled around his eyes.

'They don't trust you, Anka – any more than you trust them.'

With horror, Anka realized the First Servant was smiling.

He waited for the door to open and the guards to come in.

# Part II: The Tower

## 8: The Yawn

Patrick Cormac stumbled onto the reeking verge and away from Red Kilmun. His lungs burned with pain, but his mind was quick with exhilaration. Out of Phadraig and away into the Wastelands for the first time in a dreary decade! Karnel Dearg would come out after them, but they wouldn't be caught now! The plan had worked to perfection; his departure was precisely timed. Phadraig was already in the past, and now they'd have to move as fast as possible after the golem.

But though the Company made the crossing safely, its rigors had reminded them of their respective conditions, of what lay ahead. Until their collective strength and alertness were fully returned, Patrick knew they'd have to move with caution and trust Gnorl's judgment. Least affected by the crossing, which was routine to him, the big trapper was already onto the golem's trail. Here it was plain, stamped firmly in the oily ash. Patrick looked around for the others. Scalaman choked and spluttered, his face scarlet, taking Iubhar's support, staggering with him, throwing away his useless makeshift mask. And the reeling Songmaker's grin was a fixed apparition, starved of air. Behind them all the vapors of Red Kilmun spat and hissed; Patrick heard the thread of a Fallen One's death-shriek – it ripped thinly through a sudden wavelike roar. On the other bank many still queued numbly for their attempt at the crossing; many would fail it like that one. The Fiststones required steadiness and capacious lungs. Patrick's triumph at escaping prison was muted.

But he knew the crowd of Fallen Ones on the other side was to the Company's advantage. They'd hold up the pursuit. They'd almost held up the Company in their numbers. Once into the Fringe and out of sight of the Gate, the Company had moved ahead of them to the Fiststones.

The way to the south was open without having to cross the river.

But the route rumored to lead to the Savior of the Fallen Ones made the crossing necessary. So that the majority would attempt it.

Patrick dismissed them from his thoughts. He joined the Company by the crags.

Gnorl squatted by the base of a trunk which crawled with red ants. He jerked a thumb at the prints and marks in the ground.

'Ten minutes – no more. Mother lay *here*; old woman made divination *there*. Then they went into the ravine.'

Toes of his pitted black knee-boots digging into the soil, the tracker stood, swatted crawling ants from his leather-covered backside. The heat was growing, and they discarded and rolled up their cloaks, strapping them to their packs. As yet, only one Fallen One had appeared on this side of Red Kilmun, and had staggered off blindly. The Company busied itself, checking weapons, equipment, food, and water, using the activity as an excuse. As individuals, they were uncertain of each other and especially of Patrick Cormac. Ten years was a long time; they didn't know what they were caught into this time. Iubhar's face was sour as he checked the charge-meter of the powertube he'd filched; he couldn't read Patrick's mind. He knew only that it was an arrow in one direction, the protection of the one-eyed child. That the Company lived again for that reason alone. Now Patrick stood off from them, adjusting the straps which bound his torchblade to his right calf, half in and half out of the boot. And Scalaman was suspicious, unsure whether it was Patrick Cormac or the High Witchman in front of him. They weren't together, and none of them knew what to say. Even the Songmaker was silent, pulling on his old black tunic with the cat's eyes on the chest. In the dark, the eyes glowed realistically, and had frightened many out of their skins. Once the Songmaker had put a whole encampment to flight, with his sirena and the eyes. Ducking in the shadows here, there, the sirena howling like a whole pack of hungry predators....

But Liam sensed the distrust as well. It made him angry.

'Why are we all locked up in our pretty little heads, each wondering if the other's the same as he was?' His demand was caustic, but it was interrupted by a volley of raw coughs which had him cursing Red Kilmun before he could continue. Tolerant amusement curled Gnorl's lip. He stood, waiting for the others to get themselves organized, broadsword across his shoulder – he thought the ancients' powertubes were effete.

Looking a trifle haggard, the Songmaker persisted.

'... None of us are the same. Only the conditions. That we adapt to the Wastelands before the Wastelands adapt us!' He took a step toward Patrick. 'So why so shy of us, Patrick? I'll concede your humanity, even though you're crazy!'

But Patrick didn't smile till he turned away, toward the High Towers gleaming high above the Burning River. He shucked off the disguising hooded cloak. The Songmaker saw the crested ring which held his hair at the nape. His eyes lit up, his cheeks went wide, he swung around on the others. 'Ah, for a moment he had me worried! You see – we're different, but we're together again. I'd give you a rousing song I thought of while crossing Red Kilmun, but we haven't the time – I'll sing it to you tonight instead!' His grin was infectious; only Scalaman scowled as Liam patted his shoulder-slung sirena. The Songmaker's eyes fastened onto Scalaman's umber tunic – it was well-cut and padded, of superior material.

'Scalaman, how will you dress in the grave? With style

and conviction? In codpieced splendor? Or will you at last learn to be like the rest of us practical beings and dress to suit the occasion?'

Watching the river, Patrick grinned despite himself.

'The material is tough, resilient!' he heard Scalaman splutter. 'It'll wear as new a ... year after your eyes have gone blind!'

'Ma-licious!' pronounced Iubhar. 'A hit for both sides. A draw! Scalaman, you'll fast remember how to trump him!'

Scalaman didn't know whether he should laugh, or not. He felt very uncomfortable; it was a miracle he made it across. He firmly believed himself to be insane, to be going with these madmen again. He'd thrown away a comfortable life ... or *relatively* comfortable ... and of course, Khassam was coming ... from the north....

An uncomfortable thought occurred to him.

'... Which direction are we taking ... Patrick...?'

Patrick turned. Three more Fallen Ones had made it; two approached them. Time they were going. 'Whichever direction the trail leads,' he said, shrugging. 'If all goes well, we will meet them waiting for us with the golem. As to the route...?' He shrugged again.

Iubhar found himself wondering if Patrick was telling them everything.

'The child,' Scalaman insisted. 'What's this child?'

Patrick paused, but his eyes were candid, and he stroked his beard.

'A changeling of sorts, sent, foretold. He must live. And we will never know why.... Scalaman, don't come if you don't want to. Go back now, if that's your wish....'

'No, no,' protested Scalaman, his pride insulted. 'I will come!'

'But for a moment you looked at me as if ...' Breaking off, Patrick laughed. 'My apologies, it's so strange to be standing here, I forget I must seem strange to you! Rest assured, I'd have been among your most regular guests, if not for the Onerous Burdens!'

'His omission of emission was due to prior commission,' Liam assured Scalaman rapidly. 'Now, are we friends? Do we go?'

Gnorl followed the trail into the ravine, set a purposefully slow pace past the family of prowlers. Even so, the others found it difficult to maintain. It wasn't until they were well out onto the mud steppes that they found any kind of rhythm. And after an hour of plodding through the desolate landscape toward the rolling hills ahead, they were drenched in sweat and aching all over. Scalaman limped, his expression utterly woebegone.

'You're lucky there's no wind,' Liam commented without sympathy.

The others saved their breath as Phadraig fell farther behind and the hills ahead grew closer. Patrick looked back frequently, but saw no sign of pursuit until almost midday. By then, they were onto a shelf of flinty rock which took them from the plains of mud up into the straggly vegetation on the low hills. Pausing to refresh themselves, they saw the sun glint on insect movement, far back.

'An hour behind, at least,' said Patrick with satisfaction.

But except for Gnorl, they were exhausted. Even Liam was morose.

'Where's the Witchmother? Why didn't she wait for us?'

'Because she might meet Karnel Dearg instead of us, you idiot,' he was told by Scalaman, who looked up from the sandy ground to Patrick. 'I see we're going north,' he said bluntly. 'Into the Yawn, the Swamp Forest, and Khassam. I think we're mad.'

Then they started off again, Gnorl in front, sword always on shoulder, head ducking and weaving for signs as the trail grew harder to follow. Silent except for the sound of their breath, they moved into the afternoon. Except for the heat, they were lucky, and knew it. No wind – and no attacks.

The Wastelands bided their time; these low hills seemed almost innocent. Once they were overrun by packs of mew-hounds, but the species seemed to be migrating away from this increasingly blighted area. The Company padded steadily past spiky bushes and trays of scree beneath the dragon clouds which grew on the afternoon, and they found their second wind.

Late in the afternoon, the trail curved past a great hollow, some hundreds of feet from rim to rim, a concrete dish between two hills, now overgrown and cracked by subterranean action. The place was old and silent, heavy with sense of the ancients. They detoured the rim, passing the remains of concrete structures which were broken by time and the elements.

'This is where the ancients listened to the sky!' Liam informed Scalaman in a hoarse whisper. 'An ear, which heard eternity....'

But Scalaman refused to respond to his provocation. And soon, the giant dish was out of sight behind them. The sun was reddening lower as they stood in the lifting breeze on a last hill and looked at the endless black horizon before them, flat and unchanging.

'The Swamp Forest.' Patrick drank water from a canteen. 'Well, we'll be through it in forty hours. I hope the golem's feet are sure. We don't want to wait for Karnel Dearg. Let's go.'

They started to slide down the final hill into the Yawn.

Though none of them said it, all felt cast down by failing to meet with Gaidhealla here. With Karnel Dearg behind, it meant they'd have to follow the trail into the Swamp Forest in the evening. The vast swamp was preferably entered in the morning, if at all, so that only one night had to be endured within it. An evening entry meant two nights – if they were lucky enough to get through the first one.

Within ten minutes, their spirits were dulled by the descent into the black-rimmed Yawn. This huge rift split the land from coast to coast, east to west, straight as a die. The slab of land had fallen an average of three hundred feet during the convulsions of the Great Forgetting. Great waves had rushed in through faults at both coasts while the ruptured earth hurled up steaming muck and detritus; further convulsions threw the faults together again, blocked off the new sea-passage as soon as it was formed. The liquids clashed and mixed, initially surging, spreading across the Yawn and beginning to stagnate as the planet settled again. As it receded through the centuries from its initial high level, leaking away through a thousand different cracks in the floor of the Yawn, new life bred. Now a forest grew from the bitter pools and shadows, its canopy of olive foliage concealing them and their inhabitants from the sun forever. Gigantic black boles thrust up from the stagnant swamp from this side to the other; smooth, branchless, and separate up to the meeting of their flowering topmost canopies, one hundred and fifty feet above the water. The Company slithered down the treacherous slope of the Yawn to the slimy rocks at the edge of the shallows. The sun was lost, save for a few slant beams which fell past the more widely scattered swamp-trees at the periphery. Insects danced in the sallow beams which failed to penetrate the blackness of the waters. Patrick shivered. It was chill and dank, and he unstrapped his cloak, clasped it around his neck; the others were doing likewise. The trail here was quite lost; the silent waters before them were quickly lost to the gloom beneath the trees.

They had to find the nearest connection between the Green Walkways and the shore of the swamp.

It was impassable by boat, mostly because of the Green Walkways themselves, a knotted, tangled skein of vegetable fiber which had grown to cover much of the swamp's area. The Green Walkways were alive. They were the body and the nervous system of one plant which extended across the surface of the waters, always growing, hooking delicately vibrating scout-fibers out across new areas, anchoring the new panels of the vast web in a balanced mesh of horizontal tensions. The expansion was irregular. When each new panel was knitted and knotted up to the frontier established by the scout-fibers, it paused for a few years, storing up nourishment from the waters and growing more thickly green. Then fresh-budding scout lines would snake out laboriously on a front ten to fifteen feet wide, seeking the next anchorage across the waters. The Green Walkways had first overgrown the western end of the Yawn, and the waters at that end were now leached of nutrition and buried beneath acres of rotting fiber. The plant constantly needed new water; it had grown pathways to the eastern end of the Yawn in a matter of centuries, leapfrogging along either shore before connecting up and beginning the growth toward the center. In the not so distant future, the plant would be spent and starving, and there would be no life left in the smothered swamp.

The swamp's denizens – fish, reptiles, giant worms, other creatures which had never been named or identified – were apparently aware of the threat which the plant represented to their future. The giant nervous system grew more slowly now. Too often, the new scout-fibers sent out by established panels were destroyed before they could hook themselves to a new vantage point. So the swamp itself would live a little longer, but eventually the hungry plant would smother it. In the meantime, there were many large lagoons where the plant hadn't yet reached, especially in the center of the Yawn. But even these were defined by green paths, if not yet by voracious lawns.

This was convenient for travelers who wanted to cross from one side of the Yawn to the other. Whatever creatures in the swamp thought, humans regarded the Green Walkways as benign.

The Company had to stumble some distance through the stinking shallows, past boulders big as houses, before they came to the nearest connection between the Green Walkways and the shore. The panel was a dimness in the gloom beneath the trees forty feet from the rocks. It was anchored by loops curled around outlying trunks, the end of a local network. Spotting it first, Gnorl grunted with relief and immediately splashed off through the shallows, hands on sword and eyes vigilant roundabout. The others covered from the shore, but he waded waist-deep and pulled himself up onto the final panel of the path without incident, hooking his fingers through the knotted green fibers. Even where the underside of the three-inch-thick mat touched the water, the fibers felt dry when they weren't, their texture fuzzy, as though they vibrated continually, imperceptibly, and were aware of being touched. Gnorl didn't let it worry him. Pulling himself up, he strained his eyes for a sign of the golem's passing. . . .

Waiting, Patrick was tense. If the gaunt man found no sign here, they'd have to go on – or back – until they found the point of entry the golem had taken. If they lost the trail here, they'd never find it again. If they didn't find it soon, Karnel Dearg would be on top of them. Then he saw Gnorl standing, waving something. And heard his bellow, bouncing off the cliff behind them.

'This is the way!'

Wasting no time, they entered the sour-smelling water, waded as fast as they could, alert for telltale ripples approaching. One by one, they scrambled dripping and filthy onto the platform. Scalaman needed Gnorl's jerk. He regarded himself and the others with disgust.

'Dreaming of a scented bath?' asked the Songmaker.

Scalaman snorted, turned too sharply, and almost lost his balance.

They'd been baked, now they were freezing. Patrick examined the piece of cloth which Gnorl had found and held up – left for them by Gaidhealla, without a doubt. He nodded, rubbed his hands, his face, attempting to show good humor. 'Move quickly, and we might stay warm.' But he was more exhausted than he dared admit, even to himself. And his thoughts were not completely under control. This place with its decay imposed phantasms on his mind.

Iubhar watched him from behind as the Company moved off into the Swamp Forest in single file. They were swiftly enveloped in the damp gloom; tree trunks more than fifty feet distant merged into misty background. For a time, they moved without interruption, each with his own thoughts. Iubhar was still disturbed by the expression he'd read on Patrick's face.

*He's full of doubt. He wonders if he condemns us all for something fantastic and unworthy, if he has escaped Phadraig at all . . . and if ever he'll escape himself. . . .*

But Iubhar could think of nothing positive to say. His mind was oppressed. He thought of his woman, and angrily suppressed the little voice of guilt that whispered from the spaces beneath the vaulted trees.

They walked steadily, now adjusted to the slight, continual trembling of the Walkways. Even the Songmaker fell victim to the increase of dreariness. He tried to conjure heartening notes, then reslung his sirena after several harassing failures. Now the Swamp Forest occulted them completely. There was nothing but the black water, the black boles, and the constant effort of walking at the point of balance along the zigzagging green paths. The plume of their breath became constant, with Gnorl reading a bruised fiber here, a snapped one there, until the remains of filtered daylight unfixed into shrouding mist. Iubhar realized he was almost asleep.

'Patrick, we must find a place to eat and sleep,' he insisted. 'More of this and I'll walk right off the path. And the rest of you are so tired you won't see or hear me go.'

Scalaman muttered vehement agreement, hunched and shivering still beneath cloak and hood. But Patrick was determined to continue as far as possible, to satisfy his own driving urge, and to put as much distance as possible between them and the pursuit. He stopped and turned, halting them all except for Gnorl, who continued scouting on up the path to a fork of three joining paths at the next monster black bole.

Patrick's voice was obstinate and tired, the voice of the High Witchman in its inflexibility.

'My torchblade will light the way. And Liam can keep us awake with his songs.'

He bent to pull the smooth cylinder of his torchblade from its bindings above his sodden boot. He flicked. Blinding light whipped out, speared a bole and set it smoking. Quickly, he adjusted; now orange cascaded, throwing a high tent of light all around. 'There,' he said with sharp satisfaction. 'Now we can go on a while before we rest.'

Iubhar was stiff.

Liam and Scalaman flashed glances which agreed.

Commotion interrupted the ugly feeling, the path rocked violently, there was a threshing of water up ahead. Patrick, closest, spun around and focused a long beam up the path where Gnorl had disappeared. He caught a flash of sinuous motion up at the junction of the paths around the huge trunk, fully twenty feet in diameter. Scrambling closer along the rocking path, he threw a brilliant light on a water-worm's rearing, segmented coils – on Gnorl, flat on the fibers beneath it, unable to penetrate its armored hide, in danger of being swept off as the worm heaved more coils onto the Walkway, submerging it and threatening to snap it beneath its weight. Cold waves swept across the bucking path, which shuddered of its own accord.

Patrick scrambled for handholds, ten feet away from the blind casting of the worm's mottled 'head'; Scalaman was swept off into the water, howling with indignation. Liam snatched up Scalaman's abandoned crossbow before it went too, then a headful of hungry teeth appeared and headed straight for the man who owed Liam money. Hanging on, the Songmaker notched up a quarrel, yelled at Scalaman to get out of the way so he could get in a clear shot. Iubhar trained his powertube grimly into the dark. The path was sinking lower; thirty feet away Gnorl was scrabbling against the tree trunk as slimy coils heaved closer to crush and sweep him off. He swallowed water, cursed, roared with anger, convinced he was dead. But then Patrick studded his tightbeam focus. The worm's head gouted, blue flame licked the air, bits of worm rained onto the waters which heaved and surged as the creature slipped back, shuddering, off the Walkway. Patrick turned, to be dazzled by the close-range flare of Iubhar's powertube.

The beam gouted violently inside a gaping pink mouth about to close on Scalaman, who struggled three feet out, glaring with popeyed fury at the Songmaker. Liam shut his eyes and triggered the wavering crossbow. The quarrel flashed, Scalaman ducked, the quarrel reappeared, imbedded in the flailing, brown-spotted flanks of the mortally wounded predator which fell away from Scalaman. The Songmaker was looking relieved as Patrick turned away to help Gnorl. The big man lay dazed in several inches of water at the junction of the frantically vibrating Walkways with the bole of the tree. The last coils of the worm slid, feebly, into the water, leaving the slime of its life-fluid everywhere as Liam and Iubhar dragged Scalaman to safety. Blood was spreading on the water, attracting hungry interest; ripples were arrowing from every direction. Scalaman spluttered and gasped. As soon as he had his breath he attacked Liam, snatching back his crossbow. 'You idiot! Were you trying to kill me? If I hadn't ducked, you'd have taken my head off! Why didn't you charm the creature with your cursed sirena? I could swear you meant to kill me, and not the creature!'

'Of course I meant to kill you, you owe me money!' snapped the Songmaker with angry sarcasm. 'As for your crossbow, it would have sunk to the bottom if I hadn't snatched it up in time. By the way – your beautiful tunic – it's ruined.'

And he turned away, leaving Iubhar to hold back Scalaman.

Gnorl pulled himself up without assistance from Patrick, but he needed the support of tree and broadsword together before he could stand. Shaking his head, he reached slowly into a waterproof belt-pouch, and extracted a pinch of paper from which he shook out and swallowed a white powder. After a moment, he nodded his thanks.

Patrick refused to accept them; he stood, damning himself.

'I let you go ahead,' he said. 'My judgment was at fault.' His voice was harsh.

Gnorl stared for a moment, then shrugged. 'Why blame yourself? All are at fault. All are still alive.'

All five gathered by the tree at the center of the complaining Walkway junction. The waters about churned as the worm and the brown-spotted predator were torn to pieces by their cousins and brothers. Liam and Scalaman ignored one another. And Iubhar was concerned by Patrick's silence. After a while, the disturbances died, and peace returned. By now, it was completely dark. Patrick adjusted his torchblade, producing the orange glow. His face was sullen, tight-lipped. Iubhar could see he was busy torturing himself.

'The trail, Gnorl. Which path?'

The trapper's reply was curt.

'Don't know. Destroyed. What of your intuition?'

'It fails me.' Patrick shook his head, his features almost ugly. 'I only know we must follow as hard and fast as possible. But we'll stop for the night as soon as we find a cradle or some other safe place.'

He took the lead, the orange cascade held above his head. They followed close, cautious, their ears alert to every ripple and sound from the darkness. If the trail was lost, they could only follow what appeared to be the most direct route. Soon they passed a trunk which formed the junction of eight of the paths, which had knitted together well out into the surrounding lagoons. Colored marking dyes had been used to paint directions on this trunk. The Company passed it onto a Walkway much more broad and thickly matted than the one before. The orange cascade glowed steadily; soon it lit up a mound of fibers which heaved twenty feet above the water.

'Cradle!' he called back, relief entering his voice.

Gnorl was already scrambling up, sword in hand.

Hardly able to move their legs another step, the others followed him to the relative safety of the mound.

Cradles were formed in areas where the fiber-growth grew unacceptably dense, demanding so much nutrition from the underlying liquids that the plant as a whole began to suffer from malnutrition. When and where this occurred, the plant began a struggle against itself, with the result that the weakest, least virile panels in this conglomerating web were pushed up and away from the life-giving swamp by the stronger panels, which annexed their areas, growing underneath. This process, repeated many times over the same area until the sheer mass of dead fibers resisted any further encroachments, resulted in the cradles, which were as safe and dry as any place could be in the Swamp Forest.

They ate cold meat and biscuits; they didn't dare to attempt a fire, which would have burned away the entire cradle and landed them in the water. They were not in the mood for talk or song. One by one, they unrolled soaking blankets, wrapped themselves side by side, and tried to get some sleep, their bodies aching and chilled. Each took their turn on guard, squatting silent in the pitch-blackness, Patrick's torchblade beside them if light should be suddenly needed. Nightsounds drifted and echoed, but nothing came to join them up the mound of dead fiber. After many interminable hours, the blackness began to lessen, ever so slightly. Gnorl went down to the Walkway, bent, with his head to the green of the living fibers.

Returning, he prodded the others awake.

'The Witchmen come,' he said.

Frozen, stiff, unable even to complain, the Company moved on as the light grew, chewing tasteless mouthfuls of breakfast as they did.

They had little sense of reality on this second morning. There was nothing but the endless vistas of black waters and fencing trees which soared up to the hazy, sun-mottled canopy overhead. Down here, the Wind did scarcely more than ripple the protected waters. And it seemed like Phadraig had never existed, that they had always been on the Green Walkways. They moved mechanically, without any real conviction that they would ever leave this place. After two hours on the same broad green strip, another junction; this time, six new forks to choose from. They waited for Patrick, who went into intense concentration before pointing out the continuation of the path they were on. And some way along it, Gnorl muttered triumphantly, ducked to pick up something small which was lodged in a crisscross of fibers. Grinning, he dropped it into Patrick's hands. Patrick examined it with relief. It was a withered flower, stem snapped off close to four lemon petals. Iubhar, Liam, and Scalaman crowded close. They recognized the common flower from the thorn bushes which grew extensively near the great concrete dish they'd passed the previous afternoon. Whether purposefully dropped or not, it indicated that they were back on the trail, if they'd ever left it. Their mood improved, the Company continued. But the passing of the hours returned them to the same leaden state, placing one foot in front of the other, endlessly. And the Witchmen were gaining. Though they weren't in sight, Gnorl deduced from the vibrations transmitted through the Walkway that they were little more than a half hour behind. Grimly, they moved, the day doing its best to penetrate the mournful canopies above. With afternoon they came onto a single strand of the system which crossed a vast, treeless lagoon. The sun blazed down upon them, upon the fields of lilies and water-plants which throve there; the smooth waters reflected the uneasy movements of the sky as in a negative mirror. When the surface was broken by splashing, gouted into gleaming shapes not fifty feet away, the five jumped into compact body, prepared to defend themselves against another of the great worms, stranded on the Walkway, the nearest trees too far away. But the activity was caused by a family of silver reptiles at play, not at all interested in the Company.

Relaxing slightly, the Company continued without a break. In time, they left the lagoon, and were again beneath the shrouding trees. Now they'd been in the swamp for a twenty-four-hour eternity, with the constant tremor of pursuit pushing them on, and on. Patrick felt remote, and unable to communicate the thoughts on his mind. Behind, Iubhar was wondering if his leader thought about Salamander. It was true she was on Patrick's mind. But the immediate situation was more pressing. He felt like an athlete called on to give his supreme performance when completely out of training. On the roof of the Central Tower the morning before, it had seemed so straightforward, prophesied, and Iubhar's skepticism had amused him. Now, he fought not to share it himself. The High Witchman had fled Phadraig, to become Patrick Cormac again, in the Wastelands, as of old.

And the mission had seemed straightforward too.

Now Patrick Cormac felt like a naked, unpurposed man.

He was confused by too much thought, too many possibilities, alternatives, and unknowns. His intuition was out of training. Perhaps Iubhar understood. But he couldn't expect the others to appreciate his fallibility. They compared him with a memory ten years dead. They expected him to be as he had been – young and full of energy. But his youth was gone.

And his certainty also seemed to have deserted him.

The decline of his morale was reinforced by the new region they entered late in the day. They were surrounded by individual trunks so close-growing as to form a sullen wall. These trunks, more slender than the previous giants, were stained with wort and lichen, infested with drab creepers which coiled on the water. The air was foul, insects droned, were snapped up from the turgid water. The Company was soon so stung and bitten that previous miseries seemed inconsequential. But they couldn't stop.

And they had the prospect of another night ahead of them in the endless swamp. Here the swamp was shallow, and rocks began to thrust diagonally from the yellow-stained waters. They might find safety on one of these rocks for the night – if they could afford to stop. If the Witchmen behind knew how close they were to their quarries, then there would be no rest or safety tonight.

Suspiciously without event, the second day withdrew itself.

The Company saved its breath and concentrated on putting one sodden foot in front of the other, over and over again, forever.

## 9 : The Land Beyond

The golem took them out of the Swamp Forest with the rising of the sun of the third day. Thus far, Cuyahogan had been faultless, tireless. But Salamander was dying, had never more than half recovered consciousness during the crossing of the swamp. When they stood on dry land again, Gaidhealla had yet to make up her mind – whether to wait here for the Company, assuming they had the trail – or whether to continue. The worst of it was that Salamander couldn't be her prime concern. The child's safety was more important than Salamander's survival. But unless a foster-mother could be found, Salamander's survival was important to the baby.

Khassam ahead, the Witchmen behind. The problem had occupied her mind through two days and nights. Two nights – she had compromised. Cuyahogan could easily have continued through each of these nights, beaming the darkness with its night-vision, sufficiently fast and sure to evade attack from the waters. But she didn't want to get too far ahead; she couldn't afford it. On each of those nights, she ordered Cuyahogan to set them down on one and another of the cradles. Through them, Salamander slept, the one-eyed child slept, Gaidhealla shivered and tried to sleep, with the golem standing guard over them. The child had accepted Cuyahogan, and no longer wailed when the golem took them up. The old woman made sure it was kept warm and dry, but she knew the swamp was doing none of them any good. On the second night, they were attacked by something they never saw. The golem met it, sent it yowling back into the splashing waters.

On this third morning, they reached the opposite shore, climbing out of the Yawn onto a tongue of flat plateau which sliced deep into the Swamp Forest. In the north, the better part of a day distant, a range of black hills, and behind them, she knew, the Scarp. There was a tower on one of the nearer hills, though invisible at such a distance. A reclusive eccentric had once lived there, harming nobody. She'd heard only rumors of the present inhabitant. They referred to the Infernal Priest: they were melodramatic, and probably untrue. Nevertheless, it was the way they must take. Salamander needed rest. They needed a sanctuary for the night. For the land ahead was the land of the Banissen Saturna. And Khassam's vanguard must also be somewhere ahead, somehow to be avoided. Whatever the nature of its inhabitant, the tower was preferable to the hostile land. Possibly they would get an unpleasant reception. But Gaidhealla had trust in her own knowledge and in the golem's powers of persuasion.

She wondered one last time whether she should wait here for the Company. Every step taken lessened the probability of their meeting.

But Salamander's drawn white face decided her.

And there were herbs which grew in the land beyond.

Besides, the Company had its own ordeal to overcome. If Patrick and his friends succeeded in following them to the tower by the night, they'd have proved their value to the child. Then possibly, together, they might slip through the broad front of Khassam's advance, perhaps through one of the tunnels which riddled the Scarp.

But if the Company failed to win through and find them, then it wasn't going to be much use anyway. She wondered if the scrap of cloth and the flower had been found. She wondered if the Company lived. She wondered where the Witchmen were. Then she ordered Cuyahogan forward.

*

Karnel Dearg was proud and unimaginative. Thought of failure rarely entered his calculations; he was accustomed to the success brought by taking no chances. Perhaps his respect for the Wastelands had been dulled by the soporific of Council politics. He took fifty Witchmen, and the golem's Keeper, and three hunter-trappers to guide them. He didn't really expect to have to listen to their advice.

The squad descended arrogantly to the Fiststones, pushing aside the Fallen Ones who blocked their way and held them up.

The squad re-formed on the other side with a good deal less self-assurance, and minus three of its number. Karnel Dearg raged up and down their ranks, furying at the incompetence of a unit which allowed a seventeenth of itself to be destroyed so gratuitously. The trail was clear, and the squad was double-marched up the ravine, past straggling Fallen Ones who were forced aside beneath the fronded trees where the prowlers lurked. But their pace declined through the broiling day; the sun was in steep decline when they looked down on the mires of the Swamp Forest. The Witchmen muttered among themselves, casting uneasy glances at the somber graveyard ahead. They were unsure of the Witchgoddess' protection at such a distance from Phadraig. They were unwilling to descend into the Yawn. But Karnel Dearg refused to let them rest, refused to listen to the trappers' advice. They shrugged and withdrew, and privately resolved to quit the suicide squad at the first available opportunity.

They moved out onto the Green Walkways, into the gloom, flaring torches held above every fourth head in the single file. The Witchmen dream-marched until Karnel Dearg was forced to let them rest, his trackers insisting that it was quite impossible to follow the trail farther. On the other hand, they said, if the squad stopped here, exposed on a single Walkway strand, by morning they'd be decimated.

Word was passed back that they'd continue to the nearest

cradle, or knitted lawn sufficiently wide to hold them all. Scarcely able to move their legs, the Witchmen stumbled on, no longer caring what might live in the evil waters at their feet.

They reached the junction where the battle had taken place. The path was torn; gobs of the giant worm floated on the still-rippling water. The Witchmen defiled past, one by one, uneasily fingering the growth of their chins, drawing the Sacred Symbol's double curve on their foreheads. A sudden surge came from the water, teeth gleamed against torchlight, another gob of the worm was gone.

'They tire; their pace slackens!' barked Karnel Dearg down the exhausted line. 'What are you frightened of? The Witchgoddess protects us if we are brave!'

He was prudent enough to qualify his exhortation. Karnel Dearg had problems. The trail was leading them north, directly toward Khassam's presumed line of advance. In Council he'd expressed his opinion that the High Witchman was defecting to Khassam with Phadraig's secrets. Now, the night dark, he wondered uneasily if they were being led into a trap, if perhaps Anka hadn't been right. The protection of Norm Purity was one thing in Phadraig, but another altogether out here. They came to the trunk which formed the axis of eight radiating paths. The paths had knitted together into a lawn which extended out for a hundred feet on every side of the trunk. Here they stopped. Karnel Dearg called the trappers and his lieutenants.

'Let them eat, then sleep. Five hours. Ten men will be awake at all times; the rest will sleep close in the center.'

The night was uncomfortable, dangerous. Fifty-five men in one group radiated a wide beam of nervousness which attracted grateful attention. When the morning came, the roll was short by another four – all of them sentries. The Witchmen applied cold razor to chin on order, prayed to the Witchgoddess without much spirit, ate, re-formed, and marched out on the Walkway indicated by the trappers.

Not far ahead, Gnorl picked up the vibration of their

coming.

The second day was worse than the first. The Servants of Norm Purity moved steadily across the baking lagoon and into the chill, insectile afternoon, without once catching sight of their prey ahead. And Karnel Dearg hounded his sullen trappers for information:

'How far ahead? When will we catch them? Will we catch them before we leave the swamp? What do you know of the land beyond?'

The trappers grunted monosyllabic answers. refusing to commit themselves. 'Not far.' 'Soon.' 'Maybe.' 'Not much.'

Falling evening half saw attack by a violet-striped creature with frills of crimson gauze double-ridging its scaly back. It lunged out from behind a trunk. Powertubes flamed energy, and it was dead, but so were two more Witchmen. They passed the second night on a cold shelf of rock without having caught up with the Company. None of them slept, not even Karnel Dearg, a skilled catnapper. And none of them died, though the rock was infested with blood-sucking insects which caught them as they dozed, nipped them wide-awake again. Tired and deathly pale, they shaved again next morning, prayed with emphasis, feelings mixed. They were almost through the swamp – but was Khassam just ahead? Orders were barked, and they started off again through thinning trees. Now the light was better, brighter, and the short blast of Wind was stronger, rippling the more open waters. But though long stretches of the Green Walkways were visible ahead, there was no sign of the Company. Before midday, the tongue of high plateau which cut into the Yawn was visible through the last of the trees. Here, the heat was clammy, the surface of the deep water proliferant with puffily-flowering green bladders, mats of lilies which pushed against the Green Walkway, red-and-black dragonflies, mosquitoes. The humid air droned and hummed as the tongue's black cliff grew nearer at the end of this last, single stretch, which grew increasingly slender. Karnel Dearg lifted his eyes to the edge of the land above them.

'Where are those glasses?'

He snatched the magnifying eye from a lieutenant, and hastily trained it to the vegetation on top of the cliff. And in the narrow well he saw two bared heads in the instant before they turned and moved away. One of the heads had flaxen hair, held at the neck. The other had a sharp face, with a bristle of red-brown hair. It was all he could make out. But it was enough. There was no time to be lost. He threw his arm up and pointed, bellowing back down the line: 'There they are! We can be there in ten minutes! We must double our speed!'

Through his impatient excitement, he misjudged the distance, the capabilities of his exhausted men, and the capacity of the Walkway as its width narrowed down. After ten minutes, scarcely a third of the distance was covered. A further ten minutes brought the cliffs closer.

But even the vanguard was still well out from the base of the tongue when a drone began to grow from the northern sky.

The drone grew louder, the column halted, looking up in consternation; it was a sound the Witchmen recognized.

High in the air above the tongue, the formation of gleaming silver dots appeared, heading south, toward Phadraig.

The *eala*.

Even as they watched, five dots detached themselves from one side of the parent formation and began to descend to where the Witchmen were trapped. For a moment, they stood still, as though hypnotized. Then a man howled with fear. And Karnel Dearg shook his fist at the cliff-top; he blazed with anger.

'Traitors! You led them to us!'

Cut and bruised, Scalaman pulled himself up over the top of the cliff, and lay panting with relief on flat ground in sunlight. The climb had been another nightmare which he could have avoided by staying in Phadraig. It hadn't been made any easier by the way Liam bounded up like an exuberant boy. Scalaman's head pounded; he was fed up.

'How do you know we're still on their trail? Why didn't they wait for us here? Why do we go north, right into Khassam?' he demanded, shivering resentfully inside his sunken, shredded tunic. Iubhar warned the Songmaker with an eye not to make any comment. 'Witchgoddess rot this cursed land!'

Scalaman got to his feet and scuffled morbidly around the rock shelf. 'What are you grinning at?' he muttered at Liam. 'Don't think I've forgotten!' He glowered, his face seemed to have lost flesh already, and he grimaced with hatred for the sallow, apathetic vegetation up here. 'Gnorl, how do you know they came up this way? This ground's impossible to read!'

The black-bearded man looked up speculatively from his customary crouch of rest. 'I see what you cannot.' He pointed roundabout. 'Here – see. And here. This broken fern.' He stabbed a direction with a broken fingernail. 'North – to the hills.'

Patrick turned from his consideration of the black range ahead.

'When did they pass?'

'Three hours – perhaps three and a half. Cuyahogan stood *here* – the old woman walked about. . . .'

'Deciding what to do, perhaps,' Patrick scanned the northern horizon. 'It's an ugly land,' he said thoughtfully. 'We all hoped to meet them here. Her reasons must be good. I remember a tower on one of those distant hills – a sage lived there – but I've heard nothing but evil of the present occupant. I think it's there we'll find them, if we make good speed today.' His expression was grim; he jerked his thumb toward the black hills. 'No tower could be more evil than these lands after dark. You'll recall the hypocritical innocence and mimicry of life in these parts. Perhaps you'll also recall the Banissen Saturna?' And his grin was tight as he pushed back his hood and went to the edge to look out over the swamp, two hundred feet below.

'Crass ghouls, savages!' spat Scalaman from the bushes where he'd gone to relieve himself. 'Inhumane, abnormal, and bestial!'

Liam's grin was wide. For some reason, perhaps because they were back in the sunlight, he felt good.

'You do them an injustice! For a start, their metaphysical system is most interesting. Any race which justifies its slaughter of all strangers on the grounds that strangers suffer from wanderlust, and that wanderlust is a form of demonic possession, must be spiritually interesting. That this race then proceeds to worship wanderlust as a demon of unpronounceable name is little short of amazing. It implies their pragmatism, duality of attitude, and possibly even a sense of humor!'

Gnorl grunted, polishing his sword-blade. Scalaman was silent behind the bushes as Iubhar tamped down and lit his briar, relaxing while he could. He checked his supply of weed, wondering when he'd get the chance to renew it. Somehow, the thought of deprivation was almost more alarming than any other prospect.

Liam went to join Patrick at the edge. His grin was easy and artless; his rough-cut bowl of hair covered a brain satisfied with the immediate present. He opened his mouth, but was cut off short.

'Look ... I saw something, a flash of sun on metal, perhaps....'

They withdrew quickly. Scalaman reappeared, and Gnorl got up.

'Did they see us?'

'Possibly. Why wait to find out?'

The Company started along the tongue, sheer walls falling into the Yawn on either side, scabby lichen beneath their filthy boots, ferns brushing their drying legs. It was almost midday, and the sun shone without prospect of interruption. Patrick heard Scalaman mumbling complaints about the heat, the Songmaker, the mission, the Witchmen, the world. Patrick grinned; he was glad the bedraggled masochist still complained – it was a connection with the past. Scalaman's life was an agony of sensitivity, despite which he persisted in bruising himself against every sensual rock he could find, from bed to battlefield. The day Scalaman stopped complaining, that was the day to worry about.

In a few minutes they left the isthmus and the Yawn behind, and entered a varied, attractive land. Smooth emerald lawns rolled up and down gentle slopes into the hazy eastern middle-distance; past experience made them stay well clear. Gnorl followed the trail without difficulty, though the ground was hard as they entered fields of prickly purple scrub. A few minutes more, and they found their way barred by another obstacle. Liam and Scalaman were disputing fiercely when Patrick raised a warning hand.

'Snowtrees . . . be careful now!'

Liam fell instantly silent. Now they walked between two hillocks on suddenly apathetic lichen, and picked their way into the snowtree grove which extended across their path. And they found themselves sweating in the white of winter, their course crisscrossed with the crooked, poisonous albino branches of the petrified dwarf trees. They took careful, well-judged steps. Even Liam's mouth was tight as they navigated this eerie elfin land of snowlight beneath the sun.

'Why did they come through here?' hissed Scalaman. 'Why court this danger? There's no cure for the snowtree touch; the whole body rots and crumbles. . . .'

Eyes intent, he ducked and twisted, clearing one low branch by an inch, pulling himself around the next, streaming with sweat, receiving no answer until he joined the other four in a small clearing at the center of the grove. The ground was covered with lichen, except for a patch where a creeping carpet of anaemic but flowering weeds similar to liverwort was growing. Gnorl and Patrick crouched, examining the weed. Gnorl sounded perplexed. 'They stopped. Girl lay on her side, here. Old woman gathered flowers....'

Patrick plucked several of the sickly purple flowers, crushed them in his fist, then examined the pulp. Then he nodded, his expression cleared. 'She stopped to make a salve for Salamander's wound. This flower has healing properties; it purifies the blood....' He was silent. Then he threw away the pulp with disgust. 'But it is fiery, and only to be used in extremity....'

The others were silent, not knowing what to say.

Iubhar glanced past petrified branches at the cobalt sky. 'Listen!'

The rest of them heard it. The growing sound.

Simultaneously they saw the pattern of shining dots which seemed to rise through the crooked shawl of deadly branches.

'*Eala* ... more than I've ever seen.... Where did Khassam find them...?'

Patrick seemed slightly dazed by the sight, pale face staring.

'Phadraig's ruin,' observed Scalaman miserably.

'Into cover!' snapped Iubhar. '*Liam* —'

'Look how perfect their pattern is!' the Songmaker was lost in momentary rapture, his head thrown back against the hooked neck of his slung sirena. 'The sun flashes on their grid; diamond facets are projected on the air, like gateways into other worlds!'

Scalaman, scuttling for cover, turned about and scolded: 'Your poses fool nobody, you idiot! You'll give us away!'

'Genius usually is idiotic,' the Songmaker retorted. But he moved fast enough, pushing as far as he dared beneath the scanty leafless snowtree cover.

'There are twenty-five,' Gnorl confirmed for Patrick, who squatted beside.

'When they appear over Phadraig ...' Iubhar was pale with anger.

But Patrick was wondering where the Witchmen were. The roar in the sky grew till the air overhead was full of the metal machines; their thunder rolled and crashed across the land. The Company stood out when the formation had passed; they watched them dwindling to the south, over the Yawn. They saw five machines to the east of the grid peel off and descend, sunlight spinning on their vanes....

'They've seen Karnel Dearg and his men. They won't be off the Walkway yet.'

Patrick's words were confirmed. The Company plainly saw the black eggs tumbling from the bellies of the hovering machines.

Then they heard the sound of muffled explosions.

'Unnatural, abnormal energies! It's hideous!'

Scalaman was vehement, and Iubhar nodded sharp agreement.

'It's the times,' said Patrick Cormac, without any sign of emotion.

'But ... Phadraig ...' Scalaman was disbelieving.

'Phadraig is dead.' Patrick met Scalaman's furious gaze. 'Our former life is dead. Nothing can change it. We have another purpose. If Khassam lusts for the ruins of Phadraig, let him have them. They're no good to him or anyone else. We're not fighting Khassam unless he gets in our way. Our mission is to safe-conduct the child wherever the Witchmother of the Third Eye has decided. Nothing else, no former hatreds or allegiances, must affect this purpose.'

His voice was sharp against the doubt and suspicion he read in four pairs of eyes. Even Gnorl was forced to burst out against him.

'But how can you not feel pity on those poor...?'

'Old ways die hard,' said Patrick, 'and they'll kill you faster.'

And Scalaman voiced the same suspicion that Iubhar had.

'Patrick ... did you know that ... did you expect the *eala* to come and attack the Witchmen...? Did you ... plan for it...?'

Scalaman immediately regretted the stumbling question.

He found he couldn't look away from those wide, burning eyes.

'What do you think, Scalaman?'

His voice was too quiet. Scalaman had to answer.

'Perhaps you ... dreamed it ... as you dream other things....'

'If that were the case, I would have told you!'

'Yes ... yes....' And Scalaman looked down.

The drone of the *eala* died away to the south. The clearing in the grove was silent, filled with suspicions. Then Liam laughed.

'Of course, Patrick, we believe you, as much as we believe ourselves. Which, in my case at least, isn't very much. I'm ever doubtful of what I tell myself. But while we're worried about our mutual honesty, won't you tell us, what *is* this new principle that we're running after and trying to serve?' Standing easy in the center, he brought his sirena around and struck a curling question mark. 'We have a prophesied changeling which, in three days of life, has caused many deaths. What benefits does it promise in future atonement?'

Patrick's face was a mask.

'There is no atonement. They die because they are dead.'

'Then what about Salamander? Do you care if she dies?' Iubhar's outburst was raw with the pain he felt.

Patrick stiffened. For a moment it seemed he'd hit out at the smaller, wiry man. Gnorl stood watchful beside him as a breeze crackled the branches of the snowtree grove. Patrick closed his eyes. 'Do you too think I've lost my humanity, Iubhar?' His whisper was tight through his teeth. But then his eyes opened, and his rage burst through. 'How do you think I can retain my humanity if I let my mind dwell on death and suffering? It comes to all of us! Death is necessary for life to be! The Witchgoddess isn't as Norm Purity would have her. At times, our planet reels through the sky as drunkenly as we upon its surface, pulled by other sources and us with it, so that we struggle for our lives, and try to react to the changes before they kill us! The child's a change, a signal, an unknown direction, which will kill us or lead us to new perceptions – but Phadraig is the past, it's a corpse, it's dead! Cling to its memories and we will die too! Ignobly! Pathetically!'

Without waiting for reaction, he pushed past Liam and left the clearing, moderating his temper as he approached the snowtree branches.

After a moment, looking at each other, the others followed.

The Company pushed on into rolling land, past the innocent-seeming lawns, past snowtree groves, through more friendly woods, and down to a grassy savannah through which a clear river flowed from the black hills ahead to the Yawn behind. They stripped off their muddy clothes and plunged into the water to clean and cool off, leaving Gnorl on guard on the bank. He took his turn when Patrick came out, dripping, his body gleaming pale and muscular in the sunlight. Gnorl stripped except for the amulet hanging from a thong around his neck – the dog-tooth of a mewhound – and the waterproof pouch belted around his waist. He was weather-burned dark, his broad frame matted with curling black hair. Nodding curtly, he dived into the water without ado and joined the others, leaving Patrick watchful on the bank with one hand close to the torch-blade as he dried. Several times already, one or another of them had suspected movement from shadows, behind bushes, in waving seas of waist-high grass. But no enemy, animal or human, had been caught in full gaze. If they were watched by the Banissen Saturna, Patrick knew they were safe until nightfall. The tribe rarely attacked strangers in daylight, finding no reason to make a present of their lives to ferocious, wanderlusting madmen.

Patrick watched the four of them in the water and ate, frequently checking the flat lands behind and around. He wanted to relax, yet he knew he couldn't. Despite the swim, he felt ill-tempered, isolated, and confused, his thoughts scurrying out of reach. As yet he hadn't grown back into the feeling of physical command; he'd been locked so long in a bureaucratic cocoon where intrigue and suspicion were more appropriate than fast reactions and honest thinking. He watched the lithe Songmaker taunting Scalaman about the dimensions of his paunch, but he couldn't smile – he felt isolated from them. He knew the isolation was at least partly of his own creation. But try as he might, he couldn't break down the barriers which had been confirmed by his outburst in the snowtree grove. Scalaman distrusted him, Gnorl would be won over on his own terms alone, even Iubhar was unsure. He revised his thoughts. Only the Songmaker took him less seriously than he took himself. But Liam had always distrusted premature judgments involving his own point of view. Perhaps the Songmaker's vivid imaginations gave him so many perspectives that he was constitutionally more tolerant of others than most people could be.

Patrick regarded the black hills ahead. They seemed no closer. He knew this was the illusion of their color and of the haze which lay around their lower, greenmantled slopes. In fact, he could see the nub of the tower toward which the trail led, a black dot atop the basalt crags of the nearest climb. They should be well up the slopes by dark, and needed to be. Breeze soughed in the grass behind him; he turned, but there was nothing there. The sound he'd heard was in his mind.

He was pulling on shirt, boots, and leggings as Liam and Iubhar, laughing, pulled themselves out onto the grassy bank. The Songmaker took a look at his face and shrugged, reached for his sirena as Scalaman followed them out, his hair rat-tailed, grumbling about sharp stones and cut feet. Iubhar quietly filled their canteens from the river. He thought he knew where Patrick was. Thinking of Salamander. A sadness on his mind, a presence he couldn't reject. Iubhar knew Patrick was cut to the quick by their exchange in the snowtree grove; they'd hardly spoken since.

Gnorl came out last, with something silver and wriggling in his hand.

He threw the fish back in the water.

For there was no time to gut and cook it or to lay traps. The Company followed the trail again, leaving the river after another half hour. It fell through rapids between the hills. They began to climb through the endless long grass toward the hill ahead, hands on their weapons, eyes skinned and jumpy, the trail of trampled stems easy to follow – too easy —

'Many feet followed the golem,' Gnorl growled, 'at a distance.'

'How far ahead?' Patrick demanded.

'An hour . . . not more. . . .'

Then all five were whirling in reaction to sound which burst in front of them, Gnorl whipping sword from shoulder, Scalaman slotting quarrel to crossbow, Liam swinging sirena around. . . .

Frightened faces and leaping legs filled the air before them.

Patrick Cormac lowered his torchblade and laughed with relief.

The herd of green-dappled deer fled. But thereafter Scalaman kept his bow at the ready, quarrel in the groove, until they were out of the grass and climbing toward the lower, forested slopes of the hill. They passed a roughly-tended field of maize, and continued watchfully.

'They are nomadic between Scarp and Yawn,' said Patrick, 'but sometimes they stay in one place long enough to raise a crop.'

His voice was cautious. Iubhar realized he was apologizing for his mood. He clapped Patrick on the back, but said nothing. Soon, they were beneath the first trees with the sun thickening in the northwest. Their feet muffled by the mossy loam, they passed under a cathedral vault of riotous vegetation which swarmed with chittering life. Multicolored butterflies with silver eyes on their wings drifted on the cloying, overbodied air; slant sunbeams splashed on the rocks which burst vertically from the clinging humus. Patrick followed Gnorl again, his thoughts restless around a sense of imminence. Salamander. Twenty-one years younger. But they were bound by the same mesh, or mess, of fate....

The Company, tiring, dragged itself up the steepening slope through the thick, tearing undergrowth, up natural paths which the golem had followed, its oversized prints clearly displayed.

A wavering howl drifted from the flank of the hill.

It was answered by another from the undergrowth, closer.

Then the close air was reverberating with hungry clamor.

'Mewhounds...!' breathed Scalaman, forgetting about his feet.

'Back to back, each guard the one on your right!' snapped Patrick.

Then the slavering white-whiskered creatures were upon them.

## 10: Lawns of Green

'Lie flat!'

Karnel Dearg had bellowed the order down the line of stranded Witchmen as the five silver machines roared overhead. The three trappers glanced at each other, then dived off the Walkway and started swimming for the shore, estimating that the dark water was a safer place to be. They were hardly noticed in the confusion; white faces stared up, frozen, at the horrible metal birds which hovered above them, above the highest trees. Some had heard Karnel Dearg and fallen flat, digging their faces into the fibers, but most of the Witchmen were standing hypnotized as black eggs came tumbling down from the *eala*, unable to understand what was happening.

The black eggs plummeted into the water, almost all at once, straddling the Walkway.

Five high fountains rose and sprayed the Witchmen.

Then the world was destroyed.

They were hit by fists which exploded from the swamp, smashing them through the gouting air, and ripping apart the Walkway.

A shudder ran through hundreds of miles of the organism.

The *eala* turned away and rose to rejoin the main formation.

A silence fell over the swamp, broken only by feeble splashes, the thin cries of the wounded and drowning.

Blood spread, and soon attracted attention.

The tongue of rock was reached by eighteen Witchmen and two of the trappers. The third had been dragged under by something which reached from the bottom of the swamp and coiled around his ankle.

Not even the explosions had made it let go from its hold.

Karnel Dearg wasn't among those who reached the shore.

The golem's Keeper had been killed instantly by the blast.

The surviving Witchmen knew they were Fallen Ones. The two trappers left them to their lamentations, and began the climb out of the Yawn, bent on self-preservation. They knew they'd need all of their skill.

When their shock receded, the Witchmen began to follow. But the trappers were no longer there when they pulled themselves over the top.

Without speaking or seeming to notice each other, they drifted away down the tongue, sense of community lost. Several drifted for the whole day, shadowed by creatures which never put in an appearance, scouted by grinning sons and daughters of the Banissen Saturna. These people were overwhelmed by the sudden influx of madmen who needed exorcism in the name of the dread demon, Phanphaecanh. A filament of his essense lay in the loft of the Infernal Priest, whom they both feared and despised....

Scouts padded behind several stumbling Witchmen, grinning with anticipation.

One of the Witchmen came to the snowtree grove, and entered it; a trembling finger touched a branch, the black spot spread immediately, and he could only collapse and watch the withering, first of his arm . . .

The last nine stayed loosely together, striking a hopeless course to the west, by instinct more than mutual agreement. They passed another who slept of exhaustion in the middle of a pleasant lawn, but they didn't see him there.

They drifted through the blazing afternoon along the edge of the Yawn, past dormant prowlers, over soothing parkland which called them to lie down and sleep. But they continued, erratically, already asleep, dreaming what they saw, the sounds they heard, heavy breath, a muffled scream. And they found that they'd stumbled into night, and there were only eight of them left. All around, the Wastelands were astir. They found themselves awake, standing huddled at the center of an enormous lawn, its border everywhere lost to darkness. They found themselves, wanting to live.

'We should stay here,' said one shivering man, 'where we can watch in all directions.'

'We'll freeze to death!' another muttered.

'We'll get warmth from the powertubes,' answered a third.

'Listen to the night!' interrupted a fourth, with horrified wonder.

That settled the matter. The Wastelands were alive with challenge and response. The Witchmen huddled around the dim radiant heat emitted by the powertubes stacked in the center of their circle. Each avoided the eyes of the others, avoided himself. Stars appeared intermittently through the scudding wraiths of cloud; the wind was chill and damp. The lawn began to move. The Witchmen failed to hear its whispering beneath the wind. They didn't realize that they were sinking into the creature which began to draw itself up around them. It lowered them subtly within itself, without tilt or jerk. One or two of the Witchmen wondered where the wind had gone. They looked up in confusion, for they still heard it in their ears, whispering louder. And blackness, deafening, whispering all around, no sky above. Warned too late, they were on their feet, powertubes in their hands, a torch held up. Light flared on the grass of the lawn which had drawn itself around them so they were trapped in its folds, inside a hollow, diminishing gourd. The grass was growing orange and stretching for them from all sides: not grass, cilia, lashing with orange hunger. Back to back and still on their feet they studded their weapons frantically, burning black swathes of charred cilia, but it was too late. They were pressed close, deafened by the whispering; the walls of the digestive gourd glowed intense nacarat, and folded in upon them. The whispering climbed to a sudden shriek, then silence fell. The lawn's gracious carpets had uprooted from the dry earth below, and slid in over the center, in waves like a concertina. Now it was piled up in the middle around its central root, a triumphant digestive mound beneath the sour Wastelands sky of night.

## 11 : The Idiot Daughter

The juice of the purple flower coursed like fire through Salamander. She groaned, stirred, then fell back to restless sleep in the middle of the snowtree grove. And Gaidhealla's eyelids drooped; she needed sleep herself, much more of this and she'd lose her sense of judgment. The center of the snowtree grove was as safe a place as they could find, immune from attack except from the air. She told the golem to stand guard and wake her after three hours, or immediately it sensed anything or anybody approaching, or if Salamander awoke. The child was fed and half asleep in the shade of the poisonously beautiful grove; the old woman knew she should watch over her daughter, but it was physically impossible. She slept. And the golem wakened her after more than two hours. Salamander had recovered consciousness, stimulated by the fiery herb. But not wholly. Gaidhealla felt her forehead; the girl's temperature was high. And though the wound was uninfected, the old woman was pessimistic.

For, though Salamander recognized her, the girl wasn't in the present. She didn't seem to know that she was a mother or had ever been pregnant. Eyes were open in her milk-white face, she talked, but weakly, and with the voice of a seven-year-old. Gaidhealla realized where and when the wounded girl's mind had fled. Salamander was watching Kalnakill's forces blast open the Southern Gate, watching them sweep into Madadhmachair with fire and sword, forcing their way along the Culane and up into the Chahd.

She was watching the Company Chatachain drive them back.

She saw Patrick Cormac as he was before Council took him.

Gaidhealla stroked her forehead, wondering sadly if she'd admit the present Patrick to her reality. If they met. If the girl didn't die

The golem took them from the grove through rolling, varied land.

It held Salamander in the crook of its left arm now, where Gaidhealla could watch her, soothe her, try to talk with her.

They were passing through a wood when she heard the *eala*. She ordered the golem to wait in shadow until they were gone. Soon they were into the wide stretch of gently-waving grass and skirting the clear waters of the river. She knew they were being watched and followed, every inch of the way, but she thought daylight attack unlikely. She wondered how they'd be described. A monstrous white un-man and a babbling girl, an old woman and a one-eyed child? Were they fit as sacrifices to the Demon of Wander-lust?

Late in the afternoon, the tower was clear on the crags of the hill before them until they came beneath the trees. Cuyahogan attacked the slope as the sun began to slip. The child was hungry again, and it began to wail, while from the other arm, Salamander was talking steadily, without inflection or expression. Gaidhealla couldn't stand the combination; she told the golem to stop in an open glade with a good view in most directions.

The girl was completely unaware of the baby at her breast; she had neither, she was seven years old.

'Mother, today we learned the History of the Seers, how Maelnagar the Maker of Outcries was drowned to death in a barrel of liquid from Red Kilmun when Crowcar was High Witchman. The teacher said that Maelnagar was wicked, he spread false doctrines and alarmed the people.

But why did they kill him so cruelly? Mother, I've overheard you talking about Maelnagar, and you don't think he was wicked, do you? When the teacher said Maelnagar was evil I wanted to say that you said he wasn't, but I remembered what you said about talking to people who wouldn't understand, so I didn't. After all, he's only got a double white cord, and he's not a very good teacher, he gets angry when I make mistakes. If Maelnagar was drowned for telling people about their mistakes, why isn't my teacher drowned? He's always going on about how stupid I am, and saying if I don't love the First Servant I'll be a failed mother someday like that fat lady I never saw again. ... Mother, what happened to her ...?'

Ashen-faced, Gaidhealla took the baby from her, held it up.

'Salamander, he's your baby ... he's born of you....'

The girl interrupted her piping monologue to answer sweetly.

'Don't be silly, Mother; little girls can't have babies!'

Then she was talking about her hateful teacher again, and the old woman turned away with tears on her cheeks, overwhelmed by pity. But the child was content, its eye closed. Her face was very bleak as she looked at it in the failing light. She knew its mind was ancient, not the mind of a newborn baby except for its frustration at physical needs and limitations. It was difficult to think of the polypheme as a 'he'; one of the many new genders current in the more tolerant Wastelands was needed. But perhaps none of those would do, either.

She realized the forest had gone completely quiet.

She spoke to the golem in a low voice concealed by Salamander's stream of words.

'Cuyahogan, take us up, swiftly. We're surrounded by Banissen Saturna. Protect us, burst through them up the hill to the tower on the crags above. Now!'

The golem lifted Salamander, was taking up Gaidhealla and the child when the attack came. Small, knobbly-featured men were around them on all sides, appearing like ghosts from the declining light. Cuyahogan accelerated, knocking aside a thrusting spear. Gaidhealla saw close-set brown faces go past in a blur, and the golem leaped for a rock-shelf six feet above the clearing, landed on its feet and left the Banissen Saturna clear behind. The twenty warriors stared, momentarily dumbfounded. Then they rushed in futile, token pursuit. Their squat necks were hung about with rattling greenstone pebbles; they were naked except for ragged strips of cloth wound around their loins and trailing up over their shoulders. As they ran the wind rushed through holes bored in the greenstones, setting up a thin wail to complement their discordant, infuriated howl. The golem fled up the rocky mold of the trail; the Banissen Saturna abandoned the chase. A hoarse voice hurled its execrable accent in the golem's wake:

'We meant no harm! We are not fools; we have heard of Phadraig's monster! To the Tower of the Priest if you must, there to meet the Patriarch of Demented Feet, Phanphaecanh. Surely he'll absorb you, and the monster too. Be warned, we are friends, you seize death!'

Then Cuyahogan took them out of earshot. They were high up the slope, the dark woods cackled with frustration, from far down the hill drifted the shrilling of a pack of hunting mewhounds, and the night was coming to life. The golem burst up from the topmost trees, climbed intermediate strata to the smooth, gleaming basalt which slabbed up above them, reflecting the light from Cuyahogan's eyes, a dark mystery, a cracked maze. Salamander had fallen silent, her face calm. But Gaidhealla watched as the black tower came into sight over the brow of the hill. Now the final slope flattened out onto the summit plateau; the tower lay not two hundred feet away, boosted off the bare rock by the flat circular building around its base. The tower's summit was outlined against the deepening indigo sky. As they came closer Gaidhealla thought she saw a wavering glow above it, a blue radiation almost the same color as the sky behind. Either the roof didn't exist or it was transparent; the site was ideal for observing the sky. She'd heard this place lay at the junction of two leys, energy-paths of the Witchgoddess, and that, in the ancient past . . .

She caught herself. The air was unnaturally cold. She remembered the fading taunts of the Banissen Saturna. What did they mean? Her mind wasn't clear. The child began to wail, the sound thin and dismaying. It seemed to Gaidhealla that they'd entered a field drained of its natural energies. She found herself yawning, again and again. But the golem didn't appear to be affected. It bore them swiftly into the lee of the tower. The surrounding ground walls were built of monolithic basalt. The unwindowed tower above was black and solid against the sky's deepening violet.

'Circle the building, Cuyahogan.' The golem obeyed. But Gaidhealla saw no door, window, or gate. Instead, they met two dismal men sitting on a rough-and-tumble of rocks on the other side of the tower. They looked as though they'd spent their lives there. They showed no interest or fear, not even looking up when the golem beamed their faces with light. Gaidhealla recognized them as Mountainmen of Kor. Khassam employed this nimble, sparrow-faced race as scouts. They were thin, dressed in furry rags, with yellow complexions, their black hair greased up into whorls and spikes which indicated status and clan prerogatives. They didn't want to talk, or open their mouths, except to yawn.

'You scout for Khassam? Where is his army? Why are you here? Who owns the tower? Have you lost your tongues?'

The scouts made no attempt to duck the light in their faces. One of them shrugged fatalistically. He muttered something to the other in their own language, and looked up cynically. 'None of it matters. Some are trapped outside the Tower; others are lured within. It makes no difference; the end is the same.'

'Who goes in? How are you trapped?'

His gaunt rictus was distantly related to a smile.

'You'll go in, lady of Phadraig. As for the trap, try walking down the hill again. You'll find yourself going in circles when you thought your line was straight. Try it, before you call me a liar.'

He broke off to yawn hugely, infectiously.

'The golem's not affected!' snapped Gaidhealla, angry.

The scout shrugged and turned away, to stare gloomily northwest in the direction of his own land, lost forever beyond the Scarp and the Jerezid dominions.

Gaidhealla told the golem to descend the hill as far as the trees.

The golem plunged obediently down the side of the rocks.

'You see?' asked the scout, before them again. 'I told you.'

She ordered the golem to descend in a different direction.

'Give up,' said the same scout, jerking a thumb, 'and go within; accept the Priest's hospitality. The door is open. Farewell.'

Gaidhealla was weary and despondent. She turned her head. It was true. Misty blue light shone through a gap in the wall. One of the blocks of basalt masonry had been dematerialized. They were clearly invited inside. Gaidhealla faced the dilemma as best her heavy mind would let her. They couldn't escape the hilltop, not even the golem. Local space was twisted into a spiral around the vortex of the tower. Every outward direction led back to the same place. She had heard of this kind of trap before. But she hadn't been expecting it. She turned back to the scouts. 'Won't you come in as well?'

'We prefer to starve on the open rocks,' came the reply. 'Here at least we can watch the changing colors of the sky, and feel the wind, and imagine that the mountains before us are those of Kor. . . .'

She realized they would not help. Not because they were hostile scouts for Khassam, but because they were Mountainmen of Kor.

'Perhaps we should wait out here for Patrick to come,'

she mused.

The door gleamed invitation.

She realized she was curious to meet this Priest who had a demon as guest. And Salamander would suffer if they stayed on the rocks. She turned to the golem's face. Its cheeks and forehead glimmered blue.

'Enter the building, Cuyahogan.'

Salamander started to talk again. But her voice was changed.

'Where are we . . . what happens . . . where is Phadraig . . . ?'

'It is sanctuary for the night,' replied Gaidhealla, soothing.

'I hurt . . . I hurt. . . .'

And she struggled against the golem. The baby started to cry.

Holding them firm, the golem moved into the misty blue, stopped, facing an inner wall parallel with the outer circle. Blue-hazed corridor curved away in both directions. The golem stood on a circular mandala composed of thousands of minute tesseracts set in the basalt. The design was unstable, aspiring to an epicenter. The old woman felt drained of energy; Salamander's head slumped onto the golem's chest. Behind them, the outer block was rematerialized; simultaneously the opposite block of the inner wall faded out.

They were met by lustrous pearly light.

'What is this evil dream?' groaned the girl, weakly.

'Through, Cuyahogan. . . .'

Gaidhealla heard her own voice as if from far away, and again the golem stood on a tesseracted mandala of different, more disturbing design.

The old woman looked down through the pearl mist; belatedly, she understood, and she whispered:

'Step aside of the design, Cuyahogan, avoid all others, they sap our energy. . . .'

The pearly light sparkled and danced with mercurial abandon.

Again the blocks switched; the one-eyed child stared into redness.

This time, the golem stood aside of the third mandala.

The fourth corridor was yellow-lit, but the color jarred. And instead of a mandala, they were confronted by the hideously ugly image of a squatting blue demon. It had seven pairs of arms and legs. Its neck was strung with skulls eyed in onyx. Its head was a nest of crawling things. And crushed beneath the central trio of seven-toed feet was the image of an imploring traveler, complete with cloak, staff, and satchel. The circular border design was skillfully wrought in garnet, chalcedony, and beryl.

Gaidhealla knew they shouldn't have come here.

They were about to enter the lair of a madman, it was clear.

The final switch of blocks took place. The new entrance granted them passage to the ambulatory hall which circled the base of the tower. It was fifteen paces from the entrance to the base; the tower was twice that in width. All was shrouded in gloomy olive miasma. There was no sound, no sign of movement. The golem stood, awaiting Gaidhealla's command. Salamander moaned, but the baby was still, its eye wide open, mouth moving. Gaidhealla jerked, caught herself. Appalled, she realized she'd fallen asleep for an instant.

'Cuyahogan,' she whispered, 'flash a waking signal in my mind every half minute. Do so now!'

Her weariness was shredded by the bright inner light. But the resulting clarity began to fade almost immediately. The cold crept in her bones. 'Cuyahogan,' she whispered, her green eyes wide behind lank strands of disheveled hair, 'slowly, walk around this hall . . . start to the right. . . .'

She was shivering as the golem began to pad silently over the smooth black flagstones; she was riddled with the sadness which was tangible in the olive soup. Her mind and sight were blunted; dimly she made out the meaning of the faded tapestry hung continuously around the outer wall. It was a grotesque cavalcade of humans, beasts, birds, and beings which never existed – vaguely she identified basilisks, manticores, the immortal Simurgh. But her eyes were blurring, her thoughts were congealing, the slabbed roof was pressing down....

Cuyahogan flashed light in her brain. She shook her head, rubbed her eyes, held the child tighter in her cloak, sensing the fearful currents which emanated from it. Salamander was slumped, asleep and drained against the golem's other shoulder. Round ... around ... around ... it was quieter and more oppressive than a catacomb; there was no door into the tower from the attic where the blue light glowed, no sign of life. The thick air blunted Gaidhealla's eyes, her lids drooped, she fought, and she saw —

'Cuyahogan ... stop ...' she croaked.

The golem had almost walked past the table placed by an alcove in the outer wall.

The table was set for ten, silver on crimson damask. There were four chairs to a side and one at either end, neatly placed. The table was flanked by ten tall bronze candlesticks, five to a side, and each stood on three semi-human feet radiating from the stem. The twenty slender candles were trimmed, but unlit.

The olive gloom crawled heavily; she couldn't be sure if those feet were bronze and inert, or ...

The golem's signal lit her brain.

And she felt the presence of a watcher in the alcove.

The jadestones swung from her earlobes as she jerked her head.

Something huge, wobbling, shaking at the limit of olive vision.

The child's eye perked open. Gaidhealla strained her eyes. She summoned authority to her voice.

'Who are you? Come out!'

Silence fell in the wake of derisive echoes. Growing dull and pessimistic again, she waited for an answer. A great shadow shifted in the depths of the alcove. It exhaled a sudden gust of breath.

Then it began to titter.

The sound was empty, a soft breath at first, but it grew, grew into a high-pitched, unremitting *teeheeheeheeee* which shredded the old woman's nerves with its multiple echoes and its utter lack of emotion. It came from a vast pair of lungs and a mind which was void. Gaidhealla fought not to shriek, not to sleep. She was giddy and chill, as the lunacy screamed through her from every side; unconsciousness was the only refuge, but the golem flashed her mind alert again. She couldn't stand any more. 'Cuyahogan ... into the alcove ... confront this ... maniac....' Unaffected, green-glimmering, the golem moved smoothly into the alcove. Gaidhealla wanted to clap her hands to her ears, but she had the child to hold, and the child was staring at the great bulk before them, quiet, apparently interested and without fear.

In front of them, the open mouth shut abruptly.

The vast face about and above it stretched into a simpering smile.

Gaidhealla stared with horror at the enormous, flabby body in its tent-like shift. The woman – it took Gaidhealla some seconds to recognize her as such – lay like a stranded whale amid mounds of faded brocade cushions on the enormous bed at the back of the alcove. Her body heaved continually for breath, the features of her face scarcely surfacing above the folds of flesh which rose to a white hairless dome.

But she smiled, though it was a travesty of a smile.

Her eyes were smiling at the baby. They were guileless, innocent eyes, like two blue flowers stuck in a great ball of dough. They were sad eyes, though they didn't know their own sadness. Gaidhealla was captured by them, and began the long fall into their twin pools of emptiness, her mind drowning....

*Flash.*

She was alert again; there was another sound.

It was the baby.

Cooing, chuckling with pleasure, reaching out its stubby arms for the great mass of flesh. Gaidhealla understood. She was frightened. The Priest was malign – and powerful. She didn't know if she had enough resources of her own to withstand him. She had to make him reveal himself, find his weak point. She found herself staring into blue flowers again. They implored her to give over the baby into her arms. Now the baby stared steadily up at her as well, and she shut her eyes and turned to Cuyahogan.

'Cuyahogan, leave the alcove.'

The baby started to bawl with wretched disappointment.

The tittering began again.

Gaidhealla shouted hoarsely: 'Priest, show yourself! My daughter dies and I am weak, but you drain our energy and torment us! Are you a host ... or a cannibal? I will not ... go to sleep ... and the golem will not set us down ... until you ...'

She lost her words and her thoughts to cacophony and lethargy.

The waking bolt flared again, and she was furious; she opened her mouth to call out again at their unseen captor. But her words were killed by the breath which came on the air, the breath which formed words squeezed from melancholy, not loud, but somehow sounding everywhere, leaving a leaden decay in her mind.

*'Daughter ... be still ... be quiet....'*

The mad laughter stopped.

The child whimpered and fell silent.

Gaidhealla dragged her eyes to the base of the tower.

*He's up there; the voice is a projection.*

Then the air breathed again. And it breathed for her.

## 12 : The Priest's Story

In a dim, dreaming corner of her mind, Salamander knew what was happening. Her personality floated, unattached, as it had done since she fell at Gaidhealla's feet in the alley. Her mind, in self-protection, had withdrawn and gone adrift out of time, unaware of what her body underwent at Red Kilmun and in the Swamp Forest. It was the fire of the purple plant which bridged the gap between mind and body and began to draw her back. But only so far. She was unable to accept bodily reality all at once; she approached it gradually via childhood memory. The day of the Company's great triumph came first; the day wore on and she'd come closer to reality, with classroom memory of Maelnagar and the subject of failed mothers. Though she was still ten years from the present when the Banissen Saturna closed in, her recognition of it was accelerating, and the drive back toward life developed momentum.

Something in the miserable atmosphere surrounding the tower harmonized with this drive. She'd surfaced long enough to realize she wasn't in Phadraig and to ask frightened questions of her mother, who'd supplied a large measure of the drive to return.

And though as they entered the atmosphere soon depressed her back to sleep, it was sleep rather than coma: a strange state of mind in whch something of her dreamed she was awake. She still floated, but now so close to reality that, if she should ever awake fully, she would know tolerably well what had happened.

She dreamed she was helpless and weak, in a stiff, cold body held by the golem which had pursued her. But it wasn't the cause of her fear.

She dreamed she was trapped in a gloomy place with her mother ... with ... some unknown creature, and she was afraid of a sepulchral breath which whispered abysmal sadness in her.

And she dreamed she heard her mother speaking, but in waves, from peaks of clarity which faded into dull, lethargic troughs, before the next peak broke.

But each new wave was weaker than the previous; the breath was increasingly insistent, more terribly sad and leaden....

'... Old woman, why your anger? I make you welcome. The table is set. But I cannot show myself, for it is my fate to radiate a sadness which none can bear. You have borne my sadness since you saw my tower; it is my sadness which makes you ... want to ... sleep ... sleep.... Oh, my sadness is unbearable, and all ... must ... sleep ... but you withstand it? I believe the creature sends bolts into your mind ... oh ... be assured I would lessen my sadness if I could. The prospect of fair company and pleasant conversation is so ... sweet, so ... rare, so many of my guests go to sleep ... go to sleep ... your monster does not sleep ... does it obey you alone ... alone ...? Oh ... sleep ... what words will charm your monster, and give it rest ... rest ... rest ...?'

Gaidhealla's mouth was open and the secrets of the golem's control were marshaled on her tongue; she wanted to sleep, she groaned.

'The golem ... it obeys ...'

*Flash.*

She swallowed the betraying words.

'Enough of this foul hypnosis! Show yourself! Or the golem will break into your sanctum and drag you out.'

But already the edge of her clarity was fading and the

cold draft came stealing back into her mind, weary and disappointed.

'... The strange child in your arms ... it is silent, it sleeps so innocently ... oh, innocence ... the child wants the arms of my daughter ... and her sadness would be lessened if she could hold the innocent babe, if just ... for a minute ... oh, let them sleep together, and lay down your sad daughter ... refresh yourself at my table ... then rest ... you are tired, so tired ... the child – it has a name...?'

'It ... it has no name ... it ...'

'No name? No name? It sleeps, nameless? So strange ... so strange ... oh, respect my misery; let me name the child ... Alhazuer ... the name I would have given my son ... he was never born; he sleeps forever, Alhazuer ... sleeps in your arms ... I scent him ... I scent him....'

*Flash.*

Gaidhealla realized her initial peak of clarity was less this time. And that the being behind the whisper could catch her with questions at her most dull before each new flash. She had to order Cuyahogan to ... adopt a new, irregular warning system. But words were breathing in her head again. And she couldn't remember what it was she'd been about to do. Except that it was something to do with Cuyahogan. She struggled to remember. Or was it something to do with the Company? She couldn't think. She shook her head, trying to clear it of the maddening whispers which grew, so she could hear or think of nothing else.

'Condemned ... I am condemned to live and die alone, hopelessly longing for friends and ... lovers ... with nothing but my idiot daughter, the greatest of many sadnesses ... and there is Phan ... Phan ... impossible, I am miserable, confused, so baffled by life ... but Phan is my friend, so far as mortal may associate with elemental. Phan forbids me to meet you, for fear I would become less sad, less bound to him. I cannot object, my will is not free, and Phan is my master ... but at least I can tell you my miserable history ... the sad tale.... Eat; there is food on the table; lay down your daughter by mine ... let her sleep ... let my daughter take Alhazuer ... you are a good woman, I can sense it; have mercy ... mercy ... and eat, then sleep ... sleep. How I wish I could sleep, forever, dreamless ... forever ... oh, my life was destined for bathos, and bathetic it is ... laugh; you will find my story absurd ... relax; tell your monster to lay you down ... oh, absurd—

'I was fathered by Ranulph; it was the first of my misfortunes. My mother died giving birth, and he never took another wife; his one true wife was the sky and its signs. He wished to train me in his ... wisdom. He moralized endlessly. He was an ethical dullard who refused to profit from his powers. It was sad, but I could not respect him ... and I was so lonely, so lonely; it was unsafe to leave the Tower, and guests never came ... never. There was nothing to do but sleep ... sleep ... down ... lie down ... I thought so much about sleep I forgot how to do it, oh ...

'I thought I was glad when my father died. I believed myself alive for the very first time. I left this hateful tower. I deserted the stars for living elements. I evaded the Banissen Saturna. I traveled, and I acquainted myself with many beliefs in many lands, believing that I searched for reasons to explain my ridiculous existence. But the more I traveled the more I realized that my father had been right after all to shut himself up; the world offers nothing but confusion and distress. I realized I wanted oblivion. I wished to lose myself, to sleep ... sleep sweetly ... dreamlessly ... unknowing ... forgetting ... I wanted to lie down ... lie down ... forget ... surrender....

'But it was too late. My juvenile thirst for purpose had trapped me in laughable, tragic paradox, for my unconscious quest for sleep ... sleep ... had led me into knowledge, and learning, and lust for life, though this lust was nothing but a desire for its opposite. Insatiably, I sought satiation. I fed ... feed ... I drank ... drink ... I traveled through my twenties, my thirties, and my forties ... far beyond the Jerezid lands to the Black Lakes, to the western mountains where, alone, I sought out Phadraig's legendary Savior of the Fallen Ones and found an idiot box which repeated the same meaningless benediction, over and over, over and over. It did not tell me how to sleep. I threw it over the cliff in a rage, and returned to the plains more miserable than before, again among people who knew how to sleep, how to laugh, how to cry, how to ... forget ... oh, how to forget....

'Disguised as a merchant I came to Phadraig when still young. I disputed with market-square theologians and dabbled with your Witchgoddess, but I did not learn how to sleep, not at all.... By the sea in the south I lived with those who worship the waves, but not even the sea could teach me sleep ... and in the mountains of Kor I looked upon the sealed vaults of the ancients, which Khassam has opened to the sadness of all, and wondered how long they had slept. And I learned, everywhere I learned ... In Kor, they worship one god, but those of the plains below remember the Divine Mutant ... in Lamassa, unmen sacrifice themselves before mirrors, believing their reflections will catch up their souls and give them new life as free spirits. With Jerezid sages I meditated on ancient symbols and images – I have heard the music of the ancients, preserved on shiny black disks; I have seen the moving pictures of their world projected in my sleepless brain ... and they increased my sadness, for they were like me: they too had forgotten how to sleep ... how to sleep ... but they were frantically awake together, and I am alone, always alone. There was no relief for my mind in this world. My sadness became a tangible, dreadful thing. Wherever I went people jeered and called me mad and whipped me through their streets whenever I opened my mouth, because I frightened them when I asked them how I might learn to sleep ... how to sleep ... and after many years in many lands, nobody would approach me because of my sadness, oh ...

'For all my knowledge told me nothing of how not to

know, how to forget.... I tried drink, and I forgot for a while, but the remembering was worse. I uprooted screaming mandrakes by the score; in retaliation they made me ill. I ate mushrooms which opened my mind and made me remember what I hadn't known. I tried a thousand different potions which only increased my sadness a millionfold. Now I could no longer walk among others; my passing laid a blight on their souls, reduced the greatest of warriors to tearful sleep, reduced them to the very state I craved so much ... and crave now ... sleep ... sleep is the only thing I have forgotten, and the only thing I wish to remember. You cannot guess how fortunate you are to be able to sleep ... so sweetly ... so softly....

'Scorned by fate, I returned in despair to this tower. But at the bottom of the hill I was captured by the savages. They believed me to be possessed by the Demon of Wanderlust, Phanphaecanh – and indeed I was. My sacrifice would have been just, for I would have slept ... but they were overcome by the sleep of my sadness before they could kill me. The misfortune was immense: my chance of forgetfulness was lost, and I thought of committing the sacrifice myself. But fate illuminated me with a new awakening, a new realization – all those years of futile search, and the answer lay on my very doorstep! Phanphaecanh, the Patriarch! I was ablaze with his Truth, my soul was quickened, and for a while I knew the meaning of ... happiness, though now I cannot grasp the concept at all. Entranced, I hastened up the hill, and found my tower as I had left it. My new task was revealed to me, and in ferment of creativity I embarked upon a course of spiritual elevation through the discipline of creating my flesh in flesh. For a while I thought I had lost the desire to ... sleep.... For the first time, my sadness was appropriate. I gloried in it and in Phan....'

Now Salamander dreamed that she lay asleep on a couch in an alcove, that the golem stood immobile above her, empty-armed, that she was stretched out next to the immense body of a bald woman with eyes like flowers. She dreamed she heard an endless confession in words of sodden olive melancholy; she dreamed she saw her mother, small, and slumped against cushions on the other side of the alcove, her eyes closed as if she slept ... and the old woman held loosely in her lap something which Salamander couldn't recognize – something with one eye, which was open on the great bulk of the fat woman. The woman began to move, slow, and silent, sliding from the cushions, placing feet which were almost dainty upon the black flagstones, standing like a jelly, her blue flower eyes on the child which Gaidhealla held, standing beside the unmoving golem below which Salamander lay as she dreamed of the voice which crept in her head....

'... Inspired by the Patriarch's ever-present company, I trained myself with the strictest rigor. I fasted for eight days every month; I determined a propitious hour to commence the operation; I consulted my father's books. They took on new meaning for me. I chose from the savages a virgin girl indicated as suitable by my elemental mentor ... for the savages feared and revered me after they awoke from their sleep. To them I had become priest and avatar of the Patriarch, and they learned to do my wishes, which are his, in fear of their miserable lives. And all would have been well. But I became distracted by increased sadness; the Patriarch made demands inconsonant with the purity of my inspiration. I was horrified, fearing I would be lost again. I reminded him of our bargain, but he revealed his force. I redoubled my efforts, I fought, I railed, I denied, but it was useless. I discovered I was conquered, my tastes were changed, I looked on my inspiration with loathing, and I wished only to forget it. But Phan was subtle and persuasive. He explained that we were bound forever together, familiar and inextricable, that we must live in agreement, or the relationship would not be tolerable for me. He urged me to complete the task and sullenly I agreed. But the agony of my sleepless sadness was returned, my mood was changed, and my daughter was created in desolation and error, the idiot of my confusion. Now she lives in desolation, the mirror of mine; but in her emptiness, she has never known it, and this has been her only fortune. But now fate has brought her happiness – Alhazuer. Deprive her of this dreadful happiness and for the first time she will know her sadness, thus increasing mine, and she will lose her ... sleep ... sleep ... come, daughter, soundlessly ... sleepfully ... taking him gently in your arms, come; there is ... hope ... that life will be more than echo of my sadness; there is a course to which Phan has agreed ... you have come, sent by fate, though it will not rescue me ... me....'

The very regularity of Cuyahogan's waking flashes had long since helped to dull Gaidhealla's mind. And so long as the voice continued in the same mournful tone she would be trapped in her exhaustion. But briefly it had changed, for an instant being charged with expectation and disgusted triumph. The spell was broken, and she snapped open her eyes, realizing with horror that Cuyahogan no longer held them. At some point she must have been inveigled into ordering the golem to set them down. Dazed, she saw Salamander stretched out on the couch. But where was the idiot daughter? And the child?

Then she saw the blue light irradiating the olive from the door in the base of the tower and, outlined in it, the daughter's great bulk, barely squeezing through the space to the steps beyond.

'Cuyahogan! Bring them back here!'

But even as the golem blurred the wall was solid again, the blue light was gone, and the child was taken.

'Fool! Your history is a lie; your demon is your own split mind!'

But it was useless; there was no reply. Dull again, she ordered the golem to stand still, ordered it to flash her mind at random three times every minute. Too much, and she would damage her brain. She sat beside Salamander as the first flash came. How one paid for solitude in Phadraig, locked from the real world! She had grown soft, she had listened, had ordered the golem to enter when they should have waited. Now they were neatly separated.

There was still Cuyahogan.

Possibly she could dissolve an entrance to the tower with mental force boosted and directed by the golem.

Possibly. But it would almost certainly kill her, which would do the child and Salamander no good.

Several minds linked in circuit might do it.

If only the Company ...

She refused to think it. The place seemed impregnable on account of its gloom, which invaded the innermost recesses of each private mind. She doubted that even Khassam's force could make much impression here.

'Why are you so silent now?' she burst out, flashed again. 'You were happy to jabber when it served your purpose. Take care, the child dislikes you, his spirit is the opposite pole to your demon illusions, and he may destroy you....'

But the gloomy silence persisted.

Chill, she wondered what the Priest intended.

Then Salamander moaned, twisted, she opened her eyes, and licked pale, cracked lips.

'I'm thirsty ... so thirsty....'

Gaidhealla saw that her daughter was conscious again. She felt a quick relief – it was one ray of light in the misery. She turned, saw that the table was heaped with food – meats, fruits, sweetmeats, faceted crystal decanters of mellow wine. She wasted no time wondering how it had all got there.

'Cuyahogan, bring a goblet and a bottle of wine from the table.'

The golem obeyed. Gaidhealla filled the glass goblet. Salamander's eyes were large. But before she let her daughter drink, Gaidhealla unlooped a translucent crystal from about her neck. She dangled the colorless stone in the mellow red wine.

The stone turned black.

Suppressing words, she dashed the decanter to the flagstones where it shattered, and the poison ran down the cracks and collected in a pool by the golem's feet. The old woman turned to Salamander, whose face was a restless green shadow. 'Patrick,' she heard the girl whisper, 'where is Patrick? I'm so thirsty, Mother, so ...'

Gaidhealla received two flashes in quick succession, the second jarred and hurt her mind, but they left her clear to think sharp for some seconds. Salamander might recover. The Priest was afraid of Cuyahogan, and could have done nothing against them if not for his daughter. And in the attic, the madman was set on some course which his demon approved, involving the child. There was no knowing if the Company was close; she could feel nothing in this lethargy. Even if Patrick and his men were close, they wouldn't be able to get in unless the Priest allowed it. And why should he?

The old woman realized sadly that she had little option. She had to link her mind with the golem's deadly power and attempt to force an entrance. She would give the golem instructions to carry out in the event of her death. It was all she could do. She would have to trust Salamander and the child to Cuyahogan. But would Salamander understand...?

She turned to the girl.

And realized that she'd forgotten what she was thinking about.

## 13 : Breaking Through

It was said that the mewhound didn't know if it was cat or dog, but it knew what it liked.

The pack fell on the Company. Long stiff white whiskers vibrated with blood-lust; slit eyes gleamed red in the tent of torchblade light as the five men fell back to back. Patrick narrowed the light down to a pin-thick beam which sliced through the brain of the beast leaping for his neck. Gnorl cut through the neck of a second with a down-sweep of his broadsword. Scalaman hastily notched a second quarrel, sent it deep into the mangy ocher body of a third beast snapping at the Songmaker's side. Liam fended off the body with a dirk in his left hand, kicked out at snapping jaws as he struggled to set the board of his sirena. Beside him Iubhar splayed the cat-dogs with powertube flare. There were thirty, maybe forty of the beasts coming at them with their bushy tails and flattened skulls, laid-back ears and feline stealth, mewling hideously as they circled and tried to pounce. One got inside the weapons and ripped open Scalaman's arm before Gnorl, howling furiously, laid it in two. Then grisly sound grew from the sirena, set back the creatures on their heels. Patrick flared his beam wider and burned into a circling bunch. Another fell back, impaled by Scalaman's bolt. His arm was bloody, his bleached mane a shaggy mess as he cursed steadily.

The Songmaker sent fast-thudding heartbeats into the rest of the pack, which fled, leaving fifteen dead or wounded behind.

Scalaman wiped his brow, ignoring the burning of his torn arm.

'They'll feed well tonight,' he commented. He went to retrieve three deep-buried quarrels, wiped them clean against still-twitching flanks. Only then did he let Iubhar examine his arm. There was no trace of indolence on the wiry man's face; his teeth were bare. Behind, Patrick let his arms fall around Gnorl and the Songmaker, and he grinned.

'More like it! I felt my blood thicken again!'

But the tower on top of the hill was on his mind, and Salamander.

And their heads were lifted by the commotion of angry laughter, jeers, and curses which drifted down on the air from high up the slope.

'The golem's through,' commented Iubhar, binding Scalaman's arm, 'but we're not so fast, and they must know we're here.'

'And where is Khassam's army?' Patrick murmured. 'It must pass through this area if he's taking the direct route to Phadraig.'

Weary and pessimistic, but with a sense of companionship and self-confidence returned, the Company crept up clefts and gullies, awaiting the attack as the night grew darker. But after long minutes of bruising progress, they realized they were no longer followed. They clung to shadows as three men of the Banissen Saturna came running down the slope as though it were day, casting fearful backward glances, the greenstones howling around their necks.

'What do they fear? Did the golem massacre them? Or is it the tower?' the Songmaker hissed after they were gone.

They climbed without interruption for another half hour, though there was life all about in the bushes and trees. They reached the crags and stood beneath the drifting, heavy sky. Storm flashed and muttered in the northern distance over the Scarp, but they only had eyes for the indigo radiation which crowned the black rocks. Like the golem before, they climbed up into the lethargy and came to the Tower of the Priest. Its summit was the source of the horrid blue. The Company circled it, past old bones, a human rib-cage, and found themselves yawning and depressed. They came across the two scouts. Gnorl recognized their race from their fantastic hair. He felt his blade.

'From Kor – Khassam's scouts!'

One seemed to be asleep despite the bitter chill; the other was seated calmly. 'The hill's busy tonight,' he commented without surprise. 'And so is the Priest – with his guests. . . .'

Iubhar's fingers found his onyx amulet.

'Guests? Describe them!'

Wearily, the scout described the golem, Gaidhealla, Salamander, and the one-eyed child. Then he advised the Company that they were trapped on the crags. Gnorl jabbed him meaningfully with his sword and told him to talk sense. The man shrugged, his narrow face split in a yawn.

'There's no way out by the way you came in.'

Patrick's impatience fought against weariness.

'How do we get in?'

The scout regarded him candidly.

'You enter if the Priest wishes you to enter. Unless you possess some superior power, which the look of you makes me doubt. We have been here many days, we have seen many of the local people go in, but none of them have come out. The door has been opened for us, but we refuse to enter. Death from grief and starvation is preferable to accepting the Priest's hospitality.'

Unseen by the others, the Songmaker slipped away down the slope.

'Starvation? – and you Mountainmen? Surely you can trap. . .?'

'No animal's so stupid as to set foot on these rocks,' the scout answered Scalaman, 'and the birds stay well away. Only men are stupid enough to come here.'

The Songmaker was beside them again. He looked woebegone and confused. 'It's true,' he announced. 'We cannot leave the hill!'

'Look – the blue light is growing more intense!' Iubhar grabbed Patrick's arm. 'We must find a way in, or they'll die!'

The second scout who'd seemed to sleep sat up.

'Your wish is granted.' His voice was deep, incongruous; he pointed at the wall. 'Look. The way is open. Farewell.'

Blue light from another source shone on his pinched face. The Company turned as one and saw the entrance glaring invitation. Gnorl and Scalaman eyed each other uncertainly. 'You let the melancholy overwhelm you; be strong!' Iubhar shouted at them. The Songmaker looked up at the tower, shaking his head. Patrick took a step toward the blue entrance, then looked back at the two scouts.

'We'll take them with us,' he told the others.

Gnorl and Iubhar nodded, and went to seize the scouts. The two Mountainmen looked up into powertube muzzle, along blue-gleaming blade.

'Fine weapons. Why do you point them at us?'

'You enter with us,' answered Gnorl. 'On your feet.'

The scouts were aghast.

'You're from Phadraig. But we have no quarrel with Phadraig. We were forced into Khassam's army!'

Patrick suppressed a yawn. 'We have no quarrel with you. But we'll kill you if you don't get up. You have five seconds. One ...'

'Then kill us!' challenged the deep-voiced one, chin stubborn, gaze away through the developing storm in the northwest. 'Kill us now! Our land and clans are lost forever.'

'... Two ...'

The second scout saw something almost demented in the tall flaxen-haired man's blue-lit face. He nudged his obstinate friend hastily.

'No, Tembar. Be practical! Those we've seen vanish inside the tower have been weaklings; these are strong men. Could be they'll defeat the Priest. Besides, we are perhaps cowards to choose the easy death. We're no longer bound to Khassam, if we help these. . . .'

'. . . Three . . .'

The distant thunder muttered louder; the blue light thrust back the gathering blackness of the night.

But the scout called Tembar was contemptuous of the blade at his throat; Gnorl felt swift admiration, a sense of kinship.

'Then I choose cowardice: you go with them, Idrys. I'll die here!'

'. . . Four . . .' counted Patrick Cormac, his wide eyes icy.

Iubhar's finger tightened on the powertube stud; he felt dazed.

But Idrys was on his feet, dragging Tembar up with him.

'I outrank you in the Eagle Clan. I order you to live!'

He shielded Tembar like a breathless bird, announcing, 'We will follow. Put down your weapons. We agree!'

'No,' contradicted Patrick, 'you will go in front.'

And five pushed two into the crawling blue.

'The design's hideous!' whispered Liam. 'It drains me further.'

'Don't . . . look at it, or stand . . . on it!'

Patrick was hoarse. He pulled hard on his beard to cause himself pain and keep himself awake. Blocks switched; pearl light confronted them. Tembar advanced on Gnorl's sword-point, but Idrys yawned, black eyes nervous like a lizard's. And into the red corrider—

'Hit each other, hard! We must stay awake!'

Again the switch. Now the seven-legged and seven-armed demon. They felt oppressed, trapped; Scalaman fell asleep against Gnorl, who shook him roughly awake; Liam reeled, and Iubhar hit him. The final block dissolved. Gnorl forced the scouts forward into the olive gloom. Tembar stared murderously at Idrys, who began to crumple. Gnorl jabbed him upright again. But Gnorl also felt like heavy lead. All seven stumbled into the ambulatory hall, treading on each other's feet, without eyes for the tapestried carnival or the base of the tower. Their minds were going, drifting. Patrick cursed, urged them on. He staggered; his mind was swimming.

A bolt of energy stabbed into their minds.

And Patrick saw the table through the gloom. He sensed the alcove behind it, and he swallowed his fear, pushed forward, torchblade at the ready, wondering at the bolt of waking energy.

Dim, vague shape, approaching—

Up jerked the lean barrel of his torchblade.

'No, Patrick! It's Gaidhealla!'

Her desperate voice froze his finger. The shape in the gloom before him merged with his memory of the Witch-mother; they faced each other. It was Gaidhealla. But her face was utterly haggard, with new lines he'd not seen before, and gray was spreading in her raven-black hair. Patrick stood frozen in front of the Company.

She saw him with great relief. He was cloaked, filthy, his eyes slightly mad, long hair lank and streaked with dirt.

They embraced, but immediately he stepped back trembling.

'Salamander? The baby?' His voice was strained, hardly audible.

Through the fog she saw Scalaman beside the table, reaching—

'No! Don't touch food or wine. It's poisoned!'

Scalaman, reeling with fatigue, fell back. The golem, standing motionless by the tower's wall, flashed them again. The Company stood with drawn weapons, eyes sharp and nervous in every obscured direction. Quickly, Gaidhealla explained what had happened, what she'd been about to do when she heard their stumbling feet and ordered Cuyahogan to alert them. Patrick was astonished.

'You would have killed yourself! And didn't the Priest know your intention? Why did he let us in...?'

Shaking her head, she warned them of the hypnotic breathing voice.

Then she said to Patrick: 'Salamander's in the alcove.

She may live. If any of us do.'

His face a pale mask, Patrick went to the alcove. He was followed by Gaidhealla, Liam, and Iubhar. Gnorl and Scalaman remained leaning against the tower's wall, guarding the scouts. But Gnorl's blade rested on the floor, and Scalaman's crossbow drooped. Tembar glowered with fear and fury, while Idrys fell asleep with open eyes.

Patrick looked down on the wounded girl, his expression concerned and fearful. But her eyes were open; she recognized him through the olive, through the mist of her weakness – the beard, the wide eyes, the haunted, irregular features, vague, but unmistakable. She was fired with new hope and energy.

'Patrick!'

And the voice was her own, momentarily rich with her character.

He went down on his knees and bent over her. He saw in her wan face the beauty which had deserted her in pregnancy – the archness, the quirky intelligence of her pale, parted lips, the slight uptilt of her nose, the sharp, delicate cheekbones, the expressive eyes.

Just a hint – then exhaustion claimed her, her eyes closed, and her character faded.

But in his turn, he felt the energy of hope. He hadn't expected to see her alive. Gaidhealla watched, aware her intuition was trying to tell her something. But the golem hadn't flashed them for many seconds, and her intuition was drowned. Liam squatted, Iubhar began to slump against the alcove wall, and Patrick bent to kiss the girl.

They didn't see what was happening behind them; the blue light didn't reach their averted eyes.

Then came the flash, and their alerted ears picked up sounds.

The four turned as one. Saw the blue light. Saw Gnorl and Scalaman pushing the scouts onto the steps inside the tower, their minds taken. The golem stood useless, awaiting command.

'Cuya—'

Gaidhealla didn't finish the name.

The wall was bleak, black, and solid again.

Their furious, futile reactions were aborted as the voice came breathing inside their minds:

'... Tonight is so fateful. Four more Phan needed, of specific character, and four you provide. Phan thanks you for persuading the men of Kor to enter. Oh, your friends are well-honored; tonight they will sleep ... sleep forever ... and my daughter's miserable mind will be whole. Oh, the one-eyed child has a strange mind ... Phan is entranced; he permits me to begin the work. Perhaps, if it be successful, he will permit the lessening of my awful sadness ... perhaps .... Please leave this tower in the morning ... tonight you must stay ... the storm is about to rage ... the elements are in ferment. I cannot allow you to expose yourselves to danger. I fear you can do nothing but sleep ... sleep ... forget your useless anger ... sleep ...'

They were paralyzed. The golem flashed again, and the voice was gone; they were ignored. Liam's face was appalled, and he pulled fiercely on his well-chewed moustache. Iubhar spat on the flagstones, as Patrick ran to the black wall, raising a fist as if to beat it down.

'How? How? Oh, you'll pay! You'll—'

With an oath he turned away.

Inside the tower, spellbound, leeched of autonomy, Gnorl and Scalaman started up the steps, pushing the scouts before them. Four faces were blank, expressionless, mounting step by step toward the source of the blueness which grew more intense, as though the air were innately haloed.

Gaidhealla answered Patrick's infuriated questions calmly, bleakly.

'The madman needs minds to fill up his daughter ... so he thinks. And the blue may be radiation from some unshielded, mishandled device. Phan is his split madness, a fantasy of self which he obeys in fear. He believes himself impregnable, but he is weak with the weakness he imposes on us. Now he'll forget us for his "work."'

Her contempt was bitter, her face sharpening as the golem flashed.

Patrick clenched his teeth against the sudden pain of alertness.

'The golem,' he whispered. 'All of us together, in circuit.'

She nodded. He drew Liam and Iubhar close, and explained. 'There are four of us. We'll stand at compass-point about the golem, thus balancing the strain and effort. You are ready? It's our only hope. Old Mother,' he requested with respect, 'will you order the golem to obey my commands?'

She indicated green, drawn assent.

'Cuyahogan ... eighty-four ... obey the orders of this man, Patrick Cormac.'

He opened his mind to the identification probe which fixed him in Cuyahogan's awareness. But the old woman's state concerned him. She was pallid, and not quite coordinated; when the golem flashed them again she stumbled, pain twisting her face.

'You've suffered too much already; we three will do this alone!'

But she shook her head, denying it.

'Four heads are better than three.'

'You must not destroy yourself!' Patrick insisted. 'The child needs you too much; we're expendable.'

Her eyes were direct. 'I have the strength,' she insisted.

'Witchmother, please ...' Iubhar began.

But Patrick cut him off. He knew she had the right to decide.

'If you wish it,' he said curtly. He dismissed brief concern for Salamander. She would have to stay where she was. And if they failed to break through, her condition wouldn't matter. He turned to the golem which towered fully three feet above him, a silent menace he knew he would never trust. Like the others, he knew the energies bound into sharp focus might feed back, destroying the golem's control-matrix, and shrivel their minds. The danger was great. But the child was taken, its potential was threatened, and Scalaman and Gnorl would die – '*sleep forever.*'

'Cuyahogan, stand before Patrick Cormac.'

The golem obeyed as it sent its waking signal. Gaidhealla trembled. Iubhar and the Songmaker were grave. The four exchanged taut glances. They were ready.

Iubhar took the west point, behind the golem.

The Songmaker took the south, to Cuyahogan's right side.

Gaidhealla, rigidly controlling herself, took the north.

Patrick stood between the golem and the black wall.

'Cuyahogan, hear me. Signify understanding of each point. Face the wall – this particular block, here... Enter our minds, equally in each ... now ... gently, be very gentle...!' And with the others he gasped with sudden shock. He cried out, '*Care, take care,* – humans are weak ... there ... there ... now grasp our purpose ... hold it ... amplify our energy ... direct it against the block ... let none of the energy feed back ... now, take it ... direct it exactly as we intend ... dissolve the block.'

His face was a grimace. His mind was being sucked. The four of them fought to maintain their purpose consciously, for the golem at its gentlest burned them, emaciated them, was a flaming mental fist which captured their purpose, tightened it, amplified it to a thousand fold, hurled it against the obdurate matter of the wall. They fought to stand, but the pressure grew severe as the seconds passed. Suddenly, all four staggered, their legs giving way to gravity and weakness as they were swamped by the merest echo of backlash. Minds saturated, they shivered violently, their bodies were on the flagstones, but the golem held the sum of their intention tight, blasting it against the wall. The dreadful flame in their minds was growing too intense. Gaidhealla felt herself beginning to dissolve. The Songmaker danced in chaos vibration. Iubhar was hollow, sharded, and Patrick couldn't interpret what he saw.

Much more of this, and their minds would snap like dry twigs.

Now the block of stone was growing misty, insubstantial, but their open, streaming eyes saw nothing. The fire-giant strode in them; consciousness was dissolving to chaos, into molten hell.

It was unendurable. Patrick knew they had failed. A free remnant of his mind derided him for pride, misjudgment, and useless crimes. The whole world was aflame, a shrieking torment of the damned. It was all over. It was all over.

Then existence was dark, peaceful, a trough of night.

The vampire pressure was gone; there was only the lethargy.

Gratefully, they slumped: sleep winged in.

Cuyahogan shocked their minds – and again; starting awake, Patrick cursed it for returning them to life. He crawled blindly on hands and knees; he opened his eyes. He saw the blue-misted interior of the tower before him, saw the first steps. Shivering, he pulled the fragments of his head together. Unless the Priest had forgotten them entirely, he must surely know what had happened, and would seek to rematerialize the gap in the wall. Behind him, Gaidhealla was a rag doll with a face of crumpled paper, but she managed a weak gesture as Iubhar pulled her to boneless feet and Liam staggered against the wall; she managed that as her lips worked to form a word.

'... Qu ... Qu ... Quick ...'

Patrick's head was swimming; his neck seemed to creak as he looked up at the golem. Would it obey him? They'd need its strength to drag them up the steps. Its face was a green devil, waiting....

'Cuyahogan ... into the ... the tower ... lead us up the steps.'

Supporting each other, they half fell through the gap past walls five feet thick, passing behind the golem from olive to stronger blue. The steps were a spiral fixed to the outer wall, winding around the black maw of a wide wall which had no floor – and no guard-rails. The golem pulled them past its circular lip. Patrick risked a downward glance, almost falling. No bottom was visible. There was blackness beneath the blue spawn of the air. With Liam at the rear, and Iubhar supporting Gaidhealla behind Patrick, the golem led them onto the first steps, hugging the wall as far as possible from the lip of the well.

Then tumult burst down on them, from the blue distance above.

The babble of sound was designed to drive them mad and over the edge. The melancholy drone of the Priest was prominent, but there were many other discords in it – rising whines, tortured screams, subtle little hisses which nagged their nerves. Clutching their heads, they began to stagger and reel as though drunk. Cuyahogan flashed light in their minds; the pain was greater than the relief of reprieve. The tumult had failed, and it was withdrawn as swiftly as it had been imposed. The golem pulled them up the worn, phosphorescent steps. They climbed in a daze. Time passed and they forgot it. Cuyahogan's signals pulsed in them with irregular, effective frequency, holding them above sleep's margins. They climbed, climbed, climbed until they should have reached the attic three times over. In time, a fresh flash from the golem alerted Patrick as he stood on a broken step. Something was familiar. He stopped the golem, fighting to isolate the familiarity. Then he had it.

'We've passed this step three times already! We're caught in a twist!'

They held a halting conference. Patrick forced his way alone up several steps, counting them from the broken one. He pulled his exhausted body up around the well until he was one complete turn of the spiral above the others. Pausing for breath, he looked up into the dazzling blue, and saw dim shapes a half turn above him on the opposite side. He recognized the golem. From a distance it flashed his mind, and he understood, and climbed step by step until he'd rejoined them again.

Tiring, he repeated the climb, the golem preceding him.

He counted the number of steps it took. It vanished as it set foot on the twenty-fourth. Leaning full-length on the twenty-third, he risked the downward stare again, saw the golem climbing a turn and a half of the spiral below. By the time it approached him again, he was almost unconscious, and the others were slumped against the wall on steps below as Cuyahogan climbed past them. Its flash came again. Patrick stopped it short of the step where the space-twist operated.

'Cuyahogan ... pass the next step as close to the edge as possible.'

The golem took the step and disappeared again; came up toward them.

So the space-twist field occupied the width of the step. Patrick clutched his head, trying to think through the fog on his brain.

The width, but ... the height?

'Cuyahogan ... stretch your right arm over the next step.'

The golem obeyed and wasn't switched to a lower step. It waited while Patrick fought with his mind. Then it flashed. Patrick made it lower the arm until its unflesh impinged on the upper boundary of the field.

Cuyahogan disappeared when the arm was five feet above the step.

A turn and a half below, it remained motionless, except for the continued lowering of its arm.

Patrick gestured impatiently, stepped onto the twenty-fourth, and was beside the golem. He ordered it to carry him up to the others. Without the golem, they'd be lost, dead, but it was not trustworthy, its balance was too delicate. He rejoined the other three. And Gaidhealla's face was a skull in the blue. Liam looked like a scarecrow; Iubhar's face was jaundiced. Patrick told them:

'The twist is the width of the twenty-fourth step, but the field only extends five feet above it. The golem will hand us over it.'

The golem took up Gaidhealla; the others dragged themselves behind.

Setting down the old woman, Cuyahogan took up Patrick in his right arm, and thrust him over the invisible barrier along the straight line of its left arm. He fell sprawling on the steps beyond, and scrambled for safety. Iubhar came next; together they caught and held Gaidhealla. Liam was thrown last, landing without dignity.

Cuyahogan flipped itself heels over head, somersaulted over the space-twist, and landed on its feet facing down the steps. It turned on order. Its eyes burned red through the pervasive blue. It took up Gaidhealla again. Her lidded eyes met Patrick's; each flashed what encouragement they could. They began up the flight beyond the twist, Liam clinging to Iubhar, who held Patrick, whose arms were grasped around the golem's belly. Now the weight of gravity began to increase, becoming that of a heavy planet. Even Cuyahogan slowed, appearing to be struggling. Their bodies were lead; the blue haze was a gelatinous broth. Liam felt his grip on Iubhar slipping. The downward pressure was too great, on their bodies and in their minds. Patrick drove slow words out of his mouth at the golem. 'Cuya-ho-gan . . . pulse more strongly . . . we sleep . . . we cannot . . . hold.'

Savage energy raged in them, pruned back paralysis, and gave them strength at the probable expense of brain damage. But burned-out synapses were the least price of failure. Cuyahogan dragged them, step by step. Thought was crushed by slabs of air. The blue seemed like a solid mold in which they were cast; their movement against it was a scarcely-perceptible agony, and their faces were jellied masks.

But the roof of the well – the attic floor – was close.

Patrick knew somehow that they were almost at the steps cut through the roof to the door of the attic. They were taking everything the Priest could throw. A few more steps and they'd have the madman. But the thoughts were not really formed; they were little more than flickers at the bottom of his crushed mind, which throbbed with fire and heavy pain. He wasn't conscious of his feet. Nine steps to go ... seven ... six. His head was level with the roof of the well. The golem waded into the energy torrent which poured from the door, through which nothing but glaring brightness could be seen. The blue was a howling storm, a drumming vibration which shook them apart. Behind Patrick, Iubhar retched, Liam collapsed – and Patrick lost his grip on the golem, falling on his knees.

In Cuyahogan's arms, the old woman couldn't speak.

But she was just barely capable of thought.

The moment was crucial. The Priest was at the climax of his operation. Tortured, Gaidhealla organized her thought, and threw it at the golem. Then she was unconscious.

Though the fine tuning of its reception was severely disturbed by the energy torrent which clashed with it, Cuyahogan picked up the order, laid down the old woman, scooped up Patrick, who was still conscious on the rack of its raping, reviving energy, and advanced into the attic to seek out and destroy the source of the terrible vibration.

Left on the steps, Liam and Iubhar were barely conscious. A shriek sliced the storm, and the energy grew; their bodies were being torn apart. Their very beings – and the steps – and the walls – and the tower itself – the great blocks of basalt became transparent and ebbed into nothing, leaving them suspended in emptiness, fifty feet from the crags, from a great shaft into the hill from its summit.

The Songmaker realized he was nothing but a point of view adrift in a raging storm.

The nightlands lay below and all around; they were briefly, luridly ruptured into day by lightning which speared from roiling underbellies of cloud. Thunder crashed almost immediately. Sick with loss and horrified vertigo, Liam realized that the downpouring rain was ... lancing right through him, through where his body should be, but wasn't. It didn't occur to him then that the rain shouldn't fall in such quantities here at this time of year. But before he – or anyone else – could react to the impossibility, they were back in their bodies, shaking on solid steps, hemmed by solid walls.

They were stunned in complete blackness.

The blue energy was gone, and the weight, and the lethargy.

For an immeasurable instant, silent explosions tore at their skulls; inchoate images flickered and faded away.

Then all was utterly still and silent within the tower.

On the couch in the hall below, Salamander moaned, in the grip of nightmares. But presently, the storm diminished, she slept more peacefully, her face relaxed, and her breathing became more regular.

One of the nightmares, at any rate, was over.

In the attic and on the steps, nothing and nobody moved for a long time. The waking energy no longer pulsed from Cuyahogan's mind.

The sky above the tower began to clear.

The night advanced.

## 14: The Zodiac Machine

Patrick had no time to react as the golem rushed him into the attic.

Into the raging *face.*

That was what he thought he saw, though afterward he couldn't remember it clearly. The face of the squatting blue demon which had confronted them in the yellow corridor. A grotesque, grimacing, crackling mask which occupied the volume of the attic, the apparent source of the blue energy. A crawling of shifting shapes which flickered and flowed, eyes into bulbous nose into slash of open mouth which wavered wide as if to swallow him. It was an inferno of energy, of spectral, flowing colors, from the dull red depth of cheeks to the high-frequency violet of twisting eyes which burned his flesh and mind as Cuyahogan plunged into gaping shreds of mouth. Though his mind was blasted, Patrick realized the face had no physical substance at all.

Into the crackling, flesh-stripping energies —

Straight at dim shapes molded in the very midst of the demon.

An instant before passing out, he understood that the energies forming the face sheeted up from grids in a black machine in the shape of a horseshoe. Cuyahogan plunged between the horns of the horseshoe; Patrick was barely aware of a body beneath its feet, of two bodies in front of the golem on the floor within the horseshoe's shoulder-high bank of sleek paneling where the neck of the face should be.

One of the bodies, tiny, was active in robe and helmet at a console in the depths of the machine. The light was lurid, the pandemonium monstrous, and Patrick was splitting apart. He gasped, 'Don't ... kill!' as the golem dropped him, slammed into the robed figure, into the console. The pandemonium rose to a terrible shriek. The energy-head began to writhe even more frantically, color surging up the spectrum toward invisibility, shredding, taking floor, walls, and all bodies with it, so that Patrick Cormac was no more than an empty mote stranded in the storm.

Then he was back in his body in the blackness, unconscious, and everything was utterly still.

A baby's wailing broke by degrees into his mind. At first he didn't know where he was; he imagined he lay in his bed in the Central Tower of Phadraig. The sound was thin, persistent, incomprehensible; what was a baby doing here? He dragged back his eyelids and tried to focus. He found he was looking up into a clearing sky; cloud-wraiths dissipating even as he watched, he recognized the Sleeping Giant, though the constellation was still half veiled. He frowned. What had happened to the roof? Was this dream, vision, or mad sorcery? For the clouds and stars were not all that floated in the sky – he also saw a circle of twelve occult symbols multicolored against the heavens. In another minute he realized he was looking up through a transparent circular dome. And the symbols – the signs of the ancient zodiac – were designs in the dome of colored glass thread.

The baby. The baby was bawling somewhere very close, demanding his attention. The baby. He began to remember. He was cold and heavy. He searched for his limbs and tried to work out how to roll over onto his stomach so he could push himself to his feet. His feet? Hadn't Cuyahogan been carrying him as they burst into the ... the attic? Where was the golem now? What was this black shining wall in front of him? In front? His muscles and nerves were reluctant to coordinate with his brain, and he couldn't recall what was up, or down, or this side, or that. The physical recovery was slow; his brain throbbed viciously as memory returned and the baby fell silent.

But the weight, the blue, the torment was gone.

He managed to turn and half lift himself onto his elbows.

Gentle starlight glimmered through the shallow dome. His eyes began to adapt, to make sense of various dark shadings about him. He fumbled for his torchblade, set it clumsily, and lit up the scene with low orange flare. It showed him meters, verniers, glass eyes ranked on the curved panels before him. He understood that he lay in the well of a machine built like a U.

The sound of a body shifting, to his right —

He met the masked face of a tiny, robed body on the floor beside him. Discolored eyes gleamed through slits in the grotesque blue mask, which reminded him of a . . . face . . . which vaguely oppressed his memory. Patrick held the torchblade closer, his own face tight. The dwarf was wounded. Left hand clutched bloody right shoulder. The hand – Patrick drew involuntary breath – the hand was in an advanced state of decomposition, with fingers of discolored and lumpy glue.

Above the crumpled body Cuyahogan was bent, motionless.

The golem's left arm extended down to unsheathed slivers of nail.

The arm was pointed at the dwarf; two of the slivers were missing.

Patrick made the connection between missing slivers and bloody shoulder. His mind was working again. He knew he was looking at the maniac called the Infernal Priest. Shriveled, pathetic dwarf! His anger rose; he forgot about the silent golem. With a sudden movement which flooded his head with waves of sick pain, he jerked the mask from the face of the dwarf. And recoiled instinctively.

For the degeneration of the hand and the horror of the

mask itself had done little more than hint.

The face was a ruined, sore-ridden misery. The flesh was decayed, mottled and eaten away, a tracery of ridged veins. The mad canceled eyes seemed precarious in their sockets, as though about to fall out and dangle in the hollows of discolored cheeks.

But Patrick had seen more physically horrible sights.

It was the expression that made him draw back.

The demented, self-torturing grin, the permanent rictus.

No wonder the dwarf had refused to show himself. It wasn't a face to inspire affection or confidence. Patrick stared for a frozen instant, then flung away the mask and pushed the dwarf so the grotesque face was undermost, and the body a sculpture of shock.

Patrick looked past the golem's legs, and saw two eyes like flowers.

Then for the first time he saw the baby – One Eye.

The child's body was a dim bundle swaddled in great doughy arms between enormous breasts.

But the eye was open – it was watching him.

His first reaction was one of wrath. This creature had almost killed Salamander; it had led them into this desperate situation. For a moment, his higher intentions were drowned in anger, in human reaction. He managed to control himself.

For he knew very well that it was no child at all.

The eye radiated an utter lack of childlike quality. It was deep, mysterious: like a hole into another time or dimension.

Weak and heavy-headed, he found himself entranced against his will.

Looking into the blackness of the eye was like looking into another reality which rendered his own world and preoccupations irrelevant.

An eye which would see what none of them would ever see.

It was a telescope, a microscope, a chronoscope, a crystal

ball.

The mind behind the eye was beyond his understanding. It inhabited a different universe of perception, ethic, and intention.

It was the paradigm of a new way, the autochthon of a new race, a complete original, a revolution, a ... divine mutant....

And its crying wasn't the sound of fear; it was rage at frustrating imprisonment in a body which wouldn't do what it wanted. With an odd chill, Patrick wondered how long it would stay penned in its body, how long it would *consent* to remain a child. He remembered the rumors that he was the father. This was possible, but not provable, or knowable, and probably irrelevant. He wondered if Gaidhealla knew. With an effort, he tore his eyes away. The baby wasn't helpless. The dwarf hadn't been able to harm it; the energies released here had been too gross and chaotic to affect the cohesion of its mind.

But the baby could die a physical death like any other embodied being, and its mind and potential would be stranded. Perhaps the malign dwarf had tried to be too subtle; perhaps he'd intended to decant the child's energy into his daughter's void. The vast, fat-drowned woman comforted the child, rocking gently on the floor.

Patrick flicked quick eyes at the robed body beside him.

*At least he intended to benefit his daughter....*

Then he thought of Gnorl and Scalaman; of the others.

He found his feet, leaned dizzily against the inner bank of the machine, and held up the torchblade.

The machine stood at the center of a zodiac inscribed on the floor above the well, each sign corresponding with that on the dome above.

The zodiac occupied the entire area of the attic apart from a narrow passage around its outer rim. The passage connected the entrance with four niches hollowed from the black outer wall, which was ten feet in height to the lip of the dome, and featureless. One niche held a cot heaped with shabby blankets, the second a bathtub and buckets, the third a table and chair, and the fourth a shelved clutter of books, vessels, clothes, unfinished plates of food. The dwarf wasn't a tidy housekeeper. But Patrick had no eyes for the domestic niches.

The diameter of the zodiac, area of machine included, was about twenty feet. Each of the twelve sections which radiated from the circle containing the machine was seven feet deep, over five feet wide at the bottom end, and less than two feet wide where they met the base of the machine. Each section was defined by a border studded with varieties of quartz – cat's eye, tiger's eye, aventurine, sun-stone, and rainbow quartz. But he wasn't interested in the translucent stones.

An unmoving, shaven human being lay in each of the twelve sections, feet together at the outside, body on the appropriate sign engraved in the stone. Patrick leaned over the foot-wide grid which topped the machine. He felt a tickling vibration run through him, but it didn't seem to be harmful. He looked down the outer bank, holding out the torchblade. Saw heads, cradled in shallow troughs close to the base of the machine. Curving metal hoods covered part of each bare cranium.

Twelve bodies.

All of them looked like corpses.

Increasingly grim, he rounded the motionless golem, uneasy with its presence, then squeezed past the enormous woman, avoiding the baby's eye. He bent to the nearest victim, at the mouth of the horseshoe. Vaguely, he remembered Cuyahogan trampling across a body when they waded into the ... face. It must have been this girl. She was brown, kirtled, bare-breasted, lithe arms tattooed, each with a feathered serpent. Her features were smooth, intelligent, sensuous; she was medium in height, not one of the Banissen Saturna. He could detect no pulse; tight-lipped, he felt her shaven skull, felt terminals attached to her crown, and wires which led from these into the hood which was connected to the base of the smooth black machine.

He remembered the hideous demon face, clearly, for a moment.

He searched for Gnorl and Scalaman.

Found Gnorl, sprawled across Taurus, face contorted. No pulse.

And Scalaman, slumped in Pisces, his bleached mane shorn.

The scout called Tembar was unconscious in Aries.

Idrys, the other, was a husk in Sagittarius.

The girl at the mouth of the horseshoe lay in Libra. The other seven signs were occupied by men and women of the Banissen Saturna. Patrick realized it was no wonder the tribe was so hostile to travelers. Failure to capture sufficient sacrifices meant that Phan took them instead. He examined each of the twelve. Then he stood, stiff and desolate. What could they do now? Rage and horror welled in him, and he marched into the horseshoe past the golem and, right-handed, jerked the dwarf onto stiff feet, his physical disgust suppressed. The hood of the dwarf's robe fell back to show a pitted, cratered skull; in places the bone was almost completely eroded. The man was dying, but he'd suffer more first!

'Revive these poor people or we'll kill you slowly! The misery you've experienced so far in life will be nothing compared with the pain you'll feel if you don't obey me!'

The dwarf was stiff, but conscious. Demented eyes met demented eyes. And the breath of his voice had no force and no soul:

'Revival is ... impossible. The golem interrupted most subtle transfer of essence.... Phan is driven out ... but he will return ... and you cannot increase my sadness with torture. I am impervious to more suffering, you fool, and you are still trapped....'

With loathing, Patrick dropped the ugly dwarf.

'Wormface! Murderer! Your demon's an illusion, your mind's unhinged, your Phan is the production of this machine and the delusion of your mind!'

He swung away furiously, hopelessly, almost impaling himself on Cuyahogan's unsheathed nails. He shouted: 'Cuyahogan – sheathe!'

The pallid golem showed no sign of having received the order.

*'Cuyahogan – sheathe!'*

Now his anger was mixed with alarm. Who knew what those energies had done to the golem? He stood rooted as Cuyahogan turned, regarded him with baleful, ruby eyes, waiting – for what? Final provocation?

From the floor at his feet, the dwarf breathed painfully. 'It is said . . . put not thy trust in machines of the ancients . . . for in them is sadness and damnation. I know . . . oh, I know. . . .'

A cackle welled, shredded into insane silence.

A third time, Patrick ordered the golem to sheathe.

Still regarding him, the golem began to raise its left arm.

Then another voice cut in, from the door. Gaidhealla. '*Met*, Cuyahogan, *met*, sheathe!'

The nails retracted smoothly, slowly.

Cuyahogan froze in its threatening position. Patrick Cormac sighed with relief, looked toward the entrance. And the child was silent; so was the dwarf.

But his raddled eyes were open, and his brain was working.

Liam and Iubhar had taken longer to recover consciousness, then had helped Gaidhealla up into the attic in the very nick of time.

Now Iubhar was uneasily aware of the golem at their backs as Patrick held up the torchblade for the old woman to examine Gnorl and Scalaman, the Songmaker crouching beside her in case she should need support. But now that the melancholy was gone, her mind was sharp and clear, though weak. Her thin fingers traced sensing contours on Scalaman's white forehead.

Liam thought, wryly, that Scalaman would prefer to lose his life before he'd lose his mane of hair.

Iubhar turned away to keep an eye on the golem and the dwarf.

'They're alive,' she insisted to Patrick, her voice brittle. 'Their personalities are accumulated and entangled in the machine. I know about it. The ancients used machines like these to visit each other in the mind, sometimes as many as twelve at once, to heal, or indoctrinate, or to come to agreement, or just to play. Its misused effects give rise to his belief in a demon. The blueness was the excess of energy of Mind tormented beyond comprehension ... the power of twelve, possibly many more individuals thrown together ... burned up, driven mad ... and this zodiac ... more half-understood nonsense. The dwarf's more mad than evil. Perhaps he thought he'd make his daughter whole by feeding into her mind the zodiac's spectrum of influence, like a stew of mentality ... impossible fantasy. And the baby ... why Alhazuer? Yes, they're alive – in a turbulent sense, in total confusion! A demon indeed!'

'But we were in time to stop the —' Liam began.

She was bitter, vehement. 'In time to stop *what*? The child's not harmed. But these people are as good as dead. How can we untangle them, draw them back, each into his or her own body? They're lost!'

And Iubhar watched over the dwarf, coming no closer than necessary, uncomfortable in Cuyahogan's uncertain presence, disgusted by the dwarf's. Behind Cuyahogan's back, the dwarf's daughter crooned and rocked the baby as if nothing had happened, as if they were alone together in a summer world where night never fell.

Cuyahogan.

The golem.

The dwarf thought furiously through his pain.

*Met* was the word the old woman had shouted. If only he could seize control of the golem ... Phan could be induced to return ... all would be preferable to this sad situation. *Met.* Recognition flickered somewhere in the vast depositories of his unstable mind. Once his memory had been perfect, but now it frequently misled him. *Met.*

Moldering teeth bared in perpetual grin, he searched his mind.

He had it!

The word *Emet* – 'Truth' – was marked on the forehead of the Golem of the ancient Kabbalists. To destroy the Golem, the first letter was obliterated, leaving *Met* – 'Death.'

His body was a crumpled heap of dying flesh and friable bone with very little strength left. But his mind was awake, hyperactive, in a self-cursed condition. He thought at high speed.

The name of 'golem' was fanciful in this creature but, linked with the clue of *Met,* it suggested that its creators had incorporated occult elements into its control system, for their own amusement or for other reasons, it didn't matter. He had to work out the word which would bring the golem under his control. The sooner the better. Or they'd kill him before he was ready to abandon this misery. Swiftly he selected, rejected, and considered combinations of vowels, consonants, and numbers. Enunciation, pitch, and tone – all important! His mind raced, for he had little time. These invading madmen would tear his tower apart, drive Phan away forever. They interrupted his operation, invaded his privacy, abused his hospitality, called him a deluded fool. But the golem was the only cause of their temporary superiority. His mind was superior – it never slept! He would take control of the golem and punish them fittingly. They would be merged with Phan, then their discarded bodies would be tipped through the slats which hinged each sign, to tumble down the dark well and join the derelict skeletons of many others from many times, far below. The dwarf didn't know how deep the well was, or why it had been dug. But it made an excellent dumping ground for all sorts of refuse. The old woman, the flaxen-haired, passionate maniac – they would rot with the others. And their essence would be absorbed in Phan, who would prepare a delicate precipitate of spirit to make his nameless daughter whole.

Phan!

Incomprehensible blueness.

Everything and nothing! Mighty!

The dwarf knew that soon, of course, his continued proximity to Phan's raging energies would strip the remains of flesh from his bones, and his brain would rot completely. Then he'd set the controls one final time, lay his putrid body down, his head wired into the zodiac machine, and he'd leave behind body and the misery of sleepless personality forever. He'd join Phan, rise above this abominable physical level, this obscene corruption of his own body, his own life. He would flow in the ocean of Phan! And be Mind Unchained! Soon! But not yet. He couldn't accept the gift of destruction from these self-interested maniacs. Their actions outraged him, overwhelmed him with a miserable sense of injustice. He'd done their friends a great favor, given them eternal sleep in communion with an element of the Absolute! Why then did they call him evil, call him mad, if not because of their own misconceptions? They were to be pitied, not hated. He was a magnanimous being. Always, he'd been maligned and misunderstood. He couldn't understand it. Even the child, the strange one-eyed being from whose mind emanated such strong currents. Why had it refused adoption into Phan, though it sought his daughter's arms? How did it resist? What was it? It had remained neutral and unaffected throughout the buildup of energy, up until the disruption by the golem. Perhaps it was a danger, the true cause of these ill events; perhaps he should kill it – it could be antipathetic to Phan's energies.

His shoulder bled. He didn't feel it. His body was in permanent pain of continuing dissolution. He heard the anguish of the old woman. He could no longer see very well; he could vaguely make out a wiry man who watched above him. All the time, he was considering the word. Now he thought he had it. He balanced it, considered it.

Now, he would gain control of the golem. The word was right.

But a red-haired man rammed furious eyes against his.

'Hypocrite!' shouted the Songmaker, overwhelmed with fury which outweighed disgust. 'Superstitious dunce! Is fate to blame for the hideous dissolution of your body? Or is it Phan? What of the energy released by minds trapped in this machine, the ferocity of their radiation? How long have you sat here in their lethal glow, leeching minds, crying like a crocodile while your mind and body have rotted away? Energy-addict! You understand nothing of the energies you call demon. I'll show you energy. You'll dance to energy!' The Songmaker, shadowed by the golem, unslung his sirena in one swift movement, and his fingers went into frenzies of board-setting preparation. 'You'll dance and sing! Or would you prefer the tears to stream down your raddled cheeks – if there are any tears in you!'

Behind Liam, Iubhar stood unmoving, fingering his fringe of beard.

Patrick stood, supporting Gaidhealla with one arm, holding up the torchblade. The orange glow was eerie; they watched outside the bank of the machine without interrupting. Perhaps the Songmaker might break down their enemy with his skill. There was a risk that the sirena's vibrations might disturb the golem, drive it over the edge of control. But the risk had to be taken. Dawn was not so far off.

But it was the baby's eye the dwarf was most aware of as Liam's fingers began to twist, stroke, flash. The sack-like, ruined body stirred, the word on its lips as the silence grew heavily audible.

Liam, grim, built up the most nerve-racking subsonic variations he had ever conceived. His face was like a wolf's; he'd make the maniac do the dance of epilepsy at seven cycles a second; he'd make him pray for relief from the directional vibrations. Twenty seconds of silence, thirty ... forty ... the remains of the dwarf's mottled flesh sagged, rippled, his mind crushed by misery more dull and haunting than any he'd ever felt. It was leaden, and fright began to crawl in him. The word – he must speak it out before he lost control of his vocal chords in the onslaught of subsonic depression.

The word trembled in his throat; he was afflicted by doubt.

What if it was wrong? What if Phan had deserted him?

He cursed the thoughts, the foul mental torture, the twisting of his mind, he cursed all those about him, and he spoke the word.

It hissed out between teeth, from drawn-back lips.

'*Met-Bat-A-D-D-seven-D-five!*'

Silence.

Then the golem moved.

Cuyahogan looked down on the dwarf.

The Songmaker's mouth was open; his fingers were still.

Cuyahogan's fingernails extended with an audible *click*.

Cuyahogan bent, blurred, decapitated the dwarf efficiently.

The head bounced off the side of the machine as the neck spouted blood. The head came to rest lying on its right ear. Puzzled fury was frozen on its face.

Eleven eyes were glued to the disordered golem. Neither Patrick nor Gaidhealla dared to shout commands and attract attention. The insane dwarf had done *something* to it – but what?

Cuyahogan straightened.

Twitched.

Spun around.

Lurched past the dwarf's daughter as she began to giggle.

Staggered across the brown girl's body, nails retracting, snapping out, and resheathing faster than the eye could follow.

Tripped over its feet and slammed into the wall like a falling log. Sat drunkenly, head at an odd angle, eyes glaring through the dome at the Sleeping Giant, as though it raged against futility.

Against infinity.

Gaidhealla knew that scientific dilettantes had established the original control codes for the golem about the time of the Great Forgetting. The creation of Cuyahogan had been game rather than pragmatic scientific project. They built it for amusement – and for protection. Though they liked to dream that they were invulnerable Lords of Creation, they weren't exempt from reality's unfortunate impositions.

They hadn't survived – but their creation had.

The crazed dwarf had been unlucky. He'd deduced the correct sound-combination. But it had brought him death, not control. Evidently Cuyahogan had been deranged by the energies of the misused machine. The dwarf had brought fate down on himself for the final time. And had trapped them into the bargain.

Nobody dared to move for at least a minute.

A desperate idea began to form in Patrick's mind.

They gathered in the horseshoe, picking their way past bodies with care, not for a moment removing their eyes from the golem.

'Burn out its brain with your torchblade before it attacks us!'

White-faced, Patrick rejected Iubhar's hissed advice with a shake of his head. 'It's faster than us. If we threaten it —'

Then he lit the dwarf's remains with a flare of orange. The bank of the console was spattered with blood. Gaidhealla grimaced. She felt empty, remotely sick at the joke of their situation. The light danced on scattered scabs of flesh on the ugly, staring head, on the robed and shapeless body which lay in a spreading pool of blood, on silvery fretwork as Liam, pale, reslung his sirena. He felt responsible for what had happened. He fumbled apologies which Patrick cut off with a heavy hand on the Songmaker's shoulder. Behind them the dwarf's daughter giggled, almost inaudibly. They avoided the baby's steady gaze. Iubhar and the Songmaker too had clashed with that deep eye, had felt doubt coupled with simultaneous fascination.

'What now?' Iubhar was dazed. 'How can we revive our friends? How can we escape?'

'Break through the dome, lower ourselves down the walls, starve to death on the rocks,' suggested Liam miserably. 'Perhaps the men of Kor were right after all....'

Then Patrick squeezed out the notion he'd been fermenting.

'Old Mother.' He took Gaidhealla's pipestem arm. 'Could you control this machine, feed the three of us together into the ... maze of mind? There's a chance we could separate Gnorl and Scalaman from the confusion if we enter prepared....'

She glanced sharply at his orange-shadowed face. It was stubborn, resolved in determination. Iubhar was momentarily aghast. Liam's lips came back from his teeth; a rare mood of desperate exaltation possessed him. What an idea! If they could do it, and survive ... what visions he'd return with, what strange music! Gnorl and Scalaman? Well, Gnorl wouldn't thank him, and Scalaman would probably curse him for interrupting dreams of beautiful houris with eyes like gazelles....

The old lady showed no emotion.

'I might not be able to draw you out. You might not return.'

'I know that.' Patrick swung around. 'We know that.'

Iubhar, glum, didn't contest the assumption of agreement.

'I have only theoretical knowledge,' Gaidhealla objected.

'We've got no option. If we fail—' Patrick shrugged. 'But if we succeed, we may also as one mind solve problems which escape us as individuals. Such as: how to nullify the space-twists inside and out.'

'Then let's get on with it.' Iubhar was sour, as he eyed the unmoving golem. 'Dawn's not far off. The world outside's probably crawling with Khassam's army. And the golem might go crazy at any minute.'

'Liam?'

The Songmaker nodded jerky agreement.

Gaidhealla accepted. 'To feed you in, we'll have to remove three of the people already on the zodiac.' She was sharp, controlled. 'I can't foretell what the damange to their brains will be. It may be fatal.'

'If we don't – then all will certainly die,' answered Patrick.

'Then who...?' Iubhar's misgivings were obvious.

'The Banissen Saturna on our appropriate signs.' Patrick was flat, emotionless. 'Liam, you're Gemini. Iubhar, you're Cancer. And myself in the one the ancients called Scorpio.'

*Would he suggest that if Gnorl or Scalaman shared any of our respective signs?* The Songmaker was pained. Aloud, he said: 'Then we can't afford to revive any of their friends. They might hinder us and try to kill us. I suppose it's necessary they should die on our account, but—'

Then he followed Patrick's gaze to One-Eye, and he fell silent.

*Not on our account,* he realized, *but that strange child's.*

'Salamander,' asked Iubhar, 'will she be safe?'

'She sleeps,' Gaidhealla said instantly. 'I know it.'

'... And the golem is up here.' Patrick's eyes were hooded.

They agreed, and set about it.

## 15: The Caldron

There was no time to waste. Two men and a woman were disconnected from the terminals and removed from their signs. Patrick Cormac took his place on Scorpio with an apparent confidence which he couldn't feel. It was difficult to close his eyes and relax with the golem stargazing at his feet. And this course was desperate. Even if they succeeded with their immediate objective, what destructive inner secrets would each of them learn about the others? How deep was their friendship, their union? Could it survive if they learned too much about each other? Or would it be strengthened, firmed?

And what if they got lost in the confusion and never came out?

What hellish life would they become part of?

Most disturbing of all, what would he learn of himself?

Many in Phadraig had believed Patrick Cormac's birth to have been touched by the moon. It had been argued by some Councillors that his birth under the eighth sign fitted him for the reproductive duties of the High Witchman. But others insisted that birth under the third decan of the sign suggested the potency of sex sublimated to stimulate ideals and ambitions. Gobhan had thought astrology a nonsense; he'd always believed Patrick Cormac to be a destroyer, who must be controlled.

Patrick didn't know who or what he was, or what was the source of his intuition and ideals. Uncertain of himself, he lay unrelaxed as Gaidhealla connected him with the skull-cap terminals. Through the dome, the sky was noticeably more light. There was no time to shave their heads. The Witchmother of the Third Eye connected him, then Iubhar, then Liam, her delicate fingers quick in the light of the torchblade. She threw frequent glances at Cuyahogan, but the golem continued to stare at the sky. Screened from them in the horseshoe well, One-Eye and the dwarf's daughter watched the golem silently.

Twelve bodies spoked the hub of the machine. Three more lay discarded, curled limp round feet at the rim. The three who'd replaced them lay silent, waiting, each with last moments of private thought.

Gaidhealla entered the horseshoe, ignored the mess, and studied the console with its inner-lit panels and meters. She passed a hand over one of the rectangular, close-meshed grids set in the machine's flat top. She felt faint vibration, the low radiation of the almost-dormant chaos within. She was ready. Her finger hovered, selected, prepared the linkage. She knew it could be that the twelve – the nine – were past help, that this mad scheme would only destroy three more.

Salamander. The girl was still asleep, down below.

Energy-flow. Connection. Synchronization of three minds in one.

With slow deliberation, with frequent checks over her shoulder, she began to move the single mind toward the matrix where twelve, probably many more, were trapped out of time, welded in confusion.

Propped up beside her, the torchblade flared with light. She was a silhouette, bent in concentration, her mind abstracted into the problem. Merging. Then she could do nothing but hope. They were on their own. If successful, they'd let her know.

If not, they'd have no opportunity.

It began for each of them like a dream where the dreamer hangs above his own body, conscious that he dreams, but wondering how he'll ever find his way back again. That was at first, when briefly there were three separate dreamers. They felt their time-bound personalities, the frames of reference which each termed *I* or *me*, being dissolved from the familiar dimensions, seemingly pulled through that part of the cranium which in a baby is soft and called the fontanel, at adjacent angles of the parietal bones.

Disconnected, deprived of senses, unable to prove their existence by reference to external or material objects, they died.

The three dreams of death merged into one mind which awakened to itself for the very first time. The mind of Iubhar-Liam-Patrick. It saw itself triply and was confused. What was the common denominator? There was initial battle between antagonistic elements, innermost beliefs, and views of the world. The battle was resolved when the warring mind realized that apparently hostile elements were shoots of the same plant, that it possessed a common, singular intention. It merged itself through adjacent memory-images of past events shared by all three. At first these were hazy and out of focus – triple-images of Phadraig, the Company, the golem, Gnorl, Scalaman, others – but these were gradually stabilized into a single composite. Mind interlocked on what could be resolved. Mind realized that singular triangulation offered more than plural individuals. The state presented previously unrealized clarity, objectivity, strength, and depth of perception. Where it had been split, isolated at each separate foot of a tripod, now it was unified at the apex, in the head.

Mind dreamed the intention which gave it focus and direction. The individuation of frames of reference called *Gnorl*, and *Scalaman*. Before progressing (being progressed?), the dream examined itself. It knew it faced chaotic nightmare which could result in dissolution, disaster. It required internal definition to maintain its wholeness. It needed an integral, self-perpetuating set of codes to act as beacons in the storm of random meaninglessness ahead, as anchors of mutually-supporting associations. And the dream itself had to become a life raft, a nexus defined by its beacons. Its intention was that the beacons would tend to attract shattered elements of the chaos into frames which concurred with self-aware definitions of *Gnorl*, of *Scalaman* – frames which, together as one, could dream its own tripartite self-definitions – of *Patrick, Liam, Iubhar.*

Mind dreamed it was the ancient Chinese, Chuang Tzu, who dreamed he was a butterfly. Mind dreamed he awoke and wondered if he was now a butterfly dreaming it was a man that was a Mind in a machine dreaming the universe which dreamed of butterflies dreaming....

Mind slid past reefs of distracting metaphors, images, and dreams within dreams which threatened to fragment its intention.

It fixed its chosen beacons, which confirmed themselves by cross-reference with each other in a mutually-defining web.

Mind was being consumed, as though thrown through rapids and spilled down falls into a sea of raging, random energies, of potential in permanent reaction against itself. The dream slid into vast nightmare, where total battle was the only harmony. How many individual minds were lost in *here?* It wasn't twelve, or fifteen, or just hundreds, or even whatever: it wasn't important. Sums of hypothetical individuals had no meaning; even as individuals they had been microcosms, complex unities. Here, those unities were lost, they were hypothetical frames, as possible and impossible as anything else in the universe. And here, as everywhere else, there was only the universe. With all tendency to order erased. The scramble was total. No currents persisted longer than a thought. No thought existed to perceive the currents; there were no processes or conditions for the reasoning faculty to exist. There was just the potential from which any reality might grow – if thought could only exist for a reality-structure to be conceived and perceived.

How was it?

There was no past in the machine, nothing determined.

How is it?

It's a stew, an ever-changing labyrinth.

It's a high frequency abyss, electric sheeting aimlessly.

It's humming ghosts of the Great Forgetting as real/unreal as Company and the crowd. It's Rome and Phadraig, New York and Uxmane of the Middle Kingdom. It's an endless, imperceptible present, without form to give meaning to moment. It's pregnant with the loves and hates of many societies, places, times – but none of them are ever quite born. It's music, but its scales aren't human. It's random, it's whatever could possibly happen. It's the product of a machine but the machine's the product of the energies within it, the product of potential made actual in time, called human.

It's a malfunction.

The makers of the machine didn't intend to build an agent of entropy. Their purposes were therapeutic, political, scientific, and possibly – as with the golem – deadly playful. It served their purposes; they never mapped out the totality of its potential. Or perhaps they preferred to remain deliberately blind to the teeth of the tiger while they could still swing from its tail.

The machine was already full with shredded mind at the time of the Great Forgetting.

Time didn't touch the eternity of its internal present.

In time, the machine was rediscovered by looters in the ruins of a once-extensive building over the bottomless shaft. Inadvertently, they released a manifestation of its 'godlike' power. The looters fled with a horrified tale of the demon. Within months they were dead, their bodies rotted away. Worship of the demon grew extensively in the region. A new tower of black basalt was built to house it. Many centuries passed. There were many occupants of the tower; many minds had been sacrificed to the demon; many bodies had gone down the well, which had originally been the passage through which the machine drew energy from the earth. The machine had long since accumulated enough internal energy to dissipate to keep it going through quite a few more millennia. But the energy was no longer available for conversion into order.

Ranulph had steadfastly declined to activate the machine. But his son, the dwarf, had made up for all the lost years.

Beacons . . .

The sun gleams on the High Towers, on the florid slopes of the Chahd, on the squalor of Madadhmachair.

Though their origin is lost, these ideas maintain their stability in the chaos, as a lure for potential awareness, for conjunctions of chance in patterns which, outside the machine, had? would? could? did? coincide with the frames of Gnorl, or Scalaman, or Liam, or Iubhar, or Patrick. The beacons' tendency is to establish a polar matrix, a hitching-post for identity, to draw together unrelated but appropriate elements into predefined relationships.

Patterns begin to coalesce. . . .

They come together, they form, become ordered and self-adjusting in the definitive light of the most potent beacon-image.

Wavering proto-reality solidifies —

Into the smoke, glare, stench, clamor of battle —

Into the hissing of Red Kilmun, the chaos of Kalnakill's routed forces in retreat, driven from the Southern Walls to the Fringe to the sodden, reeking ash of the Burning River's verge. A great crowd of demoralized soldiers push and shove for their turn at the Crossing; others desert to the south through the neck —

Into the Company Chatachain, advancing in its strength, in its hour of triumph, ordered and eager behind the snarling crimson banner, led by a flaxen-haired maniac who roars at the retreating barbarians through the confusion of hissing arrows, flaring powertubes, and violent death. Sweeping through the corpse-littered Fringe, trapping the remnants of Kalnakill's forces against the stinking river. Many have already retreated to safety and escape, including the Jerezid Warlord's son, Khassam, who took the pregnant Ranza with him.

Desperate, the remaining soldiers turn to face the Company and fight. Their heads are assaulted by wailing phantoms conjured from the Songmaker's sirena, necks severed by Gnorl's sweeping blade, bodies pierced by Scalaman's quarrels; they're forced backward to their deaths in the river by the onslaught of the seventy. The Warlord's guard is cut down, Iubhar to the fore. And Patrick comes face to face with an aging, squat, powerful man wearing the regal Jerezid warhelm.

Kalnakill.

A silent circle forms.

Patrick Cormac moves forward. The Warlord waits, his gray eyes haunted with failure, back to the river, on guard.

Patrick Cormac thumbs three feet of blade from the body of his ancient weapon. Kalnakill roars, charges, deliberately impales himself.

He dies.

The battle's over.

The scene is unclear, bodies half-transparent, reality's cracking.

But four around a fifth, their leader, are confirmed in mutual recognition and identification. Their realization of self is ordered and simultaneous. They dream withdrawal from the caldron, define themselves in relation to a remembered world of time. They anchor themselves and each other to ideas of their bodily selves, like balloons anchored against wind from chaos. Thus stabilized, they dip back into the caldron, forming a beacon to draw the scouts for greater strength and knowledge. Dreary crags of evening outside the tower waver, take familiar shape. Idrys and Tembar sit insubstantial on a rock. 'Come,' dreams Patrick-of-Five, 'take shape and reality; join us.'

Then Company is Seven.

No – Company is Eight.

The girl from Libra is descrambled and aware in them and they in her. Zena, an elegant vagabond, born a slave beneath the Black Wharves of Ghillechly in Aquinte, escaped from the court harem of Hlahd XIV during Khassam's campaign of conquest. A wanderer captured by the Banissen Saturna. Eight recall disputing proof of her wanderlust so fiercely that it was three years before the shaman penetrated the subtlety of her quibbling and declared her a wanderlusting casuist, fit for possession by the Demon. So her strong, humorous, sensual mind is delivered to the machine. She's drawn from the caldron, as if by miracle, but Iubhar's frame of personality is the chief agent. Eight know the two relate in many ways, their union's instinctive, their characters are complementary, and they are Eight – they are Zena gladly, Patrick morosely, Idrys philosophically, Scalaman jealously, Tembar fiercely, Gnorl darkly, Liam mischievously ... Iubhar gladly, and she – she is Scalaman knowing her body, the sensual expert comparing her fine, dark-nippled breasts with ... but she is he is she and the others, multiplex, webbed, in threat of intense confusion. In Eight he's mixed more female, sees herself with a woman's eyes and him as well, male and female in one, and amazed to know he always was ... he's a caricature, Songmaker-imagined – naked and grotesque, monstrous phallic crossbow thrusting from beetroot loins, shaven dome like a mirror above a corpulent, crafty red face. The caricature's shattered by bludgeons of abuse, by nostrils breathing flame, a clown's face laughs, frames are swirling, Eight is torn by jagged, hostile fantasies, Eight wants to make love to itself but seems bound to make war, lost in a sea of foreign points of view. For here's mind from Phadraig, from Kor's sere peaks, from Aquinte's drear sea, here's Eight struggling against the paradox of unity, here are different customs, moralities, and beliefs. Here's contrariness sprouting claws, here are fears and emotional chain-reactions growing into demons. Here are frames fighting each other for singular balance and losing, their anchor-lines cut, sliding deformed back into the caldron, here's an end —

An adjustment. A splicing of common realization, lines of communication in sudden, unexpected light. No secrets. They have no secrets. Mutual fear is moribund. All doubt and weakness is common. Eight sees itself clearly. *Phadraig and Kor and Aquinte – all people! We kill ourselves with guilt! Admission – admission is the price of the joke!*

Here's forgiveness and laughter and a measure of harmony. Here are each of Eight, nearly returned to time, to individualities, to the mission of the Company Chatachain. The scouts – dour despisers of people from plains and cities – are as integral to the Company now as the other six. Eight-in-One, time-drawn, fading from realization.

*How? How are we sound together, how are we light to see ourselves? The child, One-Eye, what are we doing, who? What can he see, what does he want of us, of people. . .?*

Elements of alarm. Caused by their imagining of the attic, of the tower, and its state in time. With opened doors and nullified space-twists. With their bodies and seven other lost ones sacklike around the machine – frames for the unknown Banissen Saturna they cannot form. With Gaidhealla watching at the console, whose imagined mind they seed with reassurance that they are. With a great, fat woman behind her on the floor, holding a one-eyed child. . . .

And this is their alarm and sumultaneity:

(The conjunction One-Eye requires.)

The single eye is a depth of dreams which consume them in their imagination of it. And they're eight individuals standing, bodies charred and minds confused, in a ghostly nowhere world of flickering mists and the whisperings of dead generations. And, above —

*We're being imagined,* thinks Patrick, alone like the others.

Overwhelmed by the image-storms raging from the roiling pupil of the eye which is the sky. Panoramic shards of future burst about them; their hearts are drained in many deaths, many alternatives. Some of the fleeting, evanescent images seem to belong to a set or a sequence, but overlapping, intermingling, and changing so fast that there's no certainty. Khassam's army, rough men of Kor, Purplefield, Lamassa, Zagrin, Phrenge, Spokane, and Aquinte, trudging from Scarp tunnels in the eye – and the shambling, jabbering mumen jam – and the Company Chatachain, descending the hill with ... Gnorl in the lead, the nameless child with the nameless woman, fading images of selected possibilities, the Company converging with Khassam's army, and ... and ... and ...

And the eye swallows them.

With a complex thought, a charge burned into them:

*You are dreamed by what you cannot see. Call me no names, call me any, take me to Khassam, let me be carried by the fat woman whose void is restful. Your own wills charge you: do this, and be discharged.*

Vacuum.

Eight dream of numb return into eight bodies.

This happened as Gaidhealla received their signal of reassurance. The old lady was empty, energies drained, and age creeping on her. She knew they wouldn't go to the sanctuary now. One-Eye. The prophesied end of her life's dedication. She had never prejudiced herself with expectations about One-Eye's nature, destiny, or effect; she'd foreseen only the birth of a very great potential. Though perhaps she had, all unconsciously, accepted the image of a baby, with a baby's limitations, requiring sanctuary in which to grow adult flesh and power. But – *see him there!* – One-Eye didn't have to wait for adulthood; he could use baby-form as well or better than any other. Her intuition that the baby was about to need them no longer was a certainty. The Company lived – that was good – but none of them were anything to One-Eye. He would use them, refuse them, and forget them.

She was shaking. She had to grip the console. Her

whole life she had spent on this cause – now it was about to shuck her off. That she could accept without distress. It was what she sensed of One-Eye that set her shaking. She could sense some approaching triumph from which people were utterly excluded. What had she helped to survive?

But warning had been implicit in Maelnagar's prophecy.

No bodies stirred yet, as a cold draft swept into the attic from doors opened down below. It stirred Gaidhealla's hair, and was drawn out through vents in the lip of the shallow, transparent dome. And it triggered the golem. Cuyahogan's eyes abandoned the dawn. It jerked uncertainly to its feet, twisted, and its gaze splayed motionless bodies, crossed Gaidhealla, came to the door. The golem staggered for the stairs, went down in jerking leaps, drawn by some unknown impulse.

Salamander! The old lady hissed with fright. She could sense the girl unconscious at the foot of the steps near the well. Her daughter must have awoken, alone and confused, and stumbled to the steps before falling. She stared past One-Eye at the door, her mind racked, until she knew it was all right and the golem had left the tower for the crags without harming the girl.

Around her, in the full dawn, eight people were stirring on the floor.

Patrick was first on his feet – haggard, mordant, abstracted.

'We take One-Eye to Khassam,' was all he could say.

The acknowledgment was heavy with inevitability.

# Part III: The Clearing

## 16: Khassam

Khassam.

The Warlord stood in dawn at the base of the Scarp's jagged heights, on a slight grassy eminence overlooking all three of the tunnel-mouths from which his motley forces poured. They formed up on the space of flat ground which quickly fell away to thick forest, to rolling, disordered land. The sun was rising, weak rays shafted along the Scarp's discontinuous southern rim, over the rise and fall of the forest before them, against the steep hills which tumbled up into sudden, random nubs of black rock. Deep triangles, spikes, and waves of shadow shaded the thick land with irregular patterns. But here, the Warlord was pleased to stand in fragile sunlight. Banners swirled as if glad to be out of the tunnels' endless dim luminosity; lieutenants barked orders, curses, and derision. And soldiers of every shape, size, hue, and attitude fell into rough, reluctant rank.

Remote, bored, but in marginally good humor, Khassam watched the activity over the bright-helmed heads of his red-cuirassed escorts. The twenty handpicked men of the Loyal Jerezid Guard were rigid at attention in a semicircle in front of and slightly below him, the knee-length hems of their blue surcoats moving slightly in the breeze, the Holy Glyph of the Jerezid Dogmas blazoned on their chests. The Glyph was a blossoming tree within an equilateral triangle of three stylized silver swords laid point to pommel. But on chest and back of his own scarlet surcoat, the Glyph was emerald and gold. Brief approval figured on his stretched yellow leather face; wide thin lips drew back from broken teeth. These were capped and embellished with alloys of several colors. The Warlord was beardless and bald, save for a hairlock which hung past his pierced right ear. The black lock was woven through with strings of tiny violet amethysts, the passionless gems of sobriety and death. Some thought he wore these for the same reason he wore the dreaded cockatrice helm which now he held against his thigh – as a calculated affectation to individualize further, to put the fear of death into superstitious rabble, into would-be advisers, ambitious lieutenants, treacherous schemers, arrogant theologians. He could trust none of them. He was permanently surrounded by rats begging for favors with their right hands, who concealed knives in their left behind their backs. But he approved of his Guard. The Guard *was* loyal – more than could be said for much of the army, which was largely culled from subject dominions. The loyalty of the soldiers – not least to each other – was guaranteed by two things alone. The promise of plunder, rape, and good times in Phadraig was one. Their fear of Khassam was the other.

The grin of his approval grew. He enjoyed being feared. He had every intention of increasing the numbers of the fearful. He owed continued life and increasing glory to his cruelty, his judgment of men (paranoid but generally realistic), and to the belief he fostered (which he firmly believed himself), that he was the reincarnation of the Divine Mutant, destined to recreate the Middle Kingdom in all of its chaotic pride and exaltation. *Chaos!* It was the only idea which could still thrill him. Often, he made his songmakers chant the lays of that strange mutant kingdom for which he felt such wild yearnings. The world was too tame, the endless success of his campaigns a predictable boredom. The destruction of Phadraig was an expectation long since assimilated in his mind as certain reality. The amethysts were appropriate in at least one respect: his human passion was all but dead. Ranza had committed suicide, had refused her love with awful finality. He felt no affection for his wives, or for his crawling sycophants. And his zoo of monstrosities at Zagrin no longer excited him. Khassam had no affections left at all – save for Ranza's sad-eyed daughter, Ninaseunta, not yet ten years old. Nobody knew what form his affection took with the girl. Nobody dared to ask.

His own son, Khapilan, was on this expedition. In chains and under arrest. Khassam knew that human affection wasn't expected to enter a ruler's relationship with his progeny. It was too dangerous.

Particularly where the Jerezid autocracy was concerned.

Though Khassam was not properly of the ancient Jerezid line.

Kalnakill his father had usurped the childless weakling who occupied the throne at the end of the line some forty years before. The dominions were in uproar and revolt, and headless tax collectors were a common sight. Kalnakill had been baronial overlord of a coastal state. In league with others he marched on Zagrin and overthrew the dynasty, preceded by proclamations promising peace, wealth, and freedom. Once in power, once the popular ferment was crushed by the Alliance, he murdered his chief rivals, discredited others, and forced them and the Jerezid priests to proclaim him and his heirs Protector of the Dogmas. Then he proceeded to restore order in the dominions, proclaiming an Age of Reform. The task was enormous. And his flair for reorganization amounted to mania. No room he lived in stayed the same from day to day. Not that he was ever in one place long. The conglomeration of peoples was vast, war was a constant, with the tribal clans of Kor, the scattered and ephemeral confederations of the plainspeople north of the Scarp and west of the Metal Forests. Peoples of many shapes, attitudes, and colors. How to weld them together into empire? Kalnakill found one answer. All these tribes and peoples, whatever their attributes, possessed the common, ancient language. Though dialects were legion and incomprehensible, the roots of each were the same. Kalnakill fostered a dangerous decade of restlessness, during which he set out to uproot the identities and local deities of each community, imposing unpopular edicts and 'educational' commissions on each people. They were backed by solid force and a technique of voluntary deportation into supposedly richer areas. This technique served to disperse tribes among each other, making it easier for the commissions in freshly-mixed communities to impose the new General Synthetic – a graduated return to the common, ancient tongue. There was general resistance. Many said they were too old to adjust to a new way of speaking. Some of these were executed for linguistic heresy. The executions were public. While deported citizens and slaves in mixed communities found the General Synthetic more convenient than the confusion of their many dialects. In ten years, many people were speaking a language close to that of Phadraig. Phadraig's Council denounced the new argot as a degenerate attempt to imitate the perfection of Norm Purity.

Khassam could remember the day the news of Phadraig's reaction had reached his father, when he was nine years old.

'They may sneer as much as they like,' his father murmured. 'But many future warriors are growing in these lands – speaking a common tongue. And when we march on Phadraig it will be with common tongue and common belief!'

Even at that age, Khassam knew that his father was over-optimistic by temperament. It was another fourteen years before Kalnakill felt sufficiently sure of his control to levy an army and leave the land to priests and regents trained in his reforms. Astrologers and seers advised against the venture. But Kalnakill would not be gainsaid in his ambition. Phadraig was a hated symbol of intolerable superiority. The army formed, the army marched, but many died or deserted before they reached Phadraig. But they would have taken the city then if not for Red Kilmun, if not for Phadraig's defense by the Company of madmen led by Patrick Cormac.

Khassam hated Patrick Cormac for having killed his father.

For having denied Khassam the doing of the deed himself.

Khassam had admired his father, was an apt pupil, and had laid his scheme. Once Phadraig was taken, he would be installed as regent. Kalnakill would return to the vibrant squalor of Zagrin. Then . . .

The old man had watched his son's academic progress with alarm and admiration. He'd decided that, when Phadraig was taken, he'd have his son tried for conspiracy and executed in advance of the fact.

But Khassam felt no debt of gratitude toward Patrick Cormac.

The retreat through the Wastelands had been frightful. Ranza, the pregnant beauty seized in his brief foray up the hill before the Company's counterattack, had rejected him completely. His infatuation was obvious. But return to Zagrin unloaded more important problems on him. The dominions had revolted during Kalnakill's absence. It was five years before Khassam felt remotely easy in his sleep. Then he turned again to thought of Phadraig. The name crawled in his gut. His annual campaigns were dress rehearsals. His power grew in proportion to the fear in which he was held. He waited for a sign that the most propitious time had come; he was patient, for he had no intention of making the same mistakes as his father.

Only months ago, the sign was received. And now nothing could save Phadraig. On an expedition against brigands in the dark ravines of Kor, a Jerezid company had discovered sealed vaults sunk deep in a mountain. There were legends about these vaults. Khassam knew he could ignore the warning of the legends: he was the Divine Mutant. He ordered the opening of the vaults. Many died of various causes before an entrance was blasted. Khassam was the first to enter. He found an eerie, enormous underground palace, a treasure trove. There were great metal birds in giant hangars. The galleries and halls were stacked with all kinds of ancient weapons and devices. And, in a freezing hall at the lowest level, he found the mumen. The legendary mumen. Their bodies were frozen naked within blocks of liquified gas at a temperature close to absolute zero.

He was unsure about the wisdom of reviving these uncertain bequests of the Middle Kingdom. He debated for several weeks. The terror of his advisers decided him. Anything to strike more fear into rebellious, treacherous hearts. Nevertheless, he delayed their animation until he was sure he could control their eldritch minds.

Meanwhile, the *eala* were drawn to the surface by prodigies of effort, and forty-five of the inert machines were transported to Zagrin. Nobody could persuade the metal birds to fly, though priests quavered the appropriate rites unceasingly. A pragmatic man suggested that what they lacked was blood – not human blood, but blood appropriate to a metal being. Chemists and alchemists were brought together into work-gangs and told to find the right blood or lose their heads. Weeks, then months began to pass without result; the summer was growing, and soon it would be too late. Khassam consented to public burnings of selected chemists to encourage the others. It was then that a man came to him with a dream of a great black lake far to the north. He said that this was the black blood on which the birds would fly. He said that in his dream, the black blood burned, and gave off an evil smell. Khassam thought immediately of Red Kilmun. And mounted a harvesting expedition to the Black Lakes. Great quantities of the black blood were transported south in caravans; the crude peoples of the region had to be suppressed for stubbornly refusing to understand why brutal strangers drained the essence of their Fire-God.

It wasn't a month before that the first of the silver machines had ascended, crazily, crabwise, roaring against the sky as frightened slaves juggled with incomprehensible controls.

Five had crashed before the principles of control were mastered.

Khassam proclaimed divine salvation for suicide volunteers to fly the machines against Phadraig. They wouldn't come back, save for a few early spying missions; there wasn't time to import any more of the black blood. There was enough for forty machines to fly one-way to Phadraig. Volunteers begged for the honor. Some were fanatics. Others were due to be publicly burned, so it seemed like a soft option.

Twenty-five had already gone. The Company Chatachain had seen them the afternoon before, and the Witchmen had felt them.

'You'll fly to Phadraig with the black eggs!' Khassam had shouted at the assembled crews at the lip of the Metal Forests. 'You will not return, you will die with the birds, your divine mission complete. You will make the birds release their eggs where the verge of the Burning River which encircles Phadraig is weak. You will breach it so we can cross without danger. Finally, you will crash your birds against the Central Towers of the cursed city. In that holy action will lie your absolution from all the sins of your former lives. You will be remembered! Tonight the priests will bless you, the Seven Rites will be conducted in your honor. Tonight, you may take who and what you want; tomorrow, you fly!'

In the morning, he had led the army toward the tunnels of the Scarp, after the gleaming birds had lifted up and away.

The remaining fifteen would follow when Khassam sent

back word that he was near the city, to complete the breaching work if necessary, and to soften up the beleaguered city with an aerial bombardment. They would obey him. They would die. They had been thoroughly trained. They were more afraid of him than of death. The frequent fires impressed the people almost as much as the myths he disseminated. It was said he could scent the identity of traitors when he wore his warhelm with the cockatrice crest. Few dared look on this brass image of a four-legged cock with thorny wings and serpent's tail ending in a hook. It was said that to look direct on the cockatrice meant certain death. Khassam accordingly admired those who could meet his eyes when he wore the helm. They were the ones he usually had roasted. He couldn't afford to spoil the odds on such a useful belief. He couldn't afford to admire anybody at all.

Now he stood single, still watching the endless stream pour from the tunnels, his frame narrow, with the hint of an imbalance, but with obvious strength and agility. A line of baggage animals, dun and dim, was prodded into the light. Soon they'd be slaughtered for meat, for they couldn't be taken across the Swamp Forest. Still more companies emerged blinking into the strengthening light. Men and mutants from Lamassa, Purplefield, and beyond.

And now came the mumen.

A grotesque shambles of shapes and shapelessness. Dwarfs and giants and skinny poles with yellow eyes. Great-domed men with voracious expressions. Paradoxical, contemptuous, unsexed beings with telekinetic powers. Hirsute and hairless, clothed or naked, self-willed individuals who loathed this world they were forced back into. Forced by one who claimed to be the Divine Mutant; did he think they wouldn't know the Divine Mutant when they saw him again?

Khassam jammed on his helm as they passed raggedly, and he stared.

Yes – they did fear him – for the time being.

For as long as the chain of control-words, different every day, could be extrapolated, like ever-changing keys which locked the mumen into some sort of obedience. The mumen detested their yoke. And they loathed each other almost as much. They were proud, boastful individuals who couldn't stand their enforced proximity to other proud, boastful individuals. Khassam knew that the mumen were united only in awaiting the day the wrong word was spoken and they were released to take their revenge. Khassam cherished this daily game of chance and danger; it was a game to play against the boring certainty of Phadraig. The mumen were marched down to wait beside the other thousands who waited behind their standards and banners, congested, impatient, nervous of the shambling mumen. And the flood still poured from the tunnels. Khassam looked south, over the rolling land they had to cover. Looked past a particular high-slabbed basalt hill, a half hour distant, to the horizon. Beyond the horizon lay the Yawn. Khassam remembered the Swamp Forest well. Two days. Of course, men would be lost. But numbers didn't matter. The army wasn't so large because of Phadraig's possible resistance. It was large so as to leave his dominions drained of men and materials to serve any rebellions in his absence. Phadraig. With Red Kilmun breached, the city would be wide open. And then – Patrick Cormac.

Patrick Cormac, the High Witchman, the soul of Norm Purity.

Norm Purity smelled no better or worse to Khassam than belief in demons or in the Jerezid Dogmas. He paid appropriate homage to the Dogmas, which provided a useful pretext for making war on Phadraig and calling it crusade. In addition, he had his claim on behalf of Ninaseunta. The sun was rising higher, brighter. Despite the problem of the mumen his humor was, he realized, good. The endless tunnels had been drear and strange, though not without their dangers. He was glad to feel the breeze and watch the preliminary swirling of the sky. Soon, the Morning Wind.

Everything and everyone must be down beneath the trees by then. And a site found for his pavilion. There to hold council and give necessary judgments, eat a meal, rest. He felt no need to hurry. He felt as though he were already inside Phadraig.

From the tunnels now came a long, trickling stream of women, camp followers, and miscellaneous wagons. Khassam heard hastily-approaching feet, and he turned. Shahn, a six-foot polypheme in buckled hide and shaggy cape, prostrated himself. The Warlord felt expansive. He bent and clapped the reluctant guard of the mumen on the shoulder.

'Get up! *You* don't have to crawl at my feet!'

Shahn rose cautiously. He knew the unreliability of that advice.

His single central eye focused Khassam flat in a two-dimensional world. But he refused to look at the cockatrice which gleamed at the front of the black helm. Shahn had seen many men and women fall before that cockatrice. He'd seen Khassam in conquering furies which were more than human.

'Mumen – in formation, but restless, Lord.... Will you give the word for today?'

Khassam grinned. Shahn was frightened of his charges; they seemed unnatural to his straightforward soldier's soul. The Warlord looked past a forest of glinting pikes to where the thirty mumen waited at the base of the slope.

'The word is *Rukh*. Accent on the final syllable. Repeat it.'

Shahn twisted his tongue, producing the correct sound.

'Good. Feed it to them. They'll hate you, Shahn, but they'll obey. Until tomorrow – eh?' Khassam giggled, lost interest, and turned away. The air was restless. The Warlord's eyes climbed the black upper reaches of the green-mantled hill before them. He squinted analytically at the glint of tower on the top. Reports had been received concerning the malignity of the present inhabitant. And two scouts sent into this area had failed to report.

He wondered what it was that worried him. Abruptly, he turned to the group of advisers and lieutenants who waited ignored behind him, their faces carefully composed and their thoughts concealed.

'Nasna! Here.'

A huge man with wild leonine yellow hair and a vestigial third arm dangling uselessly from his spine approached, and went down on one knee, eyes averted.

'Nasna. Take a hundred men to that hill; place half to mark and scout the base, patrolling in grid. Take the other fifty up the hill to search the tower.' His eyes gleamed. 'Find and bring back what I expect you to find – if you fail me, you can forget your useless slack-fingered life. Understood?'

The man kept his head lowered as he nodded, backed off, whirled, and went to mobilize his men from Purplefield. Nasna. Khassam knew that Nasna didn't fear him, though he maintained a suitable pretense.

Nasna was useful to the Warlord ... up to a point.

Khassam tested the fine, subtle currents of the air with a finger.

The Wind was almost due. The exit from the tunnels was complete.

Without looking behind, he indicated for the group of advisers and lieutenants to follow him. Solidly hemmed by his Guard, he made his way through his army. Men on every side, prodded by their leaders, fell to their knees, banners were dipped, eyes turned, clouded, or shone, and the mumen glared. Some were already among the trees, gathering deadwood for cooking fires. Patrols were going out to check on and about the Banissen Saturna. He had a strange feeling ... but he could wait for Nasna's return. Accompanied by Guard, advisers, chiefs, priests, and other acolytes, he went to the place where his pavilion had been pitched.

Coming upon the crimson bell of the quickly-pitched pavilion, he clapped his hands, feeling a sudden delight.

'Beautiful!' he crowed. 'A well-chosen, restful site!'

In this clearing, the protective overhanging rocks were fused; they glimmered richly as though enameled; they were jagged crystals.

The floor upon which the pavilion was pitched was a smooth lawn, inert and benign, protected to the north by rocks and by the high screen of thick, gnarled trees, which bent and twisted as the air hazed and the Wind swept overhead from the lip of the Scarp.

Khassam settled himself on embroidered cushions inside the large pavilion. Details of the day ahead were discussed. His advisers were nervous and unsure; not one of them would speak his mind. The Warlord's mood soured swiftly. He hurled away his goblet. Red wine stained yellow satins. 'Worthless cretins. I don't need your advice. Bring me Ranza's daughter. Wait outside – all of you – *now*!'

There was one brave man in there. He was stooped and old. Cannara Cane. Khassam hadn't dared leave him behind.

'But, Lord . . . your wives . . . if you will not . . .'

'Plague on my wives! I want the girl! You'll have to wait. I won't be long with the pretty little thing; she has sharper eyes than all of you put together! Are you going to argue? Do you deny that I am the Divine Mutant, the Eastern Fox, change and cunning, cunning and change? Do you deny that this accords with Jerezid tradition?'

He came to his feet. He minced these last words, and they sank back before him, clearly thinking he was mad, in one of his dangerous unpredictable moods. He was capering like a Fool! On impulse he drew his sword and clove the air in one violent motion, spinning the blade as he did. And he howled with laughter when one head didn't duck fast enough. 'Burak,' he jeered, 'dresses like a peacock but he's got the head of an ass.' He toed the fallen man with the serrated metal cap of his boot. 'You don't move fast enough, Burak. You're not much good to me. You were lucky; you got the flat of the blade. Get up. This time – you live.'

Khassam waggled the blade playfully. 'Next time – the edge!'

Except for Cannara Cane, the other seven made dutiful sounds and motions of amusement and appreciation.

'Now bring me the girl and get out of here!'

Burak, face disfigured by a purple birthmark, scuttled after the others.

Ninascunta was brought to him. The girl's face was pale and sharp; she was very thin, wide-eyed, lips set pallid against luminous skin. She was old already with knowledge of human beings. She was pushed inside. The flaps were drawn. Outside on the smooth floor of the clearing, advisers, lieutenants, and chiefs waited grimly. The Holy Glyph stared in emerald and gold from the crown of the pavilion. The smoke of cooking fires twisted into the clearing sky; it was hot. The woods around were thick with the breakfast ructions of ten thousand men who were tired, curt, and angry, their obedience maintained by force and fear and fantasies of Phadraig. The minutes stretched. The group in the clearing waited uneasily. Cannara Cane, the shaven, bony old priest, stared straight ahead, his face completely blank. Cruel faces of the Loyal Jerezid Guard stared back. Burak's head still rang; he was uneasily aware of the mumen trumpeting with querulous and abstract arguments among the trees behind his head. Oh, he hated Khassam, he loathed the mumen, why had he let ambition drive him from his farm? There was nobody here a simple man could trust! All these hard, scarred faces, these masks! Each and every one of them would run straight to Khassam the moment he so much as dropped an ill-timed curse, or grumbled his secret doubts about the Warlord's divinity.

Squatting, poking at a fire built against an ancient trunk which was hard as iron, Shahn eyed his motley, arrogant wards uneasily.

For, one and all, they'd just now fallen silent.

And all of them stared avidly at the hill with the tower. Shahn stretched, found a gap in the leafy screen, and peered dubiously. Why did they stare? What were they waiting for? They'd never for a moment ceased their endless intellectual bickering since the moment of their revival and word-binding, not even in the dreary tunnels.

What did they sense that he couldn't?

He soon found out.

For presently the Warlord was flushed from his preoccupations by tumult from that part of the wood in line with the base of the hill.

It was the tumult of many hoarse voices jeering, shouting abuse.

But there was a strange undertone in the tumult – fear? awe? The noise grew louder, the disturbance closer. Khassam swept out in a disordered rage, slapping the cockatrice helm to his head, shouldering roughly through the double ranks of the Guard.

'What in the sacred name of...?'

But all eyes were fixed on the source of the tumult.

Fixed on the shackled line of prisoners brought by Nasna, who came running ahead into the clearing, past the jeweled rocks at the entrance. The man threw himself prostrate, useless third arm flapping from his half-naked back. And with his right arm, he gestured behind, almost peremptory with excitement.

'Lord! – we found—'

Khassam ignored him. He strode to the mouth of the clearing, pushing Cannara Cane aside. The prisoners had been jerked to a halt by the capturing soldiers, who wore tunics with Purplefield insignia.

There were six men and four women, bound together.

One of the women was gross and bald; she carried something, perhaps a baby, swaddled in her arms.

A last breath of wind sighed in the trees.

And Khassam recognized Patrick Cormac.

The man stared back expressionlessly.

There was a long, slow moment of silence. Khassam couldn't find a reaction to fit his amazement. Fate! He couldn't believe his good fortune. The blessings of his inevitable triumph obviously couldn't detain themselves any longer! Destiny strove to belong to him! Why otherwise would the only man of Phadraig he feared and respected be delivered up to him like this, as if on a plate brought by messenger?

He roared with laughter. Good-fellowship spread across his facc.

And the cockatrice leered that this meant death.

He advanced with extended hands, feeling enormous pleasure.

'Patrick Cormac . . . my friend. . .!'

But not a muscle flickered in the flaxen-haired man's face.

It was then that the Warlord heard breath indrawn in quick horror behind his back. Unexpected foreboding pricked him, and he paused. He heard shuffling motion from the top of the crystalline rocks, above his head, and to his right.

Slowly, as if his neck were stiff, he turned and looked up.

The thirty mumen were looking at him.

They were strung out in an uneven line along the edge above.

'Get back!' he roared. 'Who told you to spy? Shahn, come here!'

But Shahn didn't appear. The mumen didn't move, nobody moved, nothing moved but slow leaves and shreds of cloud. For a long moment, Khassam studied the bizarre beings, and they studied him. His confidence faded to perplexity and then to angry alarm. He saw thirty faces, each unique, one without features at all – but he divined their single, united expectation. He sensed a cold joy which spelled the upsetting of his certainties. He sensed their contempt. His eyes grew ice-green, glared along the line, and hooked, unable to look down or away. Thus caught unawares by the monstrosities he had revived, he was forced to realize the immense gap between him and them. The mumen had lived and survived in a time of which he only dreamed. Each of them was adapted to chaos, in mind and body. They had followed the Divine Mutant, legend said – but he . . . he was the Divine Mutant, unconscious of the past, perhaps, but nevertheless with that tremendous potential. Perhaps they couldn't recognize him in his present guise? But the way they stared on him with such withering hostility . . . there had to be a mistake!

Then as one they disregarded him, and focused their attention on the gross woman in the middle of the captured Company. His tongue was freed.

'I am your master! I am the Eastern Fox! Go back to your posts!'

His orders, ignored, fell into silence. The army waited.

The mumen knew, though they couldn't see, that the one they awaited lay wrapped in the great woman's arms. . . .

Babe from the Abyss, their epitome, the Divine Mutant, their one lord and master reborn.

Their time was come again; they were reunited with the only one who could unite their tempestuous minds.

And Khassam was destiny's dupe. The fool had revived them.

The Warlord couldn't face the sudden possibility of overturning.

Face mottled with rage, he swung on his chiefs, his priests, his councillors and advisers, on his Loyal Guard, on the mumen above.

*'Rukh!'* he howled. *'Rukh!* Monsters, obey, get back! I am your Lord! Get back, or my guard will cut you down! Guard!'

But the threat was empty, ridiculous. The men of the Guard were incapable of movement. The mumen, inexplicably released, held the initiative. Khassam swung in all directions like a cornered animal. Was impaled by staring, waiting eyes. Glared at those who looked down or away, refusing to look at him or his cockatrice.

Glared at Patrick Cormac, whose eyes were level, expressionless.

Khassam realized that he was alone in the middle of his army.

## 17: The Avenging Orphan

Eight had returned to eight, regained their bodies, recovered consciousness. And each of them in turn met or was met by the eye of the smooth-faced baby in the dwarf's daughter's arms. One-Eye was beautiful but ominous too; in the light of new day, the baby's complexion was jaundice to Patrick's bitter eyes. Their infection was fatal; they were bound to One-Eye by their own wills, their own dreams.

Gaidhealla had understood when without waiting the eight left the attic, followed by the dwarf's daughter, who rose silently, calmly, with One-Eye in her arms. Gaidhealla followed without question or looking back. Above the tower the sky was hazing, for the Wind was about to blow. At the bottom of the stairs, Patrick had been the first to reach Salamander, to take her up in his arms with abstracted, distant tenderness. She was conscious, and her eyes held unanswered queries. Discarded packs were gathered in silence. The Songmaker slung his sirena without even looking at it. The darkness of the hall about the base of the tower was not much relieved by the opened doors which succeeded each other to the outside. Patrick didn't touch his torchblade. And eleven – twelve, counting One-Eye – waited wordlessly for the Wind to come and blow itself out before venturing out on the exposed crags. Those who'd been in the machine were empty of arrogance and egotism. Patrick's eyes were on the stone flags; his mind was savage, tormented by self-willed subservience to One-Eye's aims, straitjacketed by the demands of the dimly-glimpsed, immediate future. Scalaman was glum, apparently not aware of his shaven condition as the Wind roared off the broken diagonal of the Scarp's rocky heights and slammed into the tower, buffeting them inside with fierce drafts through the opened doors. And the two scouts were also oblivious of their shaven pates – a disastrous condition for men of Kor, whose status resided in the magnificence of their hair-designs. Iubhar and Zena held each other's hand; their eyes were soft for each other, but their minds were gated shut by imminence. Liam watched Gnorl, who alone seemed his usual, methodical self, checking the bindings of his boots. And the Songmaker wondered at the compelling desire he felt to serve the dream of One-Eye faithfully —

*Magic's afoot,* he thought, tormented. *I can think of no other name for this dreamy coercion.*

Wind past, they gathered outside in sad union beneath the clearing sky. They could see where the rugged forestland was arrested by the yellow-gray striations of the Scarp. Patrick pointed silently. And they saw the glinting of sunlight on ranked spears and pikes at the foot of the heights where the tunnels emerged.

And the deranged golem? The Company looked all around and down.

But Cuyahogan had already left the hill. Now Gnorl led them off the crags down the gloomy northwestern side, directly toward the Warlord's army. Gaidhealla followed them without objection. She was numb, could hardly feel the world about her; her head was bowed —

*As prophecy said she would* —

Patrick's faraway realization was fatalistic. He helped Salamander. She was dizzy and uncertain; as the horizon swam, she fought to understand what was happening. Behind, Scalaman and the Songmaker helped the dwarf's daughter down the treacherous slope. Though, in contrast to her clumsy bulk, her feet were light, almost precise, and automatically selected the best ledges and spaces to set themselves down. She didn't look where she was placing them; her bright blue eyes never left the silent baby, swaddled and hooded in her white-sleeved arms.

The Company descended beneath the tree-level, but the woods were still and silent, and the sky was empty of birds. There was no sign of the golem, or of the Banissen Saturna, or of Khassam's forward patrols. Life seemed to have been sucked from the face of the planet except for the Company Chatachain, whose descent on the far side from the sunrise was a leg-aching gloom. And Gnorl kept his thoughts to the present as the overgrown slope flattened out into a sea of pale ferns spiked by trunks of ash and elm at the foot of the hill.

Tiny globes of water which clung to the drooping ferns were shaken out in sparkling parabolas by the passing of eleven dampened pairs of legs. Not dew, the water was the catch of the previous night's freak storm. Iubhar came up with Zena to help Gaidhealla, who was increasingly exhausted. And in front Gnorl moved smoothly, without appearance of doubt. He led them from the ferns, out of the hill's dark shadow, through knotted, iron-hard old oaks. Their highest boughs were jeweled by sunlight slanting past the flank of the hill. Gnorl strode beneath them, sword across his shoulder; he led the Company to the edge of a wide glade, his eyes moving restlessly. But it was as though there were a fog on his vision, and he felt vague. Like seven others he cursed the machine. He knew it must be done – like them he was seized, charged, committed. He cursed the machine. It had shown them too much – but not enough. An incomprehensible result – without personal details. Who were the sacrifices? Where would they be ambushed by Khassam's men? Who would be taken alive? – and who left dead? The dream didn't specify. Gnorl's face was fixed hard as he led the Company into the glade which was ringed by barricades of undergrowth around the thick old trees. He had never wasted time worrying about the future; he didn't intend to start now. But it was mortally hard to ignore the stalking of foreseen fate. If only he knew where and when to expect the attack, if only . . .

He stopped, alerted by something almost subliminal —

*Here? In the open, in the middle of a . . . but I would never lead us into such a perfect place for ambush. . . . One-Eye . . . monster . . .*

He started to swing, but, before they could react to his warning —

— A *twang* behind a screen of undergrowth to their right, a *hisssss* —

— An invisible voice which roared:

'Stop where you are! Don't touch your weapons or you'll die!'

Gnorl staggered, his head was flung back, and his eyes bulged in agony against the sky. He clawed vainly at the bloody black barb which had pierced his neck right through; he wrenched at the purple-flighted shaft. Salamander cried out, started forward, but Patrick held her back; he was rigid, trembling, watching the big man die for One-Eye. Too late, seven remembered this as one of the fleeting precognitive scenes of machine-vision . . . one among many. Recalled themselves stiff as Gnorl, choking, arched and crashed to the ground, his mind gone red in anguished fury as his blood stained the grass . . . as he died.

They recalled Gaidhealla's eyes' bitter jade on One-Eye, and their own, tied in dream by the being held by the idiot daughter who smiled at the beautiful morning sky. And Gaidhealla saw them stiffen, rejecting their impulse to fight on behalf of the child. There was no softness in Scalaman's eyes. Liam and the scouts were taut. Iubhar's face, behind the hunch of Zena's shoulder, was twisted in anguish, his eyes like ice. He and they all obeyed One-Eye's intention, bound by their own wills and words to a point beyond anything they had expected.

Nasna's warning echoed through the glade. The huge Purplefield leader stood up behind the archer who'd shot the arrow.

His useless third arm flapped as he raised his left in prearranged signal. Twenty archers moved out of cover to confront the penned Company, bows taut and arrows aimed. Over thirty soldiers, all in Purplefield tunics, followed the archers with drawn swords, ready axes. The Company was hemmed by an ill-uniformed and worse-formed band of ghoulish ruffians who grinned at them with brass studs and broken teeth. Some of them fell within the definition of Norm Purity, and all of them were huge. Liam had heard that the men of Purplefield thirsted continually for the delicacy of human eyeballs, served with salad, but his mind was too bound for this gastronomic memory to reoccur to him now. The archers were sweating with the tension of maintaining drawn strings, and crowded by impatient swordsmen. Patrick looked for their leader. They didn't seem disciplined enough to wait for orders. What if the child's expectation was wrong?

'Back! Back, you orphan-eating pigs!'

A man bigger than all the rest, his hair a wild lion's mane, his face bristling with red-cheeked contempt, Nasna confronted the Company. Hands on hips he strutted, turning his back so they could see the ugliness of his unboned spinal arm. He prodded Gnorl's body with a disdainful foot, suddenly bending, thrusting his thumbs at the dead man's eyeballs with lustful enthusiasm, halting before the final twist, turning back and roaring with laughter.

'You thought I would take the eyes, heh? You of Phadraig think we of Purplefield are ... not civilized ... heh?' He prodded Patrick in the chest, and roared with fresh raucous laughter. Patrick stood trembling, expressionless, cursing himself for the willing pledge of his life to the one-eyed child. Nasna raved on in boastful triumph, aggrandizing himself in front of his surly men who wanted only to slaughter and pickle the lot of them and have done with it. He swaggered around the Company, inspecting them individually, pushing back his over-eager men. 'Naw. Nasna doesn't need the eyes. The crows can have his eyes, heh?'

He came to Liam. 'That instrument is too fine to be slimed by a decadent from Phadraig! It's destined for the high vision of Purplefield's bards. And this. What is this...?' So he continued around them, stripping them of gear, weapons, amulets, belts, and anything else which looked interesting or potentially dangerous, until he came to the huge woman, the dwarf's daughter. For a moment he stared, puzzled, then he leaned back and exploded with a fresh torrent of laughter. Some of his men cackled with him. He prodded her on the chin. 'Where is it? Where is it? Do you have a chin underneath all that fat? Have you got a brain? Can you speak? And what are you holding so tight? Answer me!'

'She cannot speak!' shouted Idrys angrily.

Nasna made a sign backward without looking around, and Idrys was clubbed unconscious to the ground. The rest of the Company didn't move; their eyes were skating ponds. And Nasna made a grab for the bundle she held; he was hung heavily with belts and weapons. Her great bulk trembled a step back in defense. Nasna roared with anger. A soldier sprang on the woman from behind, grabbing her breasts, jerking at the bundle in her arms. His black braids of hair swung as he leaped; his noseless face howled with laughter as he grabbed.

He was thrown violently on the ground by some invisible force.

He lay stunned and semiconscious, blood flooding his face from flat nostril-ducts.

For a moment Nasna looked on One-Eye before the woman readjusted the hood, still smiling emptily.

Swords flashed. Bows came up. Voices roared with rage and fear.

Nasna recovered his wits. He put himself in front of the woman.

'No! Khassam will kill us if we do not deliver these alive!'

Slowly, the bows came down. Scalaman breathed again.

Iubhar gripped Zena's smoothly-muscled brown shoulder with a tense right hand. Her breathing was fast, but controlled. She knew what to expect if these savage morons decided to disobey Nasna. Once she'd been in Purplefield, and she had counted herself lucky to have got out alive. Hot eyes burned against the thin shirt she'd pulled on against the chill of dawn, sought the contours of her breasts, her slim torso. Her fate and Salamander's would be more drawn-out than those of the men, if not necessarily more painful. She was used to pain and expectation of death. She knew why she was captured here with the men of Kor and these maniacs from Phadraig, who were so unlike the popular Jerezid image of Norm Purity's citizens. The machine had showed her, had linked her with a dream deeper than her own dreams. She was throwing away her life for a mind, an unknown purpose which common sense and all her experience insisted she should reject. She wasn't impressed by One-Eye's claims, but she couldn't resist his power to dream her actions for her. The baby was making life difficult. Of course, without its birth and interference she'd already have been dead; she wouldn't have met Iubhar, and the loss would have been mutual. The wiry man inspired her with reciprocating love; she could trust him with her life. She'd never been able to say that for anyone else. Now it didn't look as though they'd ever get a chance to merge their fires and mature their love. Lips tight, she stared angrily as a stinking villain with cast eyes bound her wrists, nipping her roughly as he did.

The Company was wrist-bound in a circle around the fat woman. Patrick demanded angrily to be allowed to bury Gnorl, but he was kicked in the stomach, fell, taking with him Gaidhealla and Idrys, who was barely conscious. Nasna strutted and shouted as his men prodded the Company from the glade. His ingenuity in having them bound around the fat woman pleased him. But he concealed worry, caused by the glimpse he'd had of the terrifying baby. None of his men had seen – he thanked the gods. And his clever orders should prevent them from seeing. They were more superstitious than himself. One look at the baby would be enough to set them all in flight, leaving the Company free. Then Khassam would have his head for certain. The Warlord wouldn't listen to excuses that Nasna's men had seen the Avenging Orphan.

Nasna had lived in Zagrin. He was civilized. He knew the Avenging Orphan was nothing more than ancestral Purplefield superstition.

Or was it?

In Purplefield, orphans were still sacrificed on the sly in times of drought. The people did this apologetically, their sense of inevitability mingled with guilt. The orphans were bought and sold in the markets for this specific purpose, since parents were naturally unwilling to sacrifice their own children. Sometimes a sacrificial orphan stayed alive long enough for the household to grow fond of the girl or boy. But drought always came again. So necessary appeasement of harsh gods was often mixed with a sense of guilt, and this sense of guilt (so the Jerezid sages explained it) had given rise to the myth of the Avenging Orphan – the immaculate god-child who would be born to take revenge on all those who'd sacrificed his avatars.

But of course, the Jerezid sages were self-interested. They wanted to plant the Jerezid Dogmas on Purplefield.

Nasna suspected he couldn't depend on their explanation.

He was alarmed as he brought the captured Company to Khassam, as the bound captives attracted jeering, pelting attention.

There was something weird about these captives, whose clothes and arrogant style betrayed several of them as people of Phadraig. Their weirdness grew from the one-eyed baby. They were altogether strange. What had they been doing, walking straight toward Khassam? Who were they? Was it some kind of trap? But Khassam had ordered him to bring whatever he found. Even before he raced into the clearing and prostrated himself at the Warlord's feet, Nasna was cynical about Khassam's chances. And was wondering how he might get out of it alive, and perhaps even profit. Because for a moment, he had sensed the power in that single blackberry of an eye. The Avenging Orphan? He feared . . .

# 18: Chaos Kingdom

Now Nasna was still on hands and knees where he'd fallen at Khassam's feet, looking cautiously around at the raging Warlord, but not up at the mumen, though he knew they were there, for the hairs on the nape of his neck told him. He didn't dare get back to his feet without being ordered; there was no telling what Khassam would do in such a rage. Pennants and banners hung limp, or fluttered briefly; anxious faces pressed close behind the nervous men of Purplefield who hemmed the captured Company at the mouth of the glittering place. Nasna waited. Cannara Cane, immobile amid trembling advisers, watched Khassam swinging furiously from the mumen to the captives again. And only Burak noticed thc thin girl, Ninaseunta, appear at the flaps of the pavilion, to watch silently without any apparent fear.

'What are you holding, woman?' shouted Khassam, impatiently bundling aside Patrick and Idrys to get at her, ignoring their eyes. The Warlord tore at the dwarf's daughter's arms, frantic to learn what threatened him.

He was met by one-eyed bottomlessness.

He was jerked into the black well, his mind seized complete without any prior warning. He stiffened, a statue. Nobody moved except Nasna, who sighed and slipped sideways toward the back of the pavilion. Only Ninaseunta watched him go, gravely. All other eyes were fixed on the Warlord, who appeared to have stopped breathing.

For he was taken to the Middle Kingdom, into the chaos

of his heart's desire, into a cyclopean world —

Into battle, battle such as he'd never imagined. The world was exploding around him. Great claps of thunder burst the sky apart, the cindered ground shook and groaned dismally, chasms were born and yawned wide for his stumbling, giddy, dancing feet, snapped shut with the sound of a god's grinding teeth. He spun, he fell, the sky flared purple and orange and ugly dark green. The storm rushed in every direction, swallowed itself, subterranean strata suffered endless dislocations, noise – there was no end to the noise, lightnings rent the rushing clouds, flame shot from the bucking ground, gouted up from a crack opened near his head, exploded with a terrible *whoouff*! Khassam inhaled reeking sulphur, his lungs were on fire, his eyelids were singed off, his hairlock was shriveled, his glaring cockatrice useless to defy this world. He was burning, burning, burning on a shaking hill, a deep-sunk valley bed, an endlessly lurid plain, his crimson surcoat in tatters, his flesh scorched. He moved feebly as clouds and darkness swallowed the orange inferno, as chill swept across the heaving, fevered land. The atmosphere cried, hissed. Something struck his helm and jerked it from his head – a hailstone, the size of his fist. Earth and sky calmed down slightly. He lay half conscious as solid ice-balls melted in fields of smoldering ash. And the sky collapsed on him.

Then there were dim figures running furiously through the pall of darkness, they held flaring torches high, and even their whispers echoed hundreds of yards through the solid silence. They saw him. Arms grabbed him, dragged him, he was examined, and incomprehensible words were hissed in his burned, bleeding face. Some part of him realized it was a variant of the Old Tongue which rasped in his shattered mind:

'Fool! Out at this hour, when the Dark One passes! We should leave you here for the mutants to feast on your remains!'

He must have passed out again because then he was *inside*, beneath a smooth-curving dome of some flexible, pastel-colored material. A tall brown-haired woman with a good figure and a worn face of lined pride was watching him alertly. She thrust a bowl of thin gruel at him the moment he was clearly awake. 'Eat,' she said abruptly. 'We must leave soon. The mutants have overrun us. We can hold out no longer. What is your family? Were you left behind at the comet's last pass?'

He shook his bandaged head and reached for the gruel, but the movement hurt. So they took him for one of their own, but the woman was clearly puzzled. She conferred with men in the background. A thin man with bright blue eyes threw questions in his face. He attempted to answer none of them, feigning loss of memory. It was true enough. He wasn't sure of his identity. He finished the miserable gruel as his hosts conferred hurriedly. Clothes were thrown at him, and he was told to walk if he could and follow them.

The refugees collapsed and folded the dome away into a single pack.

They ventured into shrieking wind which swept the floor of a bare, rocky valley. Jagged lava-slag littered the cracked and dried-up riverbed. The horizon was lurid with a gouting volcano thrust from what had been sea a year before. The party was eighteen and weak, with old men and women and three stunted children. Khassam could hardly move, and he began to fall behind them in their haste as they climbed up across a bare shoulder, frequently glancing in fear back to the valley below them, their faces blackened by ash from the tortured air. From time to time a drifting spark whirled down in crazy spirals to catch at shabby leather and be slapped out by frantic hands. Khassam fell farther behind, they wouldn't wait, and he didn't care.

Then the humans were surrounded by a raiding party of mutant beast-men from nightmare, who cut them down without haste, then cut them up into strips of meat, tossing chunks to and jabbering at their huge black-and-yellow hounds, who barked back churlish gratitude.

When they discovered Khassam, a knife was raised high –

*No!* The thought spat clear through him. *The Fox wants this one.*

So Khassam the Warlord, Protector of the Jerezid Dogmas, was taken before the Eastern Fox, the self-styled Divine Mutant, lord and master of the mumen whom he epitomized, inheritor of this terrible world of cataclysm and natural rage. The Lord of the Middle Kingdom. In whose domains none of the Old Men now lived. The last had been those who'd fed and bandaged Khassam before being cut up into strips of banqueting meat. The cannibalism was a necessary ritual, not a pleasure. The Old Men – sinners, ghouls, vampires, degenerate heirs of the Madmen, the dregs of the Great Forgetting – now every last one was hunted down and purged, erased, forgotten as thoroughly as the knowledge of a world of machines, of three-hundred and sixty-five days in a year.

Khassam was brought before the Fox.

Through a ruined city of fantastic architecture, to the shell of a giant hall where the pillars shook continually, and dust was always raining. Here and in the blocked streets outside there were restless creatures prowling, plotting themselves against the lives of others, the variety of their forms and the chaos of their minds much greater than in his ordered time. The hall was a hulking gloom of shadows, and the energy of its atmosphere was a constant scream in his bones.

He was thrown on the floor before the Fox.

Ageless, milk-white face, snow-curls, eye of pitch and yolk.

And – how did it live? Khassam's eyes bulged. He wanted to retch with horror, he was not this thing, this monstrosity, this ... head on a velvet cushion which trembled with the continual motion of the disordered earth. What was the trick? Where was the body? And how did this place, this city still stand against the ruptured earth? He was in the presence of powers well beyond his understanding! And alone with them. Alone with the staring head! Though the mumen were about and behind, their bodies were invisible, there were just their minds, pushing, probing, flighting arguments while the yellow-black eye drained his mental fluid and inspected the contents of his consciousness. Khassam was tried, and found wanting. The Warlord was unable to move; he was molded rigid as adamant, a statue frozen on the shaking floor of this vast, indeterminate hall. And he was run right through, speared from every direction by the interminable mental jabbering of the invisible mumen. They squeaked, growled, hissed, and whispered inside his whirling head –

—*think ... think ... think you and Fox are coterminous...?*

—*cunning CUNNING cunning is the important thing, Khassam —*

—*can can can can can Khassassassam con con con con nuss...?*

— *he looks concussed and so connnfused —*

— *got d-d-dust on his b-b-brain, he's t-too insane —*

— *insane, outsane, whats sane in the game, the game...?*

— *who's insanesanesane of the big bad Fox...?*

— *hoohoohoo? This dream-slice, this Khassam, this time-bound cretin, this slab of vanity who dreams he's the Fox, haaaa ...*

— *he wants to be to see to be the Scourge!*

— *and bumbles, wants to bee the Chaos-Sting ...*

— *d-d-dream-slice wants the M-M-Middle K-K-Kingdom*

— *wants wanderlands of jaundiced dunes —*

— *wants the moon, the drunken silver moomoomumen moon ...*

— *see, see, he loons for the moon —*

'Stop, shut up, you're driving me mad!' Khassam howled

in desperation, tearing himself from that other eye and closing his own. He shook his head like a dog and whirled at each new taunting thought, met nothing but gibbering shadows and giggling ghosts. He grabbed for his sword, but his sweating hand closed instead around the cold dry scales of a live, hissing, crimson snake. His eyes opened wide, fired by fresh horror; he tried to relax his grip but his fingers were rigid around the serpent. And he found himself held by the snake's jeweled eyes which danced, which shrank him, began to change him —

YOU WANT TO BE THE DIVINE MUTANT. SO BE IT.

The snake bit him.

Venom coursed like liquid fire.

He felt himself exploding.

He is the Divine Mutant. He doesn't know what he is. He's nothing but a whirling point of view, disintegrating in the overwhelming lack of signposted time and space. He's lapped by the enormous, malicious humor, wrapped up in the very spirit of the Middle Kingdom, disordered in its vicious, self-centered mockery.

He's become something far too vast for his comprehension, too huge for his blocked spirit to occupy and define. All he's equipped to perceive are the frightening reflections of his own vague conceptions, the fervid chaos he thought he desired. Chaos! His dream! His nightmare reality of dissolution. Fated and failed, he sees himself much too clear, fights to reject the visions, to accept his divinity, to force his head into the terrible aura. But it won't fit, his energy's expended, his sense of self is failing. He can't filter or channel the high-frequency currents, can't convert them to his understanding, can't make sense of them, or define or predict them! He can't make the connections, or look on what he thought he was but isn't. Chaos! Khassam the Warlord is slipping, sliding, tumbling, crashing, smashing down the drain of his fevered brain to reality at the foot of time.

*

Nobody moved to help the Warlord, collapsed between Patrick and Idrys, shaking like an epileptic at the fat woman's feet. Blood and froth bubbled from his mouth; his tongue was bitten through; he babbled disconnected nonsense in the high pitch of an adolescent; his eyes were glazed and empty. Then One-Eye looked from the lunatic to his mumen who lined the bank above. The air was tight with a nerve-snapping tension. The Company stood and waited, their expressions without any feeling. Salamander wondered at the madness, at the broken Warlord, at the silent, grotesque monsters waiting above her head, every one a complete mockery of Norm Purity. This world outside Phadraig was strange. Was she still dreaming? She pinched herself, it hurt, and she gasped. And her healing wound still throbbed. She looked anxiously at her mother. For the first time the old lady's age was plain, there was no spirit in her stance or eyes, as she stared at the ground.

Advisers and councillors looked fearfully at each other. Nasna had crept away. Cannara Cane took two paces forward. He'd caught a glimpse of the baby, though not of its eye. He was thinking that the hideous baby must be killed before it destroyed them all. He was stopped by a bolt in his mind, by a blank wall which snubbed him hard —

*Old idiot! Our Lord lives. But your wick is dim.*

The aging priest jerked up his head in a sensed direction. Found a beanpole muman with pixie ears and squashed-up, beaming features.

'What...?' he threw out in strain. 'Tell us, you ... mumen!'

His voice rang up to the tops of the trees. But there was no answering response from the mumen, nor from the woods about. The massed army was waiting. A chill wave of superstitious fear had coursed through the vast, incoherent organism of Khassam's force when the mumen were seen to move unordered. Now Nasna had returned to his men of Purplefield around the back; he told those without any view of what he'd seen, and rumors coursed swiftly in all directions. Haunted eyes strained, but it was ears which heard the querulous neuter voice of a hermaphroditic muman, drifting from the top of the bank through the trees. Some could see him at one end, and his complexion like cheese.

'Who? What? Not your Lord? Are you surprised, Cannara Cane? Are you astonished to discover that Khassam is not the Divine Mutant? Or did you know it all along?'

Another voice, a rough grating, every word as if interrupted by cogs: 'The babybabybaby. The baby is the ... the ... the ...'

'EASTERN FOX eastern fox!' sang out a third, joyous voice, a lark.

'C-C-CHAAA-OS CHIEF!' stuttered a fourth, mouth a double-wide crimson slash, hiccuping with laughter. 'O-O-OR-DER SCOURGE!'

And a fifth, a squat black barrel, neckless above filthy skins – 'Cannaaara Caaane, bow yourself downnn, the Lord is here....'

Then all thirty were gibbering and gesticulating in simultaneous ribaldry, each vying with the others. But the querulous hermaphrodite, soft and flabby in a torn, gauzy gown, out-howled all of them:

'Khassam awoke us! Our Lord calls us!'

Each word was sharp and clear, each like a different, sepulchral bell. The words split the woods, were heard in every direction. Chill fingers played up and down thousands of spines. Peals of wild merriment burst from the mumen; they hopped up and down, or stamped clawed feet, before with one accord the thirty of them leaped down into the clearing, still jabbering in midair. Some landed lightly like dancers; others sprawled heavily, ungainly, grotesque, cursing. The Guard, until now frozen with fear, drew swords in mass reflex as fear, loathing, and confusion swept the clearing. Frightened councillors scrambled out of the way of the hideous, babbling mumen. Cannara Cane stood his ground, a proud old man with closed ears. But Burak was so alarmed that he stumbled backward past advancing Guardsmen into the canvas of the pavilion, tripped over a guy rope, began to fall – an unexpected hand supported him before his balance was altogether lost.

He looked into the calm eyes of the child Ninaseunta and felt ashamed of himself. But the very air seemed to hum as the Guards converged on the mumen and those struggling to extricate themselves from the apparently drunken lurchings of the mutants. The Guards. The mumen stopped their staggerings, closed their mouths. Yellow eyes, red eyes, black eyes, violet eyes burned. The Guards, howling with pain and horror, dropped their suddenly red-hot weapons and turned to flee. The mumen cackled; the air was thick with insult and imaginative abuse which the Songmaker couldn't have bettered. The Company, bound together at the wrists by knotted loops of braided rope, with the Warlord scrabbling at their feet like a mindless creature, stood unmoving as the mumen converged on the child. But the men of Purplefield, who needed no urging from Nasna, fell back into the confused ranks of scattering men behind them. Shahn stared, shivering, from the now-safe lip of the bank above the glimmering rocks; a Guard braver than the rest who tried to pick up his sword crumpled like a paper bag the moment he touched the hilt. Rich-robed councillors huddled at the back of the clearing, or whispered of witchcraft as others tried to climb the fused, overhanging rocks. Above them, bolder men crept close to Shahn to stare, past knotted trunks, through feathered ferns, down into the clearing. And the mumen jabbered continually as they surrounded the Company, stepping distastefully past Khassam's shaking body. They cut the Company loose so they could surround the fat woman who held the one-eyed child. They came to renew their allegiance to the Divine Mutant.

Cuyahogan. The golem had rampaged off the crags and into the forest, fish-white flash here, flowing unflesh there. For a time it seemed to have no sense of direction; it swung south across a river; watched by low-lying Banissen Saturna, it veered in a wide arc which brought it toward the Scarp and back to the fast-flowing river. Up to the waist in water, it splashed upstream – then turned, came downstream again to its initial point of entry. It paused, stood without moving for ten minutes, dome brushed by sunlight beneath overhanging branches.

Cautious watchers observed the monster. It stood against the green torrent, head tilted up at the hazing sky, as if ... listening....

For what? The Wind?

But when the Wind was come and gone and observers looked again, the golem was still locked in the same, almost inquisitive fashion.

A moment later, its problems were apparently decided.

It set off upstream again, and reached its former point. Here, the waters spouted through a smooth black gorge, down from the rainbow falls which cascaded out of a slash three-quarters the way up the precipitous Scarp. The golem disappeared briefly beneath a welter of lashing waves, reappeared on the eastern bank, then reached for tiny holds in the slippery rock. Dry as soon as it left the racing water, Cuyahogan climbed to the grass-tufted bank above.

A slant-eyed Lamassan soldier with a harelip found himself confronted by the etiolated unflesh of a monster from hell.

Cuyahogan gave him no time to scream or escape.

The golem now knew exactly where it was going. It set off through the trees toward the clearing. This part of the wood was almost empty of men, though gear lay strewn all about. Outlying detachments of the Warlord's army had moved in closer to the clearing and round about it, fearfully fascinated, jostling, whispering, straining to pick up the distant babble of the mumen. At first, none of them saw the golem coming up behind. With its bloody nails extended.

Machine-vision had shown none of this, save for vague revelation of disturbing conclusion. But the mood of the experience still held to seven of the Company; simultaneously, they were participants and dispassionate observers. Not even Scalaman showed disgust as a stinking, hairy muman with great-lashed violet eyes cut him loose, as others pushed and bounded among them. The mutants' disinterest in hygiene was pungently obvious. But Salamander reeled, clapped a white hand to her sickened face, fighting not to retch. The restless mumen giggled, and pointed, and jabbered too fast for words to be made out; they murmured invocation, jesting supplication, as they came to their Lord. The Company was excluded, pushed to one side as the mumen engulfed the fat, happy, mindless woman. In the woods about, and thronging the clear rise to the Scarp, the army was about to turn into a rampaging, headless monster – but not yet, not quite yet. The nine that were left of the Company found themselves up against the gleaming faceted rocks, low and moss-covered this southern side of the clearing by the mouth.

To the Company's left, the men on Purplefield dared approach no closer than fifty feet, and thousands of unquiet soldiers stirred and watched behind them; the Scarp was their backdrop. For the moment they, and those in the woods about, and those in the clearing to the right of the

Company, were mesmerized. And the Company too. For the mumen had taken One-Eye from the woman, held him close to their slow-beating hearts. Now they broke into individual chants or paeans which howled each other down in simultaneous exploration of every audible octave. They passed the baby among them, murmuring benedictions and ... jokes? For the growth of the anarchic chanting was split frequently by crackling laughter, by insults, and back-biting comments. Shortly, the mumen began to dance.

Now nobody in the clearing moved, apart from the mumen.

Apart from Ninaseunta, who led Burak quickly into the pavilion to the back, where she lifted a flap so they could slip through into the narrow space between canvas and rock, hidden from the rest of the clearing. Nobody had seen them go, not even Cannara Cane. The girl was quick-thinking. She had heard Khassam jeer the name of Patrick Cormac. She had taken a good look at the chief of the captives. She remembered her mother telling her about Patrick Cormac and what he had done. That was before Ranza was driven mad and killed herself.

Life had been hard on Ninaseunta. But she had learned a lot.

'We'll wait here,' she whispered to Burak. He was a fumbling but well-meaning friend to her. 'When the trouble begins, we'll go to Patrick Cormac. He *might* be able to save us, but don't bet on it.'

Her face was very serious.

The mumen's chanting held the woods with spine-tingling charm.

Escape? Survival? Patrick didn't know if anybody would be saved.

With the others he watched the capering celebration of the mumen, then looked at Gaidhealla to see how the exhausted old lady was taking it. She was forlorn, dispirited, made no attempt to meet his eyes, but brooded silently.

And he felt crushed, crushed and useless. Gnorl had meant nothing to One-Eye: he was just bait. Now One-Eye had his mumen: he needed the Company no longer, the Company was excluded, redundant, and forgotten. The baby ... the Divine Mutant ... would sacrifice them as easily as Phadraig and the Warlord, if it suited him.

Patrick averted his eyes from the whirling, capering dancers, and tried not to hear the disordered frenzy of their ululating chants. He turned to Scalaman, to Liam, to Iubhar behind him, his arm around Salamander, whose wan face rested on his shoulder. 'Yes!' he muttered in a surly undertone, 'all was planned, as you suspected in the snowtree grove. The Witchmen were lured out so the *eala* might destroy them. But I wasn't the one who knew what would happen. Nevertheless, we were the agents. Khassam's finished, drained, his army is about to explode, the Jerezid dominions will fall about in uproar, and we are partly the agents. The mumen live again – Khassam was the agent. One-Eye has used us all without partiality. And these ... mumen are the only ones who know his intentions; they come from the same frightful time....'

'If he *is* this Divine Mutant.' Tembar was incorrigibly skeptical.

'But why have they returned now?' hissed Scalaman. 'To set off a new time of chaos?' His face was a pale, haunted moon.

Bunched by the rocks, the army about and the mumen before, they looked at each other.

'We were duped into becoming blind agents.' Iubhar's eyes were heavy-lidded. 'And each of us by our own will....'

'Prophecy said we wouldn't understand.' The Songmaker shrugged.

'Yes, but how do we get out of this?' snapped Scalaman. 'I have a fondness for my worthless life no matter what charges are laid on it. Are we going to be discharged, only to be murdered by these soldiers? I will not accept this fate! I refuse to ...'

'What will you do instead – dance, and persuade the soldiers that you're a terrifying muman too...? It might just work, my friend!'

But Liam's derision was tinged with sad affection.

And Zena's eyes were wide and hypnotized again by the mumen.

'Look ... look ... they'll drop him ... they're ...'

For the celebration before them grew wilder, drew their reluctant attention, mesmerized them with its whirling patterns, its wailing of triumph. The mumen capered and danced like gleeful children, round and round the fat smiling woman, and they used One-Eye as a ball – they threw him high in the air, time and time again, higher every time. They wove and twisted beneath him, caught him lightly like a feather every time, howling with laughter through the jarring discords of their chanting. Faster and faster through each other – their whirling motions didn't coordinate in any recognizable rhythms or sequences of step or leap at all – so fast they must surely collide, let the baby fall to the ground – but it didn't happen; they reeled, staggered, somersaulted and leaped high, briefly caught in fragments of sun. And the baby's burbles of delight mingled faintly with their delighted howling in a terrifying compound of unreality. Patrick stared. He felt more trapped than ever he'd been in Phadraig. Trapped in greater insight. His understanding was a naked thing, a wind-scoured peak where there had been the concealment of heavy clouds before. How could they get out of this? They were stuck unarmed in the middle of thousands of angry, scared, and ill-disciplined soldiers who would run amok the moment the mumen stopped dancing and chanting. For the moment, the Company was safe – for as long as the mumen continued to hurl One-Eye high.

One-Eye. Eastern Fox. Divine Mutant. Et cetera.

Whatever the label, his nature would remain an unfamiliar chaos.

The machine-dream showed as clearly as the prophecy

that only pieces of the chaos were knowable, like ever-changing jigsaw fragments.

Perhaps One-Eye was only a provincial player in a cosmic game, but that left the rest of them nowhere – or everywhere.

Patrick's thoughts were tinged by the heavy irony of relativity.

Nothing was ordered, nothing was fixed, everything was point of view. He was High Witchman and pawn, seer and slave, leader and blind fool like the rest of them. He was stranded high on the wind-scoured mental peak. And, high above him, so high as to be invisible and unknown – One-Eye. There was no 'good' or 'bad' in this. To judge the baby with any known morality, to claim understanding of One-Eye's motives, was like trying to judge visual perspective with both eyes shut. The perception of Eight had only served to establish the immensity of the gulf that lay between them.

Now the mumen weaved bewildering patterns around the drooling, slack-faced Warlord; the air was thick with their insane merriment as Khassam crawled in aimless circles. The army was a curious, nervous sea, pent up. And Guardsmen in the clearing eyed the Company with hate, awaiting the moment they could reclaim their swords, abandoned to the ground in between them and the dancing mumen. Their Warlord was destroyed; they would never dare to attack the mumen, but the Company was human – suitable scapegoats. Iubhar nudged Patrick, then nodded at the abandoned swords. There was a chance they might scoop up several to defend themselves with, to fight out toward the men of Purplefield and reclaim their own weapons. Patrick was withdrawn into internal judgments; he nodded remote acknowledgment.

He was thinking: *I can't complain or wail against fate. I chose to abandon Phadraig for One-Eye. Phadraig was known boredom and slow death. One-Eye was unknown excitement. And I saw more purpose and meaning in the prophecy than in all the rest of the world I knew. I saw the Company alive again; I felt my own life surge. So, we are used, perhaps sacrificed. But we use ourselves. We could have chosen differently ... except Salamander ... she was never given any choice....*

But the mumen whirled, and doubt eroded his rationalization. He could see that Gaidhealla had abandoned herself. Did she blame herself for their predicament? he wondered. Should he find fault with himself as well? Would it do any good...?

When he felt a diffident hand on his arm he turned so sharply that Salamander started back, frightened by the malevolence of his expression. He softened, tapped his head to indicate that the hatred was inner-directed. But the girl was as much disturbed by him as by the mumen whose patterns she'd watched drowsily, with mounting suspicion.

*Why does he torment himself so much?* she wondered sharply.

But her whispered question was different. And her eyes were clear.

'Why do the mumen dance?'

He was taken aback. He thought the answer was clear.

'They celebrate; they show how they despise mankind....'

She nodded archly. 'Are there other reasons too?'

Liam had been watching the seething army, the trembling, rich-robed councillors. The air was electric with the mumen's howling.

'Their patterns, their sounds suck minds, rack the army with tensions and hatreds....'

'They're charging Khassam's army,' put in Idrys, vehement.

The question *why* occurred to all at once. Eyes met; only Gaidhealla didn't join in the visual exchange of possible, horrible answers.

'We must get out of here!' insisted Scalaman, tight-lipped.

'I would be happier with my sirena back.'

They could see some of the villains who'd taken their weapons and equipment, mingled among men from other detachments and dominions. Patrick saw the mane of hair which identified Nasna, who had his torchblade. To have the least chance, they would have to stay close to the mumen, and somehow contrive to seize back their weapons. He knew it was a chimerical hope. For the army grew more restless with each passing instant of the mumen's howling dance. It was more than dance – the girl was right – it was invocation. The speed at which the mumen wove their patterns around and past One-Eye, the daughter, and empty-eyed Khassam, the patterns themselves, and the anarchic chanting constituted subliminal invocation of disorder. The minds of those who saw and heard were being disrupted. And the moment the spell was snapped—

Then there was commotion from the southwest, from the broken wood over by the base of the Scarp. Shouts of distant rage, the clamor of death broke into the mumen's dance of invocation and celebration. Restless waves went through the scattered army, the greater part of which was tight-packed between the Scarp and the clearing.

Clear image of Cuyahogan came to Gaidhealla's mind.

For the first time since Gnorl's death, she lifted her head.

'The golem comes!' Then she lowered her eyes to the ground again as Scalaman swore. And the confusion increased, heads straining, hands trembling on sword-hilts. The mumen were aware of the golem's approach. Their chants continued; they didn't stop moving. But there was an evidently defensive quality to their circular pattern. And they gave One-Eye back to the dwarf's daughter. She was giggling with delight; she had never been out of the tower before. She was happy to be given the child again. She cooed at One-Eye, who made small dubious sounds. Fear? Anger?

All around, in the trees and in the open, men were pushing, jostling, shouting frantic questions; the spell half broken, they were dazed, and some thought they were dreaming, wondering where they were, and what they were doing in this place, in this army composed of neighboring enemies. And what was the commotion, what caused that awful yell? They pushed and strained and cursed, still half-held by the whirling mumen in the clearing, by the thirty dissimilarly chanting voices. The Company felt naked, unarmed. Ninaseunta grabbed Burak's arm, and pulled him after her. They began to run along the broken wall of rock on the southern side of the clearing. Cannara Cane saw them. Patrick Cormac saw them. And saw Cuyahogan, poised white above them, deadly feet on the edge of the overhang above their heads. The mumen whirled and spun in interweaving circles. The girl sensed danger above. The overhang mercifully robbed her sight of the golem. But she could see heads all over the clearing turned to a point above the two of them. Freezing on the spot, she threw a finger to her lips, and she and Burak tried to melt into the rock.

But the golem was only interested in One-Eye. It wanted to kill. The mumen allowed it no further. They penned the menace, shaking, to the rocks above. The Company felt the sidewash of the concerted mumen projection. The Company couldn't move. Why had the golem come here? What force controlled it? Was it a danger to One-Eye? An ancient Achilles' heel? It had carried One-Eye to the tower, was reliable before the energies disordered it. What had happened since to give it this motivation?

They stared, many stared, but save for the mumen, there was silence. The golem strained forward, arched into a bow, thrusting with all its strength against the barrier thrown by the hurtling mumen. It glowed, it shivered, its ruby eyes crackled with frustration, and for a moment it seemed about to break through, to fall forward. But the mumen held it. Burak looked up and met its down-staring eyes at its most forward point, and he fainted clean away. And Cuyahogan was defeated. The golem attempted to raise its arms, to aim its fingernails. The dancing mumen never looked up. They did not allow its arms to move from its sides. They threw its feral urges back at itself. Cuyahogan's perfect face took on the ghost of imperfect expression. The golem opened its mouth. The golem cried.

Those of Phadraig were astounded. The sound was unprecedented; they had thought the golem was mute. Then the intense, apparently random complication of the weird chanting flowed into a torrent of abuse. Cuyahogan fell back, jerked upright, spun, crashed off back the way it had come, wailing into the distance past scattering men.

*This is nothing but a growth of enigmas,* thought the Songmaker.

Like many others, he clutched his head; the shrill and atonal cacophony of the mumen was racking his sensitive mind.

Then the dance was over, the chanting finished.

The mumen unblurred. For a moment they stood where they stopped, utterly without movement, not seeming to breathe at all.

The sudden cessation of whirling movement was a cold shock.

Just for a moment, complete silence and absence of motion lay on the army. There was a pause, a recollection.

Then the mumen turned their backs and converged to confer with One-Eye. And the spell was broken, deliberately broken.

## 20 : Discharges

Many things began to happen in the wake of that shattered moment. The army began to dissolve into a sea of angry, frightened individuals. Guards started to rush forward for their abandoned weapons, sensing that the mumen weren't interested, so long as nobody was so foolish as to threaten them. Patrick, Iubhar, and Idrys ran to grab up swords from the opposite end of the clearing; they had less distance to cover. Ninaseunta was pulling Burak to the rest of the Company as the three passed her, ducking and weaving past confused councillors and sycophants who didn't know where to go. Frenzied chiefs ran or climbed from the clearing to catch their own men before they mutinied. The mumen began and completed their consultation with One-Eye. The dwarf's daughter heaved herself to her feet. Patrick, Iubhar, and Idrys had grabbed five swords, and were retreating past Cannara Cane as the mumen took up their chant again. They began to dance out of the clearing toward the growing chaos of the army as Ninaseunta introduced herself with measured patience to the rest of the impatient Company.

'I am Ranza's daughter. My name is Ninaseunta. You may call me Nina. This is my friend, Burak. Can we come with you?'

Gaidhealla looked up and smiled, dreadfully tired. Liam had to laugh at the girl's matter-of-factness in this crazy chaos.

Scalaman howled out: 'Patrick, hurry. One-Eye's abandoned us!'

Tembar saw what was happening to the retreating three, and swore, and scuttled forward to help his countryman. For a brutish, blue-coated Guard had burst past Khassam's dazed followers, knocked Cannara Cane to the ground, and aimed a haymaking sweep at Idrys. The sparrow-faced man ducked backward and fell over Khassam's crawling body as the insane chant of the departing mumen swelled and rose to jagged, invisible peaks. The Guard, roaring, aimed a decapitating blow at Idrys which Patrick parried as Tembar dragged Idrys clear. Iubhar, engaging a second Guard, tossed a spare sword to Tembar as Patrick kicked his opponent on the kneecap, before half-severing the man's neck at the weak spot between cuirass and helm. He whirled and jumped aside before the man had fallen, and a blade whistled through the space he'd occupied. Iubhar, beside him, slashed, and blades rang. They were sweating, hard-pressed. Patrick jabbed, and a Guard fell back, howling. The dancing, chanting mumen were approaching the confusion outside the clearing.

'Quickly!' yelled Patrick. 'Follow the mumen!'

They disengaged and ran, pulling the others with them. Patrick threw a spare blade to Liam, who gasped as he caught it, and shouted as he turned, 'You can't even trust babies these days; the time is cursed!' They ran, eyes alert for the Purplefield thieves of their weapons. Idrys and Iubhar at the rear moved half-turned against the following menace of the Guards, who were slicing ponderously at their heels as Scalaman half dragged Gaidhealla with him. But the Guards, and all of them, were moving more heavily than they would have done in normal circumstances, as though their feet were bogged as in dreams of flight.

This was caused by the mumen. They were chanting, laughing, dancing away with One-Eye and the gleeful fat woman in their midst, as though their world was a carnival, and what happened beyond it was only a shallow ghost of their reality. They could not be harmed because they knew it was so, and trebling, soaring, grinding voices affirmed it was so, and the complete freedom of their whirling, bemusing, dervish dances drove the point home. There was not a man or woman among the thousands in the ghost-parade about them who dared to lift a finger, voice, or weapon against them. Those in the distance who could only hear were arguing about the inflated, terrifying reports they'd heard of what had happened in the clearing. Argument was leading to physical disagreement in hundreds of places as the mumen danced and wailed toward the open slope which led to the tunnels. They were clear ahead of the Company.

As if by antimagnetism, the great armed mass shifted continually to accommodate their scattered, leaping progress on a broad front of over fifty feet. The gap behind them swiftly closed as tight-packed humans surged and were pushed into the vacuum. The Company was enclosed on all sides by argumentative, wide-nostriled faces. In other areas, the army was starting to battle among itself; the infection was spreading in the wake of the mumen, who danced on, without thought of the spectral Company who'd brought their master to them. There was only dreadful joy and happiness in them. Though they didn't find it dreadful; that was a particular point of view. But in their wake, the atmosphere was leaden and horrible, infesting the mind with an ugly, squatting weight which demanded the sole exorcism of violence. The maddening weight was maintained by the distanced chanting which was continually sudden, and so sharply unpredictable that it scrambled rational thought.

The Company was ringed – by murderous men of Purplefield, hawkfaced warriors of Spokane in spiked helmets, slant Lamassan mirrormen, naked pikemen from Aquinte, by a great, confused conglomeration through which the Guards came crashing. Patrick found his own torchblade pointed at his chest, as he met Nasna's baleful eyes.

The air was darkening, hazed by the growth of wraith-like mist. And a great flock of silver birds appeared over the lip of the Scarp, came wheeling expectantly above ten thousand humans who were sliding into turmoil. For a moment, the dire, raucous silver harbingers attracted mass attention, and the Company won another instant of unbearable grace. And Patrick realized that only the Guards and Nasna's men were really interested in the Company. Others crowded and obstructed, jeered, and gave Purplefield archers no room to draw. And Patrick hissed words to Scalaman without taking his eyes from Nasna as the shadows of the giant silver birds swept over them:

'They may turn against each other. We may have a chance.'

Nasna heard, and brayed with chilling, vicious laughter. 'Hoo ... hoo ... hoo ... the child you brought – the Avenging Orphan – we are damned. We will kill you all for bringing our doom!'

From the other side, a Guardsman shouted belligerently: 'Wrong, Nasna! They are ours to kill. They brought the mutant who has destroyed our Lord. Don't touch them, you slovenly perverts!'

Voices screamed with rage, random violence was flowering, Guards and Nasna's men shouted and gesticulated furiously as the birds swept low overhead.

Gaidhealla lifted her head. 'Fools! Idiots!' she rallied weakly. 'Kill each other then – it's what One-Eye wants. Turn on each other like animals, obey him!' Patrick heard deep scorn, deeper pity in her voice.

The crowd surged, and Patrick was watching Nasna, awaiting his chance. Swords rang. Idrys saw —

'Kamur!' he howled, amazed. 'It is I! Idrys! Your brother!'

But his twin came leaping from the crowd of tumbled, kicking limbs with a snarl and a dirk which he buried deep in Idry's chest. 'Bald traitor, no brother of mine!' he howled, and spat at Idrys, who fell and died disbelievingly. Iubhar cut down Kamur as the Guards went berserk against Nasna's men, howling with rage which drowned the now-distant chanting as Patrick took his pointless chance and dived for Nasna's legs as the torchblade wavered. Dived flat and bitter, raging as he hit, grabbing lefthanded for the tarnished barrel of his torchblade as Nasna, roaring, backflung, and studded blindly with both hands behind the torchblade guard. Widebeam flared across three close-pressing pikemen of Aquinte, scorched them, dropped them in the sudden shadow of a great bird hovering, the color of the moon on a frosty night. Men scrambled in all directions, setting up fresh waves through this part of the army over the general confusion of which the waiting birds swooped leisurely through the darkening air.

Patrick seized his torchblade and reversed it onto Nasna's face at point-blank range, yelling with fury as Nasna's men fell back before the furious onslaught of the expert Guards. Zena grabbed a fallen pike, ducked a blow, and half fended a swipe aimed at Patrick's back; the pike broke, and the blade glanced across Patrick's shoulder. He roared and rolled and sprayed. The beam was low, and Nasna's face was a bubbling black-and-red ruin; he still moved, slightly.

A fresh surge from another part of the struggling army broke contestants apart, increasing the confusion, over the racket of which Liam heard the clashing, heartrending sound of his beloved sirena being abused by inexpert, disrespectful fingers. He screamed, 'Vandal!' and threw himself past bodies in the direction of the miscreant.

Iubhar was struggling desperately against three Guards, Ninaseunta holding to Scalaman behind with her eyes shut as men of Aquinte turned on their ancient enemies, the Rattle Worshipers of Spokane, before the Spokane devils attacked them first. Patrick looked for Gaidhealla as a further surge drove in a wedge which separated him from the Company. He had a brief glimpse of Salamander falling, thrusting with a dirk she'd grabbed; then he was taken on the flood. An arm coiled around Tembar's neck and pulled him low. Scalaman fended off a pikethrust aimed at

Gaidhealla, wondering where Patrick and the Songmaker had gone. Tembar was bludgeoned. Salamander was trapped beneath a still body which had her knife in it. More surges, from every direction, carried Iubhar, gashed and bloody, from the last of the trio of Guards, past Scalaman, who had grabbed Ninaseunta, and lost Gaidhealla.

'*... Where...?*'

'*... Don't know ... watch out!*'

For a random hail of arrows was descending into the chaos, fired by madmen in some other part, perhaps at the wheeling birds whose shadows were so meaningful in the thickness of the battle.

Iubhar was pierced through the leg, and bodies smashed into him. Elsewhere, a shaft hissed past Patrick's ear, buried itself a foot deep in a Purplefield swordsman. He faced another, but a bloody Phrenge Yellowbelt chose to take up orphan-stealing issue. Now all were again swept off their feet and piled over others by a new, more relentless wave of confusion. The haze was thickening, the air lay thick as custard; the sun was a wide, wavering yolk which bled ocher. The slope before the Scarp was a great struggling mass of bodies, blades, pikes, axes, powertubes, and vicious morning stars. The chanting of the mumen was completely drowned by the babble of curses screamed in many dialects and tongues; the cohesion of the General Synthetic was destroyed in the madness. Sons and fathers and brothers were embroiled in mutual hatreds; friends turned against friends as long as it remained physically possible; weapons were lost and picked up by others. Men were driven so angry they grappled barehanded when pinned on the ground by bodies above them; they screamed out the madness in them as long as they could.

The great silver birds circled lower and slower now, sweeping through the haze, their curved beaks cruel, their black-ringed eyes like maleficent jewels. But where the company was distributed in that vast, heaving confusion of the dead, the dying, and the maddened, not even they could see. If any of the Company still lived, they were lost in chaos again. In the dream.

At the spot where Khassam had stood near the mouth of the tunnels, surrounded by his jabbering, prancing mumen, held by the dwarf's daughter, Chaos smiled innocently. His eye was wide with black, sunny delight: he made happy, gurgling sounds; he made chest-beating motions with tiny, yellow-pink fists. The mumen howled and leaped in dance, throwing back wattled heads and mottled heads and heads with snaky hair, chanting joy at the wreathing mists which obscured the reaches of tumbling forest with slow-sliding fingers. Between them and the nearest of the struggling army was a bare, open space, a no-man's-land, the boundaries of a world apart. The mumen felt no exhaustion, they could not feel exhaustion, they were alive again, drawing on the energies of the pandemonium before them – drawing back the energy they'd spent to stimulate the chaos, profiting enormously by the unequal transaction. They were fully alive again! Alive in the multiplex simultaneities of their life-dance reactions – thirty instantaneous individuals who'd survived and thrived in the Middle Kingdom, who'd given history to that distant period. Thirty individuals, who formed a single whole only when their Lord was present as nexus, as the hub of their wheel, as the totality of their varied potentials.

Only the presence of their Lord permitted them to dance and sing. Without him, their hatred of each other was so intense that none could have been free and remained alive. Life! Alive again! With so much to do! The decayed inhabitants of this world were too much like the Old Men, the deluded dregs of the Great Forgetting, who'd clung to traditions and reality principles belonging to a fatally ignorant age which had worshipped its own mechanical reflections, and never understood that it might *dance* instead. United by their Lord, the mumen had freed those struggling historical hangovers from their delusions of reality – and from their machines, devices, and unnatural crutches of order. The exemplars of incomprehensible Middle Kingdom chaos had gone to rest – but now they were again embodied as they'd projected; they were self-perpetuated in time. It gave them much delight to begin the upsetting of this world's notions and sacred games. To go after the destruction of those ancient machines which had escaped the Middle Kingdom and were being used again, to destroy them by using them.

It was a great joke to have had themselves stored, side by side, in frozen enmity, with the very machines which would be rediscovered and employed to be destroyed and to destroy. And Khassam, who'd thought himself the Divine Mutant, and thus well-protected from their horror, had revived them! Had already destroyed many of the *eala* to Phadraig's detriment. Everything about this day delighted them, including the pleasant illusion that it was real. Khassam particularly delighted them. He'd thought he wanted chaos, he'd furthered chaos, and now he had it.

The 'chance' circumstances of their meeting with their newborn Lord were delightful, as was the Fox's rebirth in Phadraig – in the heart of a failing order – and the present revolt which was tearing Phadraig apart. The Company gratified them, so earnestly bound to its sacred, prophesied purpose. They rejoiced in Maelnagar – it was two hundred years since he dreamed the Fox's signal, to set a wheel in motion which spun into Gaidhealla's long-laid plans – which caused their Lord to escape Phadraig where otherwise he would have been forcibly disembodied.

The Company and Khassam had played on their skeins of the dream to perfection. And the tower which studded the sky, which was swallowed by the mist – they bowed and leaped for the part it had played. There was nothing which didn't delight them. Not even Cuyahogan could do anything but amuse them, though the golem was a menace which not even they or their Lord could predict or altogether control. Cuyahogan bore no relation to anything else on Earth in its circumstances. There had been a time when Cuyahogan was one of them – yet not one of them. Unquiet Cuyahogan was machine and sentient too. During the upheavals of the Great Forgetting the golem had somehow burst through the barriers to self-awareness, from reflection to reality. Envies and ambitions had raged foremost after the breaking of the prison bars, and the golem had stalked the heaving lands until at last it came to the palace of the Fox, whom it had tried to kill. And the Fox could not control it.

The golem was a wild element beyond the images of his dream. The mumen had almost let it go ahead. They hated their Lord as much as they loved him. Always desiring self-possession, they resented their subordination to his natural authority and power which alone kept them alive to enjoy the disorders of life. But in synergetic circuit with each other and the Fox they were joined in a condition of great power. They were his manifestations, his hands and feet; the Fox needed them for self-definition and survival too. So they came together and bound Cuyahogan with words which made them tremble, for there were sounds which could annul their own spontaneity.

Khassam had learned this from knowledge the mumen had seeded during the decline of the Middle Kingdom. If they were to come again and be revived without their Lord, then for their own protection they would require bondage – minimal, but enough to hold them from each other's throats – temporary, but enough to last until the new dawn when they should meet their Lord again.

The golem, crippled, will and sentience bound, had been taken by humans at the end of the Middle Kingdom. The humans came from across the sea and chose ancient, still-solid Phadraig as their capital. Now, a millennium later, the bound golem had returned their Lord to the mumen. The complexity of the weakened binding had been snapped in the tower. Cuyahogan was free, and would return to attack again. But for the present, Cuyahogan was rejected.

So they danced more wildly as the mists thickened, as the blighting birds swooped lower, beginning to settle on the ghostly carnage with clattering silver flaps. The mumen danced, and they sang, and they laughed around their Lord. They were giddy and drunk with the wine of chaos, with the vibrations of conflict which made them so light, so free. They could have danced until every last human was torn apart and left for the feast of the razorbeaked birds.

But One-Eye didn't want all the humans dead.

He played with a dream of some alive to spread what was begun.

He dreamed of Phadraig attacked by some, and of others returning to their homelands to foment rebellions, and of others following him through the broken Jerezid lands and far beyond, praising him, making a god of him, and of others denying him, making a devil of him, and of others yet who would seek his true name. But he would deny all names by accepting every single one, and conceal the truth in the confusion of many. It was up to people to agree on a name if they could, on a true description of his nature, on a fixing-force which could define and hold his dreams. Only if their agreement was perfect and autonomous beyond his dreams could he be made answerable to them. The conditions for agreement were not yet probable in the futures of which he dreamed: futures of suspicious confederations, shifting coalitions, great betrayals, strange magics, huge acts involving enormous energies. And now in the deadly stew before him bubbled the ingredients of these many futures, struggled the future bearers of fiery messages and crusades which would sweep the whole globe clean, present the heavens with a flickering face, a jangling note, a dissonance, a disruption of the eternal song.

His dreams were deranged through their own space and time, giants of reaction and disorder. Once, he was born in the wake of the Great Forgetting, a being on a high path, a man who fell from that path in the shadow of a very high peak. He had turned to his times to survive; from being in the world he became of it, from detachment to involvement. His will had led him through chaos to an understanding that it was all the same, that the definitions and divisions of the life-dream were unnecessary and untrue, that *he* and *she* were just such divisions, that *he wanted* to be, *could* be an imageless androgyne.... But, through some fatal caprice, he had refused to take the indicated final step and abandon himself, had chosen instead to remain divided in time, to deny what he'd known to play with images and dreams instead. Self-hate was implicit in the division; he took it out on the world by destroying to create the Middle Kingdom; he was ever-raging disappointment whose delighted play had vicious aspects. He denied others what he'd denied himself, dreamed of beings who struggled to grow as he had done, denounced and obstructed that growth. The Middle Kingdom was a livid blaze, unstable in time, but eventually subject to change. His material substance, though mutable, decayed and died, and he lost his anchor of images.

He had dreamed and now he dreamed the sometime circumstances of conscious rebirth. Now he was reunited with his mumen-filaments in the form of a male infant – a baby independent of his mother, but not altogether of space, time, and creature-needs; immensely powerful on this stage, but wrecked by his own time; stagnant in his chaos which was fraudulent in that aborted understanding lay at its everywhere.

He was a denial of growth, an obstruction blocking others, a negative feedback from the failure of near-success, a rage of desires to dislocate, then relocate, then dislocate again. He chose to stay in a baby's primal state, preferring to remain where time and space had as little meaning as possible, where everything was giant, primal, evanescent, in constant flux, where images were easily shaped. The process of decline to adulthood involved forgetful submission to self-created ideas and images of reality. One-Eye. He liked it where he was, with his mumen for limbs, and the battle for energy. The male polypheme, flickering between eternity and time, self-manipulating manipulator, the irregular dancer with many false moves.... One-Eye smiled innocently; he made happy, gurgling sounds. For now it was very dark above the slow shadows of the battlefield. From it could come any of many futures, and none of them were sure to be.

One-Eye smiled, and the mumen stopped dancing on the instant, and One-Eye dreamed that those who remained alive were burned by a thought from him which would, in all probability, hinder growth and further chaos....

Now the great silver birds rose in a mass from their preliminary peckings among the dead and the wounded; they sensed something unpleasant. They departed into the darkness, croaking with dislike. For the darkness was almost complete, the yellow leeched away, the remaining shreds of misty daylight swiftly occulting as in eclipse. It was not the moon, but a thought which drained the light from those left alive, which caught them in its dream, and stilled the final spasms of battle.

The Company...?

The Company was here and there, alive and dead.

Gaidhealla had been swept away from Scalaman and trampled in the multiple rushes. She was dead.

Thoughts had flickered for a final time as she lay crushed and broken against the ground beneath feebly struggling bodies. Her mind had cleared, and her sense of personal failure had dissipated. There was a time for everything. Even One-Eye's pattern could be understood if the terms could be found. She knew she was dying, but she was tired, and ready for the change. She had been crushed and suffocated – clamor and clashing muffled all about – but she was no longer there. She was remembrance of Phadraig, of Aurum, of her children, of this final journey; she was thought of Patrick, of Salamander, of the Company Chatachain and its ultimate destiny. She was gone, composed.

*

Scalaman had held onto Ninaseunta as the maddened rush swept them away from Iubhar. The girl was screaming inaudibly through the tumult. They were bowled over into a frenzied crush of struggling bodies. Scalaman protected her with his body, howling and hacking with a sword: a bald, loose-fleshed madman who bore no resemblance to the elegant Scalaman who'd left his brothel so reluctantly. But Phadraig was gone; now there was only rage at stupid inevitability. Successive surges had crushed both of them deep; when Ninaseunta could hardly breathe one final surge threw her halfway clear. When it was growing very dark, and she became consciously oppressed by some fearful expectation, she twisted around, and called weakly for Scalaman.

The fighting was almost over, a huge bird settled nearby, and Scalaman was there behind her.

But his mouth was slack, his head was at an odd angle, and he was dead, with an expression of querulous outrage on his dim-seen face, as though he'd heard the Songmaker taunting as he died.

Ninaseunta buried her head against his tattered cloak and cried.

Iubhar was lying not far away, and he heard her through a painful daze.

He was slashed and bruised all over. The arrow had ripped through his right leg, and infection would spread if allowed. He would live if he found reason to live. But as the fighting died of exhaustion and the darkness grew on his mind he saw the groaning shadows around him with a naked insight. He remembered what Patrick had told him on the roof of the Central Tower – it seemed so long ago. *We did not fail*, he thought bitterly; *it seems we succeeded all too well*. He heard the girl sobbing, felt the tears running down his cheeks. He was thinking that Zena could not possibly be alive, and he did not wish to remain so either. What future could there be?

And the darkness was growing into the thought.

It had taken the Songmaker only a few seconds to realize he was better off if he didn't try to move. His breathing was labored, his head hurt abominably, his mouth was salty with blood, his limbs were entangled with others which didn't move. Forcing his eyes open, he brought his dark surroundings into blurred, dancing focus. He made out his right hand, which he couldn't feel; it was clutched around the familiar shape of his sirena. And the dead body of the Purplefield thief was crumpled on top of him. The sirena seemed to be undamaged. He felt a spasm of relief, and immediately regretted the selfishness. What of the others? What had happened to the fighting? Why was it so dark? He dragged himself painfully clear, crouched on hands and knees and looked about. Dead and wounded in all directions, he couldn't take it in. He made out Tembar's body huddled nearby. And vaguely saw a bald-headed girl crawling blindly toward him, her head hung down. She wore the remains of a shirt, the shirt that Zena had worn. She was Zena, another heavy shape among many who moved and moaned. Liam had no emotion in him at all; the hate he'd felt was all drained away. The darkness was growing complete. Now he couldn't even see his numb hand. The Company. He thought of his friends and he sensed a terrible vacuum. Scalaman. Scalaman was dead. He was sad, and couldn't feel it then; he was one of thousands alone in the dark.

*You never knew how much I loved you for your grumbling....*

But the darkness was entering him, it was taking shape, his reaction was basic and desperate, and he laid back his head and screamed:

'I must be insane! Only insanity could dream all this insanity!'

*

Patrick was still on his feet as the birds lifted and flapped away into the gathering darkness. His fury was spent, his torchblade was empty, he'd fought with the blade until there was no more opposition and he staggered blindly up against the vertical crags of the Scarp. He leaned exhausted against an outcrop, wiping his bloody brow, staring in perplexity at the illusion which came to him through the murk, limping past outstretched arms and crawling, wide-eyed men.

Salamander!

It couldn't be: it was a dream, a temptation of hope, a . . .

Now it was very dark, but she was close, stumbling up against him, her eyes wild, mouth open – clothes torn, her left leg and side were bared, streaked with dirt and drying blood, her bandaged wound had bled again. Her mouth was moving, panting breathless words.

'. . . Patrick . . . Patrick . . . what have I given birth to. . .?'

She was alive, she was real! He was incredulous. The despair in her voice reflected his; with the last of the light her eyes reflected back his own horror. Then they were shaking as the dark grew absolute and they collapsed together to the ground, taking what comfort each could give before the darkness entered and separated them.

The darkness flared into shape in every head.

In every head blazed a colossal eye with a depthless black pupil.

It was an intolerable soul-scorch which lit up previously unknown territories. Thousands of distressed personalities realized that they were self-condemned; horror and ecstasy rifled their minds. They were thrown into perspective from which their reality was clearly unreal, no more than an imagery. Voices cried out – all across the slope, and beneath the trees. For all were alone with the thought flooding from the valves opened in their minds. Its common psychic denominators were differently perceived and image-clad for interpretation by every different individual. It bludgeoned their former understandings; many raved with laughter, the world snatched from beneath their feet.

There were some of them who'd been part of this way before.

In Eight there had been equivalences of understanding.

Now Liam's head was great brass voices in howling descant:

'I AM FREE TO FORGET
YOU ARE FREE TO FORGET
WE FORGET WE ARE FREE'

But in most people the thought wasn't verbalized in the instant that its energy persisted. The instant was enough for minds to start shaking apart with hurtful revelations which couldn't be held, which crushed with their intolerable weight.

And the thought was gone. The eye was gone.

Thousands had hammers pounding in their heads. They opened their eyes to the clearing mists, tried to return to a reality which seemed ... strange, somehow. Slow, they eyed bloody hands and mounded dead with numb incomprehension.

They looked to where One-Eye had been.

But the mumen had already led the fat woman and the one-eyed child into the tunnels as the birds returned, wheeling, and the sun shone hot through the dissipating mists.

# 21 : Seven Silver Ravens

One-Eye was gone. The army had ceased to exist. There were only people locked in confused mental combat with themselves. There was very little movement, very little sound except for the harsh croaking of the giant silver birds who continued to wheel, their greed temporarily annulled by caution. The atmosphere was strange.

Then, seemingly spontaneous, a wave ran through the stirring mass of survivors, and words which seemed self-generated, which ran with one low mass-voice before dying of numbness:

'Discharged ... we are discharged ... free ... free to remember what we want ... do what we think ... no more tyrants ... no more taxes ... no more ...'

And the birds wheeled lower as some began to recover their wits and start the search for lost friends. They picked numbly through the masses of unmoving bodies, turning a shoulder here, a head there, remaining impassive. Liam found Zena, and in time they stumbled across Patrick and Salamander. Eventually Iubhar limped up with Ninaseunta. They spoke in flat, distant whispers. They searched for Gaidhealla in the graveyard piles as the suspicious birds continued to hold off, but they didn't find her. Scalaman's body they brought out and buried by the Scarp, working beside many others who dug their graves and built sad fires. Liam murmured a brief remembrance. A vast sense of preoccupation hung over the sunny slope, a leadenness of spirit. Later the birds overcame their fears and descended unmolested as groups of men picked through the dead for food and equipment. Activity dwindled, fires burned low, and the birds had their fill. Many friendless wounded dragged themselves with declining strength. Bands of men drifted away in all directions, hostility muted and numb. Many went into the tunnels in the distant wake of One-Eye and the mumen.

The Company Chatachain were among the first to take this route.

To Salamander, the entrance underground was too much like her descent beneath Phadraig only a few days before. It was a second burial. What rebirth was indicated this time? Her head was swimming; she had no answer, she was white and weak like the rest of them. And like the rest of them, she obeyed the impulse to enter the tunnels, without question. It was as though the momentum of their discharged mission still persisted. They couldn't explain why they battled up into the smooth, slippery network of narrow tunnels, with only the dim green phosphorescence occasional in the walls to light their way. They moved mechanically, at first among many hundreds, who gradually dispersed into divergent tunnels, or fell back altogether. The six exchanged hardly a word as they supported each other up the constant inclines, through grottoes and past ravines. Each was obsessed with the thought of One-Eye. Each was separated in the realization that none of them knew who they were. They were stumbling ghosts; they were cold and weak apart. Iubhar and Zena gave each other support, but listlessly. Patrick and Salamander moved remote from the rest, Patrick leading in the dim burrows. And Liam led Ninaseunta in the middle as the six edged up narrow paths which spidered the walls of great shadowed galleries, foot by foot and half out of their minds – Salamander concealing the pain of her reopened wound, Iubhar dragging his leg, and all of them exhausted. Passing through a place of conjunction with other passages, high and low, the little girl fell. Liam carried her, and they continued walking until their bodies refused to move another step. It was then they had to face each other and their warring impulses.

They found themselves on a ledge above a black lake in the peripheral shadows of a fantastic grotto. The still waters merged with the jaggedly-arched roof at some point beyond their vision; close by, the lake was divided into aisles and sweeping pools by the dim-seen, glimmering configurations of the plunging rock. Time was measured interminably by the changing patterns of water dripping into hollow silence.

The Company shivered close for warmth and dumb animal comfort.

Everything was lost. Gaidhealla dead, Gnorl dead, Scalaman, the scouts . . . and they lost here, squatting in the near-darkness, unwilling to look each other in the eyes, each surrounded by five green strangers in a place of the dead, racked by the growth of unspoken horror, without appetite for food, or life. The mood grew too desperate. One of the green strangers made an almighty effort, pulled gummed-up lips apart, spoke words in a cracked voice uncertain of its volume:

'Night's come . . . we're asleep, and divided . . . we mustn't fight ourselves any longer! We're numb, dead, blind with thought, we have to feel our way out!'

And Patrick was shivering more violently, crucified on some internal crisscross of energy. He put out a hand to Salamander as he spoke.

Reactions were simultaneous, as the words triggered life.

'But what if the thought's more powerful than the feeler?'

'How can we feel our way out of madness?'

Salamander spoke fast, raggedly harsh; Zena's voice was husky, cobwebbed thick. But Patrick was silent: he had no answer. Liam stirred; he had Ninaseunta's sleeping head in his lap. 'How can we feel our way out of madness?' he asked sarcastically. 'You've hit the question which all of history strives to answer!'

'Forget history; we're trapped in One-Eye's trickery!' snapped Zena, irritating Iubhar with her fury at the Songmaker.

'Stop thinking about him and he can't affect you.'

'How do you suppose I do that?' she demanded derisively.

'How do I know?' Iubhar's voice was rough. His leg throbbed, and his temper was utterly bleak. 'He tore our innermost spirits and showed us that we sleep, wrenched us more deeply than we can reach to repair!'

Lost for hope, he flung himself back down on the rocky shelf.

Salamander felt sudden ugliness, and pushed Patrick's hand away.

'You want comfort, but have you asked about my pain?'

Patrick stared away into the green luminescence with clenched jaw.

Ninaseunta stirred, moaned with fear. Looking grim, Liam shook Iubhar by the shoulder, and hissed: 'One-Eye showed us nothing we don't already know! He showed us the riddle of how we forget who we are; he hopes to divide us and make us despair. Well, he betrayed something of himself too. Remember we're discharged. Tomorrow we'll be in the sun, to find our own direction. Now, quiet, or we'll wake the girl with our complaints. Let's sit together and find our warmth as friends. If we sing softly, we may overcome our unpleasant despair....'

And he took his sirena and began to sing, soft and slow.

Iubhar interrupted him, and snapped: 'How can you sing about love at a time like this?'

The Songmaker stopped and said, 'Because we're stuck in the very bowels of misery, my friend. What else can we do that's profitable?'

'Sing, Liam,' said Patrick stiffly from his shadow. 'Sing something we know to keep us warm and heal our souls.'

So Liam chose a song of his own which Iubhar and Patrick remembered well. He took his spirit from he knew not where, and sang:

*'Returning one day from hunting the deer*
*I was hot and so dry and thirsting for beer*
*And swear I was clean and clear of all sin*
*As I entered in that greedy devil's inn . . .'*

His voice was weak and blended strangely hollow with the sad and dripping place, but he persevered, and coaxed them from their moods with absurdity. Then Iubhar sang the chorus with Patrick and himself, voices cracked and numb. Ninaseunta stirred to the sirena, sleepily.

*'Oh your money's no use*
*And your morals are loose —'*

And they sang old songs which all of them knew. For a while they were together and took strength, dissonance reduced. Then they were silent, staring into the dripping grotto. In time, they all slept.

Awaking cold, they ate, rebound their wounds, and continued. In time, they emerged onto the arid roof of the Scarp beneath the afternoon sun. And were met by seven silver ravens, smaller cousins of the scavengers. The unknown emissaries urged the Company to the north.

But the Company set its face to the west, ignoring the harsh protest of the ravens, not looking up until the birds had given in and flapped away to the north. The six were grim and exhausted, but they kept to their chosen direction. One-Eye went north toward Purplefield, and they went toward the Abeltine Lakes, southwest of Kor, and beyond the sunset. They were thought in his dream, but the dream wasn't omnipotent – they hoped to feel their own destiny through it.

**More Great Science Fiction Books from Panther**

| | | | |
|---|---|---|---|
| DOUBLE STAR | Robert A. Heinlein | 40p | ☐ |
| BEYOND THIS HORIZON | Robert A. Heinlein | 40p | ☐ |
| STRANGE RELATIONS | Philip José Farmer | 35p | ☐ |
| THE LEFT HAND OF DARKNESS | Ursula K. LeGuin | 50p | ☐ |
| CITY OF ILLUSIONS | Ursula K. LeGuin | 35p | ☐ |
| THE LATHE OF HEAVEN | Ursula K. LeGuin | 35p | ☐ |
| THE FREDERIK POHL OMNIBUS | Frederik Pohl | 40p | ☐ |
| THE WONDER EFFECT | Frederik Pohl & C. M. Kornbluth | 40p | ☐ |

*The Classic LENSMAN series*

| | | | |
|---|---|---|---|
| TRIPLANETARY | E. E. 'Doc' Smith | 50p | ☐ |
| FIRST LENSMAN | E. E. 'Doc' Smith | 40p | ☐ |
| GALACTIC PATROL | E. E. 'Doc' Smith | 50p | ☐ |
| GREY LENSMAN | E. E. 'Doc' Smith | 50p | ☐ |
| SECOND STAGE LENSMEN | E. E. 'Doc' Smith | 50p | ☐ |
| CHILDREN OF THE LENS | E. E. 'Doc' Smith | 40p | ☐ |
| MASTERS OF THE VORTEX | E. E. 'Doc' Smith | 35p | ☐ |

*The Classic SKYLARK series*

| | | | |
|---|---|---|---|
| THE SKYLARK OF SPACE | E. E. 'Doc' Smith | 40p | ☐ |
| SKYLARK THREE | E. E. 'Doc' Smith | 50p | ☐ |
| SKYLARK OF VALERON | E. E. 'Doc' Smith | 40p | ☐ |
| SKYLARK DUQUESNE | E. E. 'Doc' Smith | 40p | ☐ |
| THE IRON DREAM | Norman Spinrad | 50p | ☐ |
| SLAN | A. E. van Vogt | 40p | ☐ |
| MOONBEAST | A. E. van Vogt | 40p | ☐ |
| THE VOYAGE OF THE SPACE BEAGLE | A. E. van Vogt | 50p | ☐ |
| THE BOOK OF PTATH | A. E. van Vogt | 40p | ☐ |
| THE WAR AGAINST THE RULL | A. E. van Vogt | 40p | ☐ |
| AWAY AND BEYOND | A. E. van Vogt | 35p | ☐ |
| DESTINATION: UNIVERSE! | A. E. van Vogt | 30p | ☐ |
| LORD OF LIGHT | Roger Zelazny | 40p | ☐ |